**EMMA VISKIC** is an award-winning Australian crime writer. Her critically acclaimed debut *Resurrection Bay* was shortlisted for two CWA Daggers and won five Australian awards, including the Ned Kelly Award for Best Debut. Its sequel, *And Fire Came Down*, won the Davitt Award for Best Adult Novel. Emma studied Australian sign language (Auslan) in order to write the Caleb Zelic thrillers, of which *Darkness for Light* is the third. She is currently writing the fourth.

## PRAISE FOR THE CALEB ZELIC THRILLERS

'Outstanding, gripping and violent... a hero who is original and appealing'

*Guardian*

'More than lives up to its hype... Fierce, fast-moving, violent... it is as exciting a debut as fellow Australian Jane Harper's *The Dry*, and I can think of no higher praise'

*Daily Mail*

'Trailing literary prizes in its wake... superbly characterized... well above most contemporary crime fiction'

*Financial Times*, **Books of the Year**

'Combines nuanced characters and thoughtful plotting'

*Publishers Weekly* **(starred review)**

'Clever, brilliantly observed... Viskic just keeps getting better. Caleb Zelic is the perfect character to explore Melbourne's diverse culture and all aspects of its society, high and low, ugly and beautiful'

**Adrian McKinty, author of *The Chain***

'Caleb Zelic lives in a genre of his own: the perfect outsider in an uncaring world. Inventive, loyal, tormented and whip-smart, he stands at the moral centre of a twisting tale of corruption'

**Jock Serong, author of *The Rules of Backyard Cricket***

'Terrific... Grabs you by the throat and never slackens its hold'

**Christos Tsiolkas, author of *The Slap***

'Outstanding... Pacy, violent but with a big thundering heart, it looks set to be one of the debuts of the year and marks Emma Viskic out as a serious contender on the crime scene'

**Eva Dolan, author of *Long Way Home***

'Adds to a bumper year for quality Australian crime fiction... The dialogue is excellent... [it] zooms along'

***Sunday Express***

'Emma Viskic is a terrific, gutsy writer with great insight into the murkiness of both criminal and heroic motivations'

**Emily Maguire, author of *An Isolated Incident***

'Accomplished, original and utterly riveting, so much so that I read it in pretty much one sitting'

***Raven Crime Reads***

# EMMA VISKIC

# DARKNESS FOR LIGHT

**PUSHKIN VERTIGO**

# THE CALEB ZELIC THRILLERS

*Resurrection Bay*

*And Fire Came Down*

*Darkness for Light*

Pushkin Press
71–75 Shelton Street
London WC2H 9JQ

Copyright © Emma Viskic 2019

*Darkness for Light* was first published in Australia by Echo, 2019
First published by Pushkin Press in 2020

9 8 7 6 5 4 3 2 1

ISBN 13: 978-1-78227-543-5

Offset by Tetragon, London
Printed and bound by CPI Group (UK) Ltd, Croydon CRO 4YY

www.pushkinpress.com

*For Dad*

*Woe to those who call evil good, and good evil;*
*who put darkness for light, and light for darkness;*
*who put bitter for sweet, and sweet for bitter.*
ISAIAH 5:20

# 1.

A children's farm was a nice change. Clandestine meetings were usually held in dark pubs, not urban pastures with good sightlines and pleasant views. Half an hour before closing time, a few families were still out wandering the gardens and gazing at cows. Crisp air and deep-blue sky, a lingering warmth to the late afternoon sun. Melbourne autumn at its best.

Caleb paid the staggering entrance fee and headed down the path at a brisk pace. The five-block drive from his office had taken twenty minutes thanks to roadworks, and everything about this possible client screamed anxiety – the anonymous email address and lack of phone number, the request they meet immediately.

A feeling of lightness despite the rush to get here: the end of a good day, in a good week, in a greatly improved year. Thank God.

Caleb reached an enclosed garden with amber-leaved trees. Fluffy chickens were scratching at the ground, their feathers moulting like snow. No self-described stocky man in a charcoal suit. No men at all. Just a mother and her bandy-legged toddler offering grass to the disinterested birds. A glimpse into a possible future: a small hand in his, Kat by his side, an afternoon together in the sun. The mother turned and said something to him. Her words were too fast to catch, but her expression was clear: *Go away weird, smiling man.*

He left.

No one was waiting on the other side of the gate, or by the barns. Looked like Martin Amon was a no-show. A bit of a surprise; the man hadn't come across as flaky in their brief email conversation. No worrying overuse of capital letters or exclamation marks, just a few blunt sentences that gave the impression of someone used to taking charge. Maybe it was just as well. Odds were, Amon was an uptight manager worried about minor fraud, but his urgency could also signal something more ominous. The exact kind of work Caleb avoided these days. He only took safe jobs now – employee checks and embezzlement cases, security advice – nothing that could bring fear and violence back into his life. A lesson finally learned after his brother. After Frankie.

He looped around the far side of the garden for a final look. More chickens here, three of them pecking at a darkened patch of grass near a wooden shed. Small lumps of something pale and glistening. A cloying smell, like a butcher's shop on a summer's day. He knew that smell, still started from his dreams with it thickening his breath.

He stopped walking.

A long drag-mark led from the birds into the shed; wet, as though someone had slopped a dirty mop across the grass. Stray tufts of down had stuck to it, stirring gently in the breeze. White feathers, stained red.

Bile rose in his throat.

Movement to his right, the mother and toddler coming around the corner towards him. The child gave him a gummy smile and offered a fistful of grass. No air to speak; no words. Caleb put up a hand and signed for them to stop. The woman froze, her mouth opening as she noticed the pallid flecks and damp grass, the chickens peck, peck, pecking. She scooped up her child and ran.

He should run, too.

Should turn and leave and never come back.

He skirted carefully around the chickens and followed the long stain to the doorway. No windows, his eyes slow to make sense of the shadows. A peaked wooden ceiling, high stacks of hay against the walls. The man was lying on his side by the door. Charcoal suit, a few extra kilos softening his stocky build, sandy hair matted at the back. No face, just a bloodied pulp of flesh and bone.

# 2.

They left Caleb to wait in the farm's cramped office, surrounded by posters of children and plump cows, half-drunk cups of tea. By the door, a bored constable sat in a swivel chair, flicking through her phone. Dark outside the room's lone window, night falling hours ago, along with blanketing exhaustion. A temptation to rest his head on the cluttered desk and sleep. No idea what he was waiting for, just that the homicide detectives had been about to let him go when they'd received a phone call and conferred hurriedly outside, asked him to stay.

Amon had been shot. A bullet to the back of the head, exiting his face. Caleb didn't know a lot about guns, but he'd seen the devastation they could wreak on a body. Had felt the hard kick of one in his hand, the warmth of another man's blood.

He started as the constable leapt to her feet. Two suited men were coming through the door, both taking up a lot of space for not very large people. A quick flash of their IDs and a few impenetrable words to the constable and she left, closing the door behind her. Both men gave Caleb the cop once-over as they crowded into the room; one smaller and clean-shaven, his mate with a brown goatee like a half-eaten rabbit. That beard was going to be a problem, concealing most of the man's bottom lip, and all of his top one. When the hell had Victoria Police started allowing its employees to have facial hair?

Beardless pulled the free chair in front of Caleb and sat, but

5

there was nothing settled about him: feet flat on the floor, eyes constantly moving. Rabbit-face perched a buttock on a low filing cabinet, even tenser than his colleague.

'Thanks for waiting,' Beardless said. 'Makes this all a bit easier.'

An easy read: clear and steady, his voice faint, but audible. Caleb almost sagged with relief – he was too tired to lip-read any mumblers.

'Sure,' he said.

'Our colleagues in homicide say you don't need an interpreter.' The detective's eyes slid to the hearing aids he couldn't possibly see beneath Caleb's dark hair.

'No.' Caleb fought the urge to check his aids were covered as he asked the obvious question. 'You're not homicide?'

Beardless paused before answering. 'AFP.'

Federal cops interested in a state crime. And cops not eager to share their names. The murder felt professional, not just the silencer the killer must have used, but also the shot to the back of the head. Organised crime, maybe?

'Why are the feds interested in Amon?' Caleb asked.

'We'll ask the questions if you don't mind, Mr Zelic.' Beardless pulled Caleb's phone from his pocket and passed it to him. 'We've had a look at the emails between you and Martin Amon. What else can you tell us about him?'

Caleb could push it, ask to see their IDs and get his homicide mate, Tedesco, involved. But that would only drag him deeper into whatever foul mess this was – and 'Make Good Decisions' was his new motto. Very new motto. Plastic wrapping just off, a new-car smell to it.

'Nothing,' he said. 'The emails are it.'

A low rumble as Rabbit-face spoke, the fur parting slightly, then closing.

Shit, even worse than Caleb had expected. No point turning

up his aids; amplification wasn't going to make the man's voice any clearer, or his mouth more visible. Had to admit defeat. 'Sorry, I can't understand you. The beard's a problem.'

Beardless gave his mate a flat look. 'We're in agreement, then – the face-fur's got to go.' He pulled a bound notebook from his breast pocket and flipped through it. 'So the first contact you had with Amon was an email saying, "I need to speak with you immediately. Utmost discretion required."'

'Yes.'

'And that was enough for you to meet?'

'It's not unusual. I do business fraud – no one wants their shareholders knowing about a light-fingered employee.'

'Had you heard of the deceased before? Someone mention him? Say he might be in touch?'

'No.'

Disappointment in the detective's expression, quickly hidden. 'Even a vague comment? No name used?'

'No.'

'You speak to him at all?'

'No.'

'Not even a few words?'

'His face was gone. It made lip-reading a bit tricky.'

A long stare for that; milk-coffee eyes, a little bloodshot. 'On the phone, I meant. You said you were running late – you call to let him know? Maybe use a public phone? Borrow one?'

'I don't do voice calls.' Caleb hesitated, then added. 'Can't.'

Beardless covered his mouth and spoke, watching Caleb carefully. It'd be the usual adolescent test, something foul and personal, probably involving a close relative. Caleb gave the man a dead-fish stare until he lowered his hand.

A little glance between the two cops, and Beardless slipped his notebook away. 'Thanks for your help, Mr Zelic, you can go now.

For your own safety we'll keep your name out of it and ask you not to mention Amon to anyone. Online or in person.'

Caleb didn't move. The cops obviously knew a lot more about Amon than they were letting on. If he pressed them they might let something slip.

'Are we going to have a problem?' Beardless asked.

Make Good Decisions. Whoever Amon was, his murder had made two feds rigid with tension. Getting involved could only lead to trouble.

'No.' He stood and walked to the door, went out into the clear night air. Didn't look back.

# 3.

Caleb was almost at the café when he saw the car again: an anonymous black sedan with tinted windows and a mud-spattered numberplate. The third time he'd seen it since leaving his office. Hard to know if it was following him or if he was just being jumpy. Twenty-four hours since Martin Amon's death, his adrenal system was still in overdrive. He adjusted the rear-view mirror, squinting in the dying light: one car back and holding steady.

Decision time.

The small shopping strip was just around the corner. Pull over or keep driving? Most of the stores would be closed at five-sixteen on a Tuesday evening; not enough witnesses around for comfort. But better than none. Past the shops, there were only factories and warehouses.

He slowed as he took the bend, then sped up and pulled into the kerb. Door half open, eyes on the mirror. The black sedan rounded the corner. It drew nearer, headlights off, the driver a hazy silhouette. Closer, nearly level. Passing. It kept going, the brakelights flashing once as it reached the next bend, then it was gone. He breathed again. Just someone taking the same traffic-avoiding route across town. Nothing to do with him, or a dead man with his face shot off.

The news reports hadn't revealed much so far. No mention of Caleb or Martin Amon by name, no possible motive suggested, just a lot of speculation. An online search hadn't revealed anything on Amon, either. Which meant the man had been habitually cautious, or using a pseudonym.

Caleb sat for another moment in the rapidly cooling car, then got out and headed for Alberto's Place. The small café fronting the street was closed, but the kitchen staff would still be hard at it, readying orders for shops and hotels across Melbourne. Pies and pastas, sausages, pastries, all made to old family recipes. He'd grab some swoon-worthy food and surprise Kat with a picnic dinner at her studio, reassure her that he wasn't backsliding. She'd been worried when he'd told her about Amon last night, would still be worried.

He ducked down the laneway to the back of the old redbrick building and stopped outside the glass door. The kitchen's high ceiling was deep in shadow, the only light coming from candles, torches and phones set around the room. They were propped on shelves and benches, their combined wattage illuminating every hand movement and expression of the workers inside. Six people, all managing to carry on signed conversations as they cooked, their Auslan only slightly hampered by their latex gloves. Weekend plans and boyfriends, grandchildren, fitness regimes. Alberto Conti prowled among them, his hands never resting as he issued instructions and tasted dishes.

Caleb shoved his hearing aids in his pocket and opened the door, moved into silence and warmth. The aromas of frying garlic and onion, roasted walnuts, oregano. He received a staggered round of waved hellos as each person noticed him, the most exuberant one from Alberto. Seventy-two years old, sinew and bone, burnt-leather skin. Not the fellow runner Caleb had initially assumed, but a former featherweight boxer.

He gave Caleb the usual rib-cracking hug, along with a slap on the back. Something was seriously off about the man's strength-to-weight ratio. Forty years older than Caleb, a head shorter, but it'd be close odds in a fight.

'The power out?' Caleb signed when the wiry man finally released him.

'No, we're being romantic.' Alberto made a suitably lovesick expression to go with the beating-heart sign. He pulled a heavy-looking canvas bag from a shelf and placed it ceremoniously in front of Caleb, a hint of real reverence in his face now. 'I've given you pork belly instead of sausages. Best you'll ever eat.'

'Kat's not a big fan of pork. You want me to check the fuses? The power's on in the rest of the street.'

'It's under control. She'll like this pork. Better than your mother could make if she slept with the butcher. With the pig.' But he slipped a large quiche into a cardboard box and added it to the bag. 'How's Kat? She OK?'

'Yeah. Good.'

'I don't understand you two. You should just move back in together. Particularly now.'

Always a moment to re-acclimatise to Deaf directness after a week in the hearing world. And to wonder how Alberto had managed to extract more personal information from him in four months than most people did in years. Decades.

'It's on the agenda.' Caleb stilled. Through the servery hatch, a glimpse of a car driving slowly along the street, no headlights against the encroaching gloom. Maybe grey, maybe black. It passed without stopping.

Alberto waved to get his attention. 'I've decided to get those security bars you've been going on about. Can you organise it?'

'Sure.' The street was empty now, no passing cars, with or without headlights.

Another wave from Alberto. 'Tomorrow?'

Caleb gave him his full attention. After months trying to

convince the man to up his security, why the urgency? A lifetime as a signer had made Alberto's face as easy to read as his hands: he was worried and trying hard not to show it.

'Something wrong?' Caleb asked.

'Yeah, I got sick of you nagging me.'

'Alberto, what's happened?' He realised he'd accidentally spoken out loud, and stopped.

Alberto's lip-reading skills were as proudly non-existent as his speech, but he'd obviously got the gist from Caleb's expression. 'You worry too much.' He patted Caleb's hand.

Leave it. Alberto obviously didn't want to tell him, and mixing friendship with business was always a mistake – another lesson learned since Frankie.

Caleb checked the street and slung the bag of food over his shoulder. 'I'll get on to the installer first thing.'

He received another hug and escaped outside with his ribs intact.

An empty laneway; no hiding spots or lurking attackers. He headed for the street. Dusk had slipped into night, bringing with it the scent of cool earth. Dinner, a few precious hours with Kat, then home; sleep the sleep of the almost content.

A darting shape ahead, the black sedan pulling across the alley, blocking his exit. The driver's door flung open.

He dropped the bag and ran. Back towards Alberto's – no, couldn't risk everyone's safety. Past the kitchen and down the laneway. The glare of headlights behind him, coming closer. Fuck. Wouldn't make it. A walkway just ahead, too narrow for a car. Sprinting towards it, his shadow racing before him, breath rasping. Headlights bright, the car nearly on him.

And around the corner. Dark. Overhanging trees and sheer fences, concrete path just visible as he ran.

*Smack.*

Reeling backwards, clutching his face.

A wire safety fence across the path, construction site beyond it. Fuck, have to climb. He hauled himself up, feet slipping as the fence swayed. Too slow, childhood meningitis stripping some balance along with his hearing.

Quick check behind him. A dim shape, someone running. Seven, eight metres away, something in their hand.

A weapon.

A gun.

Clawing up the fence, fingers gripping, pulling at the wire. Nearly at the top. Hands on the –

Slamming pain.

Skin, lungs, marrow fusing.

Down.

# 4.

Minutes, years, for his brain to unscramble. Lying on his back, the hard blow of the concrete still pounding through him, arms and legs half-numb. Panic spiked before he made sense of it. Not dying, not shot – tasered.

Light flared to the right as someone set a bright torch on the ground, the kind people kept in car boots and sheds. A waft of floral perfume as a woman came to stand in front of him. Oh fuck – Jasmine. At least, that's what he called her. She'd never given him her real name, never shown ID to prove she was the federal cop she claimed to be.

He sat up, ignoring the spasm of pain in his back, and Jasmine knelt in front of him. Mid-thirties with drab brown hair and forgettable features, a tight mouth. The stun gun in her hand was designed to look like a phone. Probably the same illegal weapon she'd used while interrogating him four months ago. She'd half-drowned him in a bathtub and repeatedly stunned him, claiming it was to keep her cover. No idea what her excuse was this time, but she'd been after Frankie then, and she'd be after Frankie now.

She checked to make sure he was looking and launched into speech.

Silence.

Shit, his hearing aids were still in his pocket. They weren't exactly news to Jasmine, but he wasn't going to fumble around

15

with numb fingers trying to put them on in front of her – like peeling back his skin to reveal his inner workings. Except she'd be impossible to lip-read without them; no faint tone, just her fast stream of words and the hard line of her mouth. A mouth that had grown even harder at his lack of response to the question she'd obviously just repeated.

Fuck it.

He reached for his aids and she thrust the taser towards him. He froze.

'I'm getting my hearing aids,' he said quickly. 'Can't understand you.'

She glanced down the laneway and gestured for him to go ahead, impatience on her face as it took him a few attempts to hook them over his ears and insert the receivers. He brushed his hair over them and faced her.

'... you ... stand ... now?' A thin thread of a voice.

He filled in the gaps: *'Can you understand me now?'* He'd probably only catch every second or so word, but it'd be enough to guess the rest.

'Why the hell did you tase me?' he said.

'I told you not to run.'

'Yeah, very helpful. If you're after Frankie, I don't know where she is. Ask her criminal mates – start with her sister, Maggie.'

Jasmine scanned the path behind them. 'They're not in contact, but ... you ... her.'

'Slower.'

'You. Know. Her. Better than anyone.'

He'd thought he'd known Frankie, thought they were friends as well as business partners. 'Frankie fucked up my life and nearly got my wife killed. Even if I could find her, I wouldn't.'

Jasmine leaned closer. Chapped lips, the remnants of dark lipstick clinging to the corners, skin stretched tight across her cheekbones. 'I'm not asking you, I'm telling you – find her. She's got documents I need. Get me them or Frankie, I don't care which. You've got two days.'

He knew something about those files, but he wasn't about to tell Jasmine.

She was scanning the tops of the high wooden fences, braced as though about to run. His muscles tensed in response. What would it take to scare a cop who'd chased a man down an unlit alley?

Sudden clarity in his fogged brain: she'd claimed she was a fed.

'Is this connected to Martin Amon?' he asked.

'Yes. I need –'

'Show me your ID.'

She darted another look down the laneway then withdrew a thin leather wallet from her back pocket and threw it to him. Inside was an official-looking seal bearing a crown and the words *Australian Federal Police*, her unsmiling photo beside it. Senior Constable Imogen Blain. Imogen – a name he'd seen written, but never said.

He noted her badge number and returned it. 'What's Frankie got to do with Amon?'

'I told you, she's got documents we need. That's why Martin contacted you. I told him –' She faltered. 'I told him you'd be able to find her.'

'Wait. You mean Amon's a cop? A federal cop?'

Her jaw worked. 'Yes.'

An oil slick of fear in his stomach: a murdered fed. Whatever Imogen was involved in, he needed to be very far from it, very quickly. There was no way she was investigating this officially – not with her furtive approach and lack of partner, the fact no one else had mentioned Frankie. Imogen was either on the outer, or not a cop at all.

'I can't help.' He went to stand.

'If you don't, I'll make your life unbearable.'

He knew unbearable, knew its rank and sweating weight. Nothing she could do could come close. 'Do your worst.'

'Fine. I'll arrest you for murder.'

Cold seeped through him. How could she know?

'Did you really think we didn't know, Caleb? You shot Michael Petronin and left him to rot on the beach. A falling-out among thieves. That's what we'll tell the jury. And they'll believe it. Particularly when they find out the victim was Frankie's thug brother-in-law.'

Petronin's mangled neck and blank eyes, the warmth of his spraying blood, the salt taste of it.

Get it the fuck together and think. She couldn't know, not for sure; there'd been no evidence, no witnesses.

He tried to keep his voice even. 'I don't know what you're talking about.'

'Really? Because someone does.' Imogen pulled a sheet of paper from her coat pocket and shoved it at him: a photocopy of a handwritten letter with yesterday's date. No police letterhead, but set out like an official statement, with the author's name and signature blacked out. Words of varying sizes sloped across the page.

*I saw C A L E B   Z E L I C kill that man on the beech last year they were aguing and C A L E B   Z EL I C had a gun and shot the man dead. I know C A L E B   Z E L I C becose I seen him round and he is deaf.*

Imogen's dry lips were moving. '. . . find Frankie or do twenty years for murder.' She stood and flipped a business card onto his lap. 'Your two days start now.'

She walked away, the darkness swallowing her.

# 5.

Early the next morning Caleb went for a run along the Yarra. A need to clear his head so he could think. Once, he would have thrown himself headlong into finding Frankie, but he was trying to be smarter these days. A steep learning curve. He ran over the pedestrian bridge and up the dirt track that hugged the river, bruised muscles gradually loosening. The smells of warming earth and lemon-scented gums, the sky a smudged grey above the trees.

The morning news had brought the unwelcome confirmation that Martin Amon was a federal police officer. Everything hinged on the information Caleb's detective mate, Tedesco, was hunting down for him. If Imogen wasn't a cop, he'd ignore her threats. If she was, he was in deep shit – even if he could find Frankie, she'd never choose his wellbeing over hers.

Frankie. Former-Sergeant Francesca Reynolds, fifty-eight years old and a mind like a serrated knife. Thinking about her only brought confusion. They'd been partners for five years, friends for longer, and the entire time she'd been secretly working for crims to fund her addictions. She'd endangered Kat, lied and betrayed him. And then she'd turned around and risked her life to save them both.

It would have been easier just to hate her.

He rounded the bend to where the river cut a broad swathe through the eucalypts. The water was shallow here, a quicksilver glint as it skimmed the rocks just beneath the surface.

'... *twenty years for murder.*'

It had been self-defence. After four months of intense therapy, he could finally believe those words. Petronin had hunted him down and tried to kill him, very nearly succeeded. But no jury would believe it. Not when he'd covered up the killing, not when it involved Frankie and her family.

He slowed and stopped. Barely sweating yet, but it was time to head back. He could do it, he could hold everything together. Start by taking the most important step.

―――――――――――

Kat was wielding a chainsaw in the large metal garage that served as her workshop. Wearing goggles and ear protectors, a bandana in the red, yellow and black of the Aboriginal flag. A bird was emerging from the large block of red gum she was carving. Powerful wings and sharp talons: a white-bellied sea eagle, Kat's totem animal. She'd done a lot of eagles this year, the first of them a sleeve tattoo that ran down her left arm with lacy feathers of ochre and brown. The ridge of the wing was a long, pale scar, a legacy of Frankie's betrayal.

Kat lowered the chainsaw and stepped back to examine her progress. He called her name, then flipped the lights when she didn't respond. A bright smile as she turned. He'd been seventeen when he'd first fallen for that smile, but a grown man could appreciate being on its receiving end and possibly grin inanely, wondering what he'd done in a previous life to deserve it.

She shoved the goggles onto her forehead and pulled off a glove with her teeth so she could sign. 'What are you grinning at?'

'You.'

'Good answer – you can stay.' Seamlessly choosing one-handed signs so she could keep her grip on the chainsaw – an impressive achievement, given it was still running. She gave him a searching stare, but there was a looseness to her body, as though she'd had a good morning and was looking forward to the rest of the day.

He couldn't foul her workspace with more bad news. 'How about I take you out for coffee?'

'I can't, sorry. Jarrah's coming over to talk about a project. You'll see him if he's not on Koori time.'

Jarrah was a fellow Aboriginal artist from their hometown of Resurrection Bay. Generous, funny, smart, with easy good looks that made him a pin-up boy for the art world. Caleb would have liked him if he hadn't hated him so much.

He attempted a smile. 'Great.'

'Thought you'd be pleased.' Not many hearies could pull off irony in sign language, but Kat definitely could. She lifted the chainsaw. 'Put the kettle on. I'll finish up.'

The makeshift kitchen in the corner was piled with off-cuts of timber and iron, lumps of wrapped clay. He found the kettle next to a tin marked *Poison*; moved the tin, filled the kettle. A few minutes to choose the right tea. Six loose-leaf blends on offer, including Earl Grey, Kat's post-sex beverage. Although she was flexible about most things in life, she had firm opinions about the correct occasion for any given tea. They were in a strictly non-Earl Grey period at the moment. Hopefully a short hiatus while they navigated the rocky path between brink-of-divorce and coupledom. A smart plan, mutually agreed-upon, but he had some tugging regrets. He eyed the Earl Grey, went for the oolong: difficult conversations.

His phone vibrated while he was decontaminating the cups: Tedesco getting back to him about Imogen.

*—I've got some interesting information. I'll be at Cooper Reserve between 2:30 and 3:00.*

Possibly the only person in the world under eighty who texted in full sentences, the sign of a man who took great care with everything he did. 'Interesting' could be good. Maybe Imogen Blain was a disgraced ex-cop or a con artist with no follow-through. Or maybe she was exactly what she appeared to be: a terrified woman willing to smash his life in order to save hers. The only accurate thing in that statement she'd shown him was his name; she'd either bribed a real witness or found someone happy to lie for a quick buck. If she was comfortable manufacturing evidence, what else was she willing to do?

He shoved the phone in his pocket as Kat came to the table. A sheen of sweat along her hairline and in the dips of her collarbones, eyes bright blue against the dusk of her skin. She'd stripped to jeans and a sleeveless black T-shirt, both loose enough to disguise the small swell of her stomach. She'd do that long after people began to speculate.

A soft kiss to his lips; the honeyed scent of her warm skin. He lingered for a few seconds, then moved away. 'You look great.'

She flopped onto a chair and used her headscarf to wipe her forehead, letting her dark curls spring free. 'Like the hot, bedraggled look, do you?'

'Absolutely.' Shit no, terrible response. Give it another go. 'I always think you're hot.'

'Seamless save, well done.' Her smile dimmed a little as she tried the tea. 'Everything OK?'

He wavered. His days of keeping things from Kat were over, had to be over if he had any hope of salvaging their relationship. She knew all his secrets now and seemed to have accepted the worst of them, even Petronin's death. But burdening her with Imogen's threats still felt like a bad idea.

She was drinking her tea, her eyes on him. She wouldn't

push, but she'd remember that he'd kept important information from her.

'I'm fine,' he said. 'But something happened last night. Connected to Martin Amon.' He went through his run-in with Imogen as quickly and clinically as possible, leaving out any mention of stun guns and Imogen's fear.

Kat sat very still until he'd finished, then touched his hand, running her thumb across the back of it. 'Are you OK?'

'Yeah, fine. She's probably not even a cop. I just wanted to let you know. Tedesco's checking now.'

'But can you find Frankie? I mean, if you have to.' Her usually fluid hands were stiff as she signed.

'Yeah, her sister'll know where she is.'

'Maggie? Do you really think she'd help?'

Maggie Reynolds was more likely to put a bullet in his brain, but she'd probably know where Frankie was. Despite a fraught relationship, the sisters seemed bound by something. History maybe, or Maggie's daughter, Maggie's money.

'Yes,' he said.

'Frankie's been gone for months. If these documents are so important, why is everyone after them now?'

An excellent question, but definitely not one Kat should worry about.

'I don't know and I don't care.'

She managed a weak smile. 'Exactly how I like my men – ignorant and apathetic.' She looked at the door, and her smile bloomed.

Jarrah was coming towards them, a large bakery bag tucked under one arm. Tousle-haired and bright-eyed, a swagger to his step. He kissed Kat's cheek, his hand lingering on her bare arm as he said something incomprehensible. She laughed.

A flame of pure, burning jealousy. Take it like a grown-up.

Do not, under any circumstances, tackle the nice man to the ground and dribble spit in his eyes. Kat didn't show any sign of reciprocating Jarrah's obvious feelings for her, and she wouldn't act on them if she did. Not while she and Caleb were trying to save their marriage.

Jarrah turned to him, flinched slightly at his expression. 'Cal, mate.'

'Jarrah.' He stood to shake hands. Just politeness, nothing to do with the fact he topped the artist by a couple of inches.

There were almond croissants in Jarrah's bag, Kat's current favourites. A deflating realisation last night's surprise picnic was lying in an alleyway somewhere near Alberto's Place.

Jarrah caught his gaze. '... loads ... join us?'

'Thanks, but I've got to go.'

Kat walked him to the door, but didn't say goodbye.

'It'll be OK,' he said.

She nodded, but didn't quite meet his eyes. 'I know. Next week – you're OK to do the new time?'

The twenty-week ultrasound. They'd almost made it that far the last pregnancy. And the one before that. This was the fourth time Kat had checked with him about the rescheduled appointment.

'Yes,' he said. 'I'll pick you up.'

She hugged him a little tighter than usual, a quick, fierce grasp. After she'd closed the door he stood still, the sun a faint warmth on his back.

*Twenty years.*

A lifetime.

# 6.

Cooper Reserve had once been an illegal dumping ground, but the local council had recently wrestled it into parkland. A surprisingly successful conversion, with well-used playgrounds and bike paths. Tedesco was standing by a food van, eating what looked like a bowl of grass. A large man with close-cropped hair; hunched over his food, he looked like one of the boulders artistically scattered throughout the park. Caleb headed towards him, checking his phone as it buzzed. The usual cold trickle of fear, but the text was from Imogen, not Kat. He shoved it back in his pocket without reading it: her threats could wait.

Up close, Tedesco's food still looked like a bowl of grass. The truck was called The Gourmet Gut and seemed to serve a kale-based menu. Trust Tedesco to find the only healthy fast food in Melbourne.

'Late lunch?' Caleb asked.

'Breakfast.' Tedesco thought about it. 'Maybe dinner. Caught a strange one.'

What would constitute a strange case for a homicide cop?

'Am I going to regret asking?'

'Nothing gruesome – guy found asphyxiated with a billiard ball in his mouth.'

OK, now he had to know. 'How'd it fit?'

'That was an early line of enquiry. Bloke had a hyperextended jaw, liked to do a little party act for his mates.'

'So it was an accident?'

'Nah, bad debt with a loan shark called Jimmy Puttnam. Jimmy usually sticks to whipping people with a cut-off garden hose, but he popped by when the vic was doing his act and decided to improvise. Pinched the guy's nose shut. Allegedly. Thirty people and no one saw a thing.'

'That was a fun story, thank you.'

'All part of the service.' Tedesco jerked his head towards a picnic table and walked over to it, Caleb following.

The detective could have discovered Imogen was a cannibal and his face wouldn't show it. Not a man who shared easily, possibly why they got on so well. Strange to think they'd only known each other a year, a friendship forged when Tedesco had investigated the murder of Caleb's best mate. Events that had brought them both pain, but about which they rarely spoke.

Tedesco pulled out his phone when they were seated, and showed Caleb the screen. A po-faced Imogen stared back at him; a plain background, like a passport photo. 'This Imogen Blain?'

So it was Imm-o-gen: short I, soft G. Good call not to say it in front of her.

'Yeah.'

'She is a fed. Done a bit of undercover work.'

Caleb had prepared himself for it, but it was still a body-blow. He composed his face, trying to work out what to ask next. He'd given the detective as little information as possible about his enounter with Imogen. Tedesco almost certainly knew about Caleb's part in Petronin's death, but it was on the long list of things they didn't, shouldn't, talk about. 'What's the word on her?'

'Smart, cuts corners, definitely someone to steer clear of. Which you already knew, given your last run-in with her.'

'Where's she assigned?'

Tedesco lowered his fork. 'Cal. What are you doing?' In his expression, echoes of a conversation they'd had four months ago. Caleb had been at his lowest point: sleepless, desperate, Petronin's death playing on repeat in his head. The detective had arrived with a six-pack of Boag's and the contact details of Henry Collins, the world's most unflappable counsellor, a specialist in PTSD. More words said in that short visit than their entire friendship.

'It's not like that,' Caleb said. 'I'm good. Really good. But Imogen threatened me – I need to know who I'm up against.'

'Threatened you how?'

'You don't want to know.'

Tedesco ate a forkful of kale while he processed the information. 'Then why? Frankie's long gone.'

Imogen's line about wanting documents felt true. Caleb had found a key in Frankie's belongings back in January, the kind that could fit a secure cabinet or safety deposit box. A few days later, she'd hiked through a bushfire to retrieve it from him. Smoke choking his lungs, injured and desperate, and Frankie had appeared out of the ember-touched air. He'd thought for a moment she'd come just to help him.

'Frankie's got evidence she wants. Documents.'

'Blain shouldn't be hunting for evidence – she's a desk jockey these days.'

*These days.* Phrasing that could only mean Tedesco had more information.

'What was she doing before that?'

Tedesco took a few seconds to answer. 'Working in a federal taskforce called Transis. People went very quiet, very quickly when I asked about it. Feels like something bad went down.'

Caleb had come across the name Transis when he'd brushed up against Imogen last time, but he hadn't been able to find anything except a cryptic reference on a now-defunct hacking forum. The hacking side of things could be worth pursuing.

'What was Transis investigating?'

'Crime.'

Very helpful. Tedesco's personal ethics were so solid, they had their own gravitational pull. If he went in too hard the detective would clam up; if he didn't push hard enough, they'd both sit there in silence until one of them died.

'Cybercrime?' Caleb asked.

'No.'

'Gangs?'

'No.'

'Drugs? Intelligence? Sex-trafficking?'

Tedesco sighed. 'Financial. White-collar stuff.'

'Thank you. Any more details I can painfully extract from you?'

'I have no further information, extractable or otherwise.'

'Could you hunt down some files?'

'No. Feds don't like sharing with state cops at the best of times, and this is definitely not the best of times. Whatever Transis got caught up in, you need to stay away. Remember the new motto – Make Good Decisions.' He delivered the words deadpan.

'I knew I shouldn't have told you that.'

'And yet you did.' Tedesco forked in a few more antioxidants and stood. 'Right, home to sleep.'

Discussion over, not to be reopened.

'Thanks for your help. Appreciate it.'

'Don't mention it.' A request, not a platitude. The detective strode towards the carpark, carefully placing his bowl and fork in the recycling bin as he went.

Caleb sat, fighting back the rising panic. Imogen wasn't just any cop, but one who'd worked undercover and didn't hesitate to use intimidation and illegal weapons. He had to find Frankie.

As he headed for the car, he checked Imogen's text.

—*36 hours*

———————

Frankie's sister lived in a money-kissed suburb to the east of the city. Victorian mansions and gleaming cars, dress stores containing three items of clothing, all grey. Even the library was tastefully discreet, with iron lacework and a polished brass sign. Maggie's house was a modern glass and timber creation that seemed to float in its lush garden. Good news in the presence of a black Audi parked in the driveway, even better news in the hip-height front fence; an intercom was always a stumbling block, but it would stop this visit in its tracks.

Caleb parked a few houses away, his ancient grey Commodore blending perfectly with the cars of all the cleaners, nannies and dog walkers. He turned off the engine but didn't get out. Maggie was a connector and broker, with more than a few ties to the underworld. She was also Petronin's ex-wife. The divorce had been ugly, but that probably wasn't going to buy Caleb much slack. When he'd tangled with some of Maggie's mates last year, she'd tried to kill him. God knows what she'd do for dead ex-husband. He sat for another minute and still couldn't come up with anything better than 'wing it'.

No one answered his knock. He pressed the doorbell and knocked again, the door rattling with each blow. It had dropped on its hinges, leaving the lock only partly engaged. Incredible how many people left these things unfixed. Like Kat and her landlord. Just took an hour to rehang a door; two, if you first had to convince Kat to let you do it. He rang the bell again – nothing.

There'd be laptops and phones inside, probably in clear sight. He checked over his shoulder, then gave the door a hard shove. It swung open to reveal a light-filled hallway. 'Hello? Maggie?'

He pressed a palm to the floor: no beat of footsteps or music. A brief wait for any dogs to appear, then inside and quickly down the hall, checking each room as he passed. Soft carpet and filmy curtains, all in creams and greys. Maggie had come a long way from the childhood two-bedroom fibro Frankie had once described in a rare moment of sharing.

A landline in the kitchen, but no mobile phone. Through to the rear of the house, a large room with ash floorboards and furniture, floor-to-ceiling windows, the eye drawn to a photo display on the internal wall. A mix of portraits and group shots, a lot of them featuring a young girl. Maggie's daughter. Petronin's daughter. About the same age as Kat's eldest niece, so around nine, with a solemn gaze and fine features, honey-brown hair. Not a single fake grin for the camera. A large photo of her and Petronin was hung eye-height for a nine-year-old; father and daughter wearing bright red clown noses, arms around each other – laughing. A weight dropped into Caleb's chest. He stood staring, then turned away.

A quick hunt around the room unearthed a mobile phone: plastic, with large square buttons, factory film still on the screen. Unlocked. His spurt of excitement evaporated as he scrolled through it – just a burner, with no contacts and only a handful of sent and received texts, none of them looking as though they were to or from Frankie. He pocketed it just in case and headed for an open door. A book-lined study with a plush couch and white-tiled fireplace, an open laptop on a desk by the window.

He was two steps into the room when the smell hit him: the same iron stench from the Children's Farm. From his dreams.

He didn't want to know, didn't want to look.

He walked slowly to the end of the couch, heartbeat spiking.

Blood.

A woman slumped on the floor by the hearth, her eyes closed, unmoving.

Maggie.

# 7.

He should leave – couldn't risk Maggie's mates or the cops blaming him. But he crossed to her. The same thin face and honey-brown hair as her daughter, a hint of grey at the roots. She didn't seem to be breathing. Blood had pooled on the tiles beneath her head, a gelatinous skin forming like overheated milk. He swallowed and knelt by her side, feeling beneath her matted hair for a pulse. Sticky, skin still warm.

Was that a beat? Hard to tell, hand not quite steady. In the corner of his eye, a small movement, the faint rise of her chest.

He ran for the landline.

---

The ambulance arrived as he turned out of the street, a cop car visible in the rear-view mirror as he drove away. He'd rung emergency services and left the line open without speaking, spent precious minutes grabbing the laptop and wiping down surfaces, scrubbing at the blood that stuck to his skin and nails. Had to be his imagination he could still smell it.

He drove a few blocks and pulled over. An urge to go for a run to burn off the adrenaline, but he was already at the weekly maximum he'd agreed to with his therapist.

The house had been undisturbed, nothing out of place, nothing broken. Maggie had probably known her attacker, invited them in. A botched murder or an argument gone wrong? More likely her assailant hadn't cared whether she lived or died. It had to be related to Amon's death and Imogen's hunt for Frankie. Couldn't be a coincidence. Jesus, what had the cop dragged him into?

He pulled Maggie's laptop from the passenger seat and opened it. A quick search of her pockets hadn't unearthed another phone, but there was a good chance he'd find Frankie's contact details in the computer. If he could guess the password. He tried some of the more obvious ones: MAGGIE, MARGARET, PASSWORD, 12345. What else? Most people stuck to pets and kids. Kids. He didn't know her daughter's name. Had gone out of his way not to know it. Not her name, or her age, or any details about her. What would happen to her now? Father dead, mother possibly dying.

He started as the burner phone vibrated in his pocket. Someone named Dale ringing. Very keen to reach Maggie – five voice calls and a string of texts in the past couple of hours.

—*Call me*

—*CALL ME*

—*Have to go. Library closing soon*

The library could be the elegant building he'd passed on the way to Maggie's. Not a bad place to discuss a criminal conspiracy: public, but with private areas; no CCTV. If Dale knew Maggie well enough to have her burner number, he might know Frankie, too. Might also have scary friends and a tendency towards violence.

Caution was definitely needed – so, stop and think. Ignore the feeling things were spiralling out of control, that an entire day had almost passed. That Imogen wouldn't be open to giving extensions.

The phone vibrated.

*—Ten mins then I'm going to police*

Caleb dropped the phone on the passenger seat and started the car.

---

A sign outside the library said it should have closed an hour ago, but the lights were on, and the door opened automatically. The place had the air of a freshly scrubbed manor, with wooden architraves and discreet modern lighting. Empty apart from a librarian at the returns desk and a couple of schoolkids sprawled on beanbags up the back, heads buried in books. A moment to indulge the fantasy: picking the kids up after work and going home to Kat. The three, four, five of them sitting around the dinner table discussing the day.

And time to shut that down.

The librarian turned as he approached, her shoulders slumping. Strange – it usually took months before women displayed that level of disappointment in him. She was younger than he'd realised, late twenties, with blue-black hair and multiple piercings, including one in her plump lower lip. Her name tag read *Library Services Manager, Dale Little*. So Maggie's irate caller was a librarian. A librarian-come-criminal? Unlikely. He'd never met a stupid librarian, and you'd have to be pretty thick to discuss illegal activities in your workplace.

She shot him an irritated look and lifted a phone to her ear. '... closed.'

Maggie's mobile vibrated in his back pocket. He pulled it out. 'This is Maggie's phone. My name's Caleb, I'm –'

'Finally. She should have been here hours ago.'

A tricky read with that plump lower lip, but doable, thank God. Always easier to go with the flow than get into a half-hour discussion about a neighbour's cousin's deaf friend. That, and the wide variety of strangely inappropriate reactions.

'Why were you expecting Maggie?' he asked.

'To pick up Tilda, of course.' She turned to yell something to the girls at the back of the room, and one of them lifted her head: the child from Maggie's photos. Twig arms and legs, hair escaping its ponytail. She got to her feet, frowning.

'No,' he said quickly. 'I'm not here to get her.'

'Well, I've got a flight to catch.' Dale called something else to the girls, who began packing their bags, Tilda moving a lot slower than her friend. '... the hell is Maggie, anyway?'

'She's in hospital. Someone attacked her.'

Her hand flew to her chest. Bitten nails, painted black. 'Oh ... right?' He translated from her expression: *Is she all right?*

'Not great. A head injury. I'm trying to trace her movements. Do you know if she was meeting anyone this afternoon?'

'No, but I wasn't supposed to have Tilda today. Maggie just texted asking me to pick her up from school, said she'd get her in half an hour. Oh.' Her hand went to her chest again. 'Imagine ... Tilda ... my God.'

'Did Maggie mention anything about her work the last time you spoke?'

She hesitated, her head ducking in embarrassment. 'I'm sorry. Could you say that again? I'm finding your accent a bit tricky. I mean, it's lovely. Is it Scandinavian?'

Heat rose up his face. Fuck: cottonwool voice. Years of speech therapy meant he rarely slipped into it, but tiredness and stress thickened his tongue if he wasn't careful.

He repeated the question, enunciating so clearly his jaw probably looked unhinged. Or his brain.

'Oh no,' Dale said. 'Maggie never talks about work.' She grabbed a leather jacket from the desk, glancing at the girls, who were walking towards them. 'Don't tell Tilda about Maggie until you know more. She'll worry.'

The full horror of her words took a moment to sink in.

'Wait,' he said, 'you're not really leaving her with me, are you? I could be an axe murderer.'

She froze with one arm in her jacket. 'What?'

'I mean, she doesn't know me. I'm just a friend of her aunt's.'

'You know Frankie? Oh good. I should have said – she's on her way.'

He stared at her. 'You know Frankie?'

'Of course. She's Tilda's emergency contact. Useless now she's moved so far away. She won't be here for hours.'

He'd stumbled into an alternate reality. Half of Melbourne looking for Frankie, and the local librarian had her on speed dial. All right, an unexpected turn of events but a good one: Frankie would come to him and it would all be over. A small price to have to babysit the child of the man he'd killed. Tiny. Barely worth thinking about.

The girls stopped in front of them, Dale's daughter chatting away, Tilda silent. A checked school uniform and drooping socks, her hair sticking up at the front. The same blue-grey eyes as Frankie. The same fondness for cutting her own hair, too – no way had a professional hairdresser hacked that lopsided fringe.

Dale was halfway through the introductions before he realised.

'... Caleb will mind you until Aunty Frankie gets here.'

Tilda frowned at him.

He gave her a reassuring smile. 'Hi, Tilda.'

The line between her fair eyebrows grew deeper.

Dale flicked off the remaining lights and bustled them outside. 'Sorry, I feel a bit shit running off, but it's Bali. A wedding. Let me know –' She turned away.

'Wait,' Caleb said, 'I haven't got Frankie's number.'

'It's an answering service. Tilda's got it.' Dale clutched her daughter's hand and broke into a jog, rushing to catch the pedestrian lights.

Tilda was looking up at him. Did she ever speak? Blink? OK, he'd babysat Kat's nieces and nephews often enough to know how to handle a nine-year-old. Tilda might have a little more emotional baggage than he usually dealt with, but he couldn't damage her in a few hours. He hoped.

He squatted in front of her. 'I used to work with Frankie. She ever mention me?'

Tilda nodded.

A disturbing thought occurred to him. 'Did your mum?'

She thought, then shook her head.

Thank God for that. 'How about you give Aunty Frankie a ring, let her know you're with me?'

'She doesn't like being called Aunty.'

So the girl could speak. And very clearly, too. Kids could be hard to read, but Tilda had the crisp consonants of a news anchor.

'Really?' he said. 'Why not?'

'It makes her feel like she's wearing floral undies and orthotic shoes.'

He smiled. 'So what do you call her?'

A slow, Frankiesque blink. 'Frankie.'

# 8.

He took Tilda to his office. His very new office, the ink on the lease only five weeks old. It was the last shop in a forgotten arcade in Collingwood, his neighbouring businesses an accountant and a cat-grooming venture that never seemed to have any customers. He'd chosen the place because it was cheap and a short walk to Kat's house, four minutes if he ran it. The office was just big enough to contain a desk and three armchairs, a couple of filing cabinets. White walls and a fake Persian rug completed the look, along with a kick-proof door and top-of-the-line deadbolt to keep out the area's more determined junkies. A strange sense of pride, given the slick city office he used to share with Frankie.

Tilda stood in the doorway, examining the room. Not scared, but definitely not relaxed – despite her phone call with Frankie, a short conversation involving a lot of 'yeps' and 'nups', ending when Tilda texted his photo to Frankie. Typical Frankie: always questioning, never assuming.

His message had come from a payphone ten seconds later.

—*Spoke to librarian. Don't tell T about M. Be there around 8*

Five-thirty now; a long time for Tilda to hang around his office.

'You need anything?' he asked.

Tilda shook her head.

'Something to eat?'

Another shake.

'Drink?'

And another.

They stood looking at each other, then Tilda headed to an armchair and pulled an illustrated book about the Cold War from her backpack. Good call, get a bit of light research done while they waited. He put Maggie's laptop on the desk and locked the door, threw the bolt for good measure. No real reason to suspect anyone was after him, but he wasn't willing to risk it, not with Tilda here. Not with the image of her mother's bloodied head still in his mind. A strong sense some recent event had set things in motion: Imogen and him, Maggie and Martin Amon. All of them buffeted by the same fallout, only him ignorant of its origins. A dangerous position to be in; knowledge wasn't just power, but also protection.

At the desk, he pulled Maggie's phone from his pocket, scrolled through its handful of texts. Dates and times, cryptic messages. One received this morning from someone called D.

—*Rhys Delaney on for today*

Maggie's reply was a simple 'OK'.

On for a meeting with Maggie? A online hunt found a surprising number of Delaneys in Australia, but only one Rhys in Melbourne. The slightly shadier side of the internet uncovered the basics: forty-two, married with two kids, no police record, a solicitor in a mid-sized law firm. Nothing more to be learned without speaking to the man. Or possibly searching Maggie's laptop. He checked Tilda was still happily reading about mutually assured destruction and tried her name in the password field. Nothing. Damn it. He tried another string of variations, then gave up: he'd have to take it to his friendly computer-whizz, Sammi.

The overhead lights started flashing: someone ringing the doorbell.

The spyhole revealed the unexpected sight of Alberto.

Caleb opened it, smiling. 'Hi. Come in.'

Alberto ventured slowly inside. 'I was in the area, thought I'd drop by on the off-chance.' He spotted Tilda, who was watching their signing with open-mouthed wonder. His face creased into a wide smile. 'Well, hello! And who might you be?'

Tilda blinked at him.

Alberto turned Caleb, his mouth pulling down. 'You don't sign with her?'

The mystified disappointment of a man who'd been born into a family where deafness was both hereditary and an identity. Where the word 'Deaf' was bestowed a capital letter and Deaf children were treasured as a gift instead of a misfortune.

'We've only just met,' Caleb told him. 'She's a friend's niece.'

'Never too early to start.' Alberto gave Tilda a little wave and turned to examine the room, looking oddly naked without his usual white apron. Oddly formal too, in neat brown slacks and a collared shirt. How Caleb's grandfather had dressed on his rare visits to the doctor: overalls traded for a suit and tie, nailbrush vigorously applied to cement-roughened hands.

'You going somewhere?' Caleb asked.

'No. Nice place. Do the floorboards yourself?'

'Yeah.'

'And the windows? New frames?'

'Yep.'

'Shelves, too?'

Caleb propped against his desk. 'What's up?'

Alberto faced him properly. 'I need help. I think someone's trying to bankrupt me.'

Bankrupt? Maybe he'd misread the sign. He'd discovered some alarming gaps in his vocabulary since first visiting Alberto's Place four months ago. Not surprising, given how rarely he'd seen his Deaf friends since leaving school. A distancing he'd have to do a bit of painful self-reflection about one day.

41

Caleb spelled the word with his fingers. 'B.A.N.K.R.U.P.T?'

'Yes. It started with a mis-delivery a few weeks ago. There's been a string of them since, all worse. We've lost two big hotel accounts because of it. Insurance won't pay, keep saying it's my fault. I was beginning to think they were right, but then the blackout last night –' His hands tightened into fists.

'What happened?'

'Someone set up an email account in my name and cancelled the electricity. We lost thousands in stock – fucking insurance won't pay that either.' Alberto shot an automatic glance at Tilda, seemed reassured by her rapt attention. 'So, will you help?'

'The police –'

'I've been twice. They talk to the interpreters instead of me, think I'm too stupid to run a business.'

The dismissive looks and pitying smiles, the feeling of sitting at the kiddie table while the grown-ups went about their business.

'I'm too close,' Caleb said, 'but I can recommend someone good.'

'Deaf?'

'No.'

'Then no. Hearies just talk and think they're listening.' Alberto sagged, exhaustion in his face. 'It's fifty years next month. We were going to celebrate, have a street party, but I don't think we'll make it. Not if we lose another client.'

Oh shit. The business supported Alberto and his family and staff; all six of them Deaf, all welcoming to someone who'd wandered in four months ago looking for something undefinable.

'I'll need all the details,' Caleb told him. 'Email me everything that's happened, including a list of anyone who might hold a grudge.'

The tightness left Alberto's body. 'Thank you.'

'Don't thank me until I've actually done something. I'll get someone to secure things for you online, but change all your passwords today. I'll come around before work tomorrow to set up some CCTV. Just in case it gets physical.' He paused. 'Payment on success.'

Alberto's chest puffed. 'I'm not a charity. You fix this, we go back to being a viable business.'

'OK, standard rates. I'll bring a contract tomorrow.'

'Well, Deaf rates. No need to be greedy.' Alberto hugged him hard enough to make him wheeze. 'It's a relief just to have told you.' He bowed to Tilda before signing, 'Goodbye, young lady. Lovely to meet you.'

She waved back with a solemnness worthy of a royal visit.

Caleb locked the door. A terrible feeling he'd just slipped onto the Bad Decision side of the ledger. Sabotage was notoriously difficult to solve, with no money trail or traceable stolen goods. Unless the saboteur did something stupid, the odds were against them being caught.

He turned for the desk. Tilda was watching him expectantly.

'Sorry,' he said. 'Did you say something?'

'Not yet. Frankie said you need to look at people when they speak because you don't hear very well even though you've got hearing aids.' She peered at him. 'Can I look at them? I can only see the little wires that go in your ears.'

'Um, maybe later.'

A flash of disappointment, but she rallied quickly. 'Was that signing you were doing with that man?'

'Yes.'

'Can you teach me some? Frankie won't show me any because she mainly knows expletives.' She pronounced the last word carefully, a gymnast executing a difficult manoeuvre on the balance beam. He'd underestimated her conversation level by quite a whack. Her confidence, too. The trick was obviously to get her onto a topic she found interesting.

'Sure,' he said. 'How about a word even Frankie won't use?'

She leaned forward, eyes wide. 'What?'

He made two fists and tapped his outstretched thumbs together.

Tilda copied him. 'What does it mean?'

'Aunty.'

A slow smile spread across her face, a transforming expression.

He found himself smiling back. 'You up for a drive? I need to see a girl about a computer.'

'Does she sign too?'

'No, but she's pretty good at saying expletives.'

# 9.

Sammi Ng was in her usual lair above an internet cafe. Sitting cross-legged on the floor, dismantling a motherboard, screws and wiring laid out on a *Dora the Explorer* bedsheet in front of her. Sixteen years old, with a perky smile and ponytail that could con someone into thinking she was sweet – someone who hadn't handed over a fair chunk of his earnings for her admittedly top-quality computing skills. Her airy workshop was filled with computers, some dismantled, others looking like they could run a space station. Or were supposed to be running one.

She looked up as he came in, Tilda trailing behind him. 'Caleb from Trust Works back to give me more money.' Her eyes went to Tilda. 'You his new partner?'

'No,' Tilda said and wandered away to examine a gutted computer.

'Almost as chatty as you,' Sammi said. 'Your mini-me?'

He smiled. 'Frankie's niece.'

'Huh. Funny to think of her having a family. So what can I do for you today? Need help logging onto Facebook?'

He lifted Maggie's laptop. 'Almost – I need to get into this without a password.'

A flash of very white, even teeth. 'That doesn't sound like something an upstanding seventeen-year-old would want to be part of.'

'Thought you were sixteen.'

'Time passes, people get older. Your mind's gunna be blown when I explain the days of the week.' She rose from the ground in one fluid movement and took the laptop. 'A hundred bucks.'

'I could nick down to Victoria Street and buy another one for that.'

'Yeah, but that'd be stolen, unlike this one, which you clearly own.' She hunted through a pile of USB cords then connected the laptop to a computer.

'Seventy,' he said. 'And I keep bringing you work.'

'A hundred and I don't dob you in to the cops.'

Seemed reasonable.

She dropped onto a chair, her fingers darting across the keyboard. A smug grin as she sat back. 'Done.'

'You're kidding me? A hundred bucks for ten second's work?'

'Ninety-nine bucks for the brain, one for the work. Any other way I can relieve you of your money?'

'Yes, unfortunately. Run a file search, concentrating on anything hidden or encrypted.'

Her eyes lit up. 'Cool. What are you looking for? Classified documents? Cyber currency?'

'Just a name, Rhys Delaney.' He thought it through. Might as well do it properly. 'Search for Imogen Blain, Martin Amon and Transis, too.' He wrote the names on a scrap of paper.

'Sweet. You want it now? For a premium, of course.'

A twinge in his eye at the thought of the bill. 'Yeah. I'm going to send you some info about a security overhaul for a client tonight as well. But go easy on padding that account, he's a civilian.'

She saluted.

Tilda was spinning on an office chair, watching him and Sammi at each revolution. She seemed pretty switched-on; there was a chance she'd know why Maggie had wanted her out of the house today.

As he walked over, she came to a stop. 'How do I sign my name?' she asked.

'That's a bit tricky because you haven't got a sign name. You have to spell "Tilda" with your fingers.'

She imitated his movements as he demonstrated, her fine eyebrows drawing together.

'That's it. Well done.' He shifted a monitor from a chair and sat. 'So, you got to go to the library today. Why was that?'

'Mum had to have a boring work meeting.'

'Boring meetings are the worst. Do you know who it was with?'

'No.' She slowly spelled her name again, then looked up. 'What's your sign name?'

'My initials.' He showed her the C and Z, and watched while she copied them. 'Perfect. Your mum's been working on some tricky stuff lately. Has she been worried about it?'

The girl's face shuttered. A definite yes for Maggie being worried and Tilda being troubled by it. Good work, upsetting a kid whose only parent might be dying. One of his prouder moments.

Sammi was coming towards them, a bounce in her step. She pointed to the door and headed to the stairs. Jesus, what had she found?

'Back in a sec,' he told Tilda and followed Sammi onto the landing. 'Got something?'

'Nothing on those people, but some pretty cool shit when I searched for Transis. A Trojan virus started up, and Mike and Cam went live.'

Context was half the trick of lip-reading. It probably wasn't Mike and Cam, but mic and cam. Worth checking the translation, though. 'Searching for Transis set off an alert, and now someone's controlling the webcam and microphone?'

'Yep. I've got the camera covered, but they're still getting audio so don't say anything you don't want them to hear.'

'Can you trace them?'

'Nah, they're too smart for that.'

'Police?'

'Again – too smart. It's a hacker.'

A hacker interested in Transis might have unearthed all kinds of information about someone like Imogen Blain. Not a bad safety net for him to have.

'Can I talk to them safely?' he asked.

'Sure, I've got firewalls like asbestos.'

It only took Sammi a few seconds to set up a messageboard, even less to choose a dollar sign as his avatar. He sat at the keyboard while she went to stand behind the monitor. A shiver of nerves, as though he was about to walk onto stage and didn't know his lines. Or what play he was in.

—I'm after info on Transis too. Want to share?

The cursor blinked for a long time, then a stylised Guy Fawkes mask appeared. Interesting choice of avatars: the guy was either a member of the hacktivist collective Anonymous or he had an inflated sense of self-importance – or both. A sentence appeared.

—*uncover cam and talk*

Checking if Caleb was a cop while gathering video evidence. Very smart.

—I can uncover the camera, but you'll have to type. I'm deaf, can't hear you

The cursor blinked for a few seconds.

—*K go*

Caleb checked there was a blank wall behind him and uncovered the camera.

—What do you know about Transis?

—*u first*

—It's a taskforce

—*something i don't know*

—A cop called Imogen Blain is involved. You know anything about her?

—*what else?*

Caleb paused, his fingers over the keyboard. He had nothing. The Guy Fawkes mask disappeared. Fuck.

Sammi's face fell. 'Oh, you scared him away.' She closed the lid and tapped it. 'Safe if it's shut, live if it's open.'

'The Anonymous icon, that genuine?'

'It's not like they have membership fees – anyone can be a hacktivist.'

'OK. Thanks.' He stood. Time to go before either of them could come up with more ways for him to spend money.

Sammi caught him as he reached Tilda and handed him Maggie's laptop. 'Don't forget your rubbish.'

'Any chance there's something you didn't find?'

An outraged expression, possibly genuine. 'What do you think I am? A fu– friggen amateur? There's nothing secret on that.'

Tilda looked up from the chair. 'You shouldn't put secrets on computers. They're not secure.' Delivered with the solemnity of a public service announcement.

Sammi nodded. 'You're smart. Don't hang around with this guy too long.'

---

It was well after seven by the time they got back to his office, the usually quick drive taking a little longer because of a politely requested toilet stop for Tilda. She hadn't spoken apart from that, but a lot was obviously going on inside her head.

Caleb parked in a well-lit street and got out, gave the area a good scan before unlocking Tilda's door. A chill to the air as they headed for the arcade, Tilda dressed only in her school uniform. Damn, something else he hadn't thought of. Nothing warm to give her except his too-large jacket. She must be getting hungry by now, too, and thirsty. Insight into why parents dragged around such enormous bags – a whole new world of things to learn.

'You cold?' he asked. 'Or hungry?'

Her face lifted to him. 'No. Do your parents give them to you?'

'Give what?'

'Sign names.'

His parents probably hadn't known what a sign name was. Only his brother, Anton, knew sign. Theirs had been a strictly voice-only household, his father's concession to him attending a school for the Deaf coming only after Caleb's abject failure to cope in the local one.

'Sometimes,' he said. 'My friends gave me mine. Deaf friends.'

Her eyes were still on him, as if she wanted to ask something, but wasn't sure she should. A first in their short but interrogative relationship.

'Would you like a sign name?' he asked.

Her mouth opened. 'Yespleasehow?'

'I'll give you one. Might take a while, though. They're pretty special, so I have to make sure it's –' He stopped as they reached the arcade. A dim shape. Someone hiding behind the firehose at the end of the walkway.

Imogen.

The killer.

He was turning to grab Tilda when the person moved into the open. Tall and angular, with short grey hair. Frankie. A very odd-looking Frankie; her usual jeans and leather jacket replaced by a floral top and long purple skirt, her spiky hair brushed flat. A rainbow headscarf topped off the Earth Mother look.

He managed to close his mouth but Tilda's hung open. She made two fists and tapped her thumbs together.

# 10.

Frankie was looking good. A bit of weight on her bony frame, her fifty-eight years sitting lightly on her face. Being on the run suited her. That, and the steady supply of smack she was probably on. It was only when she couldn't feed her habit that she started drinking and went off the rails.

She knelt to hug Tilda, an unusual softness to her expression. 'Hey, Turnip, sorry it took me so long. I've booked us into a cute motel. Thought it'd be more fun than the house.'

Cute and fun: words he'd never before seen on Frankie's lips. If she whipped out a Hello Kitty purse he was going to have to sit down.

She straightened, facing him. 'Thanks for looking after her. Got her stuff?' Casual, as though nothing hung between them. No pain or betrayal, no confusion that she'd saved him from self-destruction just months ago.

He kept his face blank. 'In the office.'

Tilda slipped inside once he'd unlocked the door, but he put a hand out to stop Frankie. 'We need to talk.'

'Later.'

No. If Frankie left, it was all over. Even if he managed to tail her, he couldn't sic Imogen onto her with Tilda around. He had to get the documents.

'It's important.' He glanced at Tilda and changed to sign. Frankie's Auslan was rudimentary, but she could usually follow him if he did it slowly enough. 'It's about Maggie being hurt. About you.'

She hesitated, then said something to Tilda and pulled the office door closed. 'Make it quick. No one knows I'm in town and I want to keep it that way.'

No point trying to hide his agenda. Frankie's sense for bullshit had been refined by thirty years on the force; more than that, she'd trained him. He gave her a quick rundown on the past two days. She listened without comment, but her breathing quickened at the news of Amon's murder.

'And?' she said when he'd finished.

'And I need the docs, or Imogen's going to arrest me.'

'On what grounds? Gullibility?'

'Murder. She's got a witness who can tie me to Petronin's death.'

'She's lying. If the cops could pin it on you they would have done it by now.'

'I'm not willing to take that risk.'

Her pale eyes met his. 'I am.'

And there it was, the fulcrum in their balance of power.

'Don't give me that kicked-puppy look,' she said. 'Do you think I enjoy living with ferals who knit their own pubes? Someone tried to kill me for the damn things, and now you're telling me a fed's been murdered. The last thing I need is some renegade cop getting her hands on them.' She yanked down the neck of her blouse to reveal puckered scar under her shoulder. A quick turn showed the larger exit wound, her skin livid white and badly healed. Jesus. Amon's ruined face slid into his mind. If it'd been the same gun, Frankie was lucky to be alive.

'Who shot you?' he asked.

'I don't know. Which is why I've organised an armed guard for Maggie and I'm not hanging around here with Tilda.'

'Then let me come to the motel. Tell me what you can. An hour – half an hour.'

'No.' She was reaching for the doorhandle.

'Think of it as absolution for past sins,' he said quietly.

She spun back. 'I nearly died dragging your sorry arse out of a bushfire a few months back. Any sins are fully fucking absolved.'

Yes, she'd saved his life, but she'd had an ulterior motive. He stayed silent, giving her guilt room to expand, a technique that had never come close to working on her.

'Christ.' She pulled something silver from her pocket and shoved it at him.

He stared at the wad of foil.

'Wrap your damn phone in it,' she said. 'The cop might be tracking you.'

---

Frankie was right, the motel was cute. Pink stucco with a large fishpond and three pink lawn flamingos. More pink inside: paint, carpet, lampshades, cushions. Plump golden cherubs clung smugly to the walls. There were two bedrooms and a kitchen/dining area that opened onto a sitting room, but it had the feeling of a much smaller space; a womb, maybe.

Frankie mouthed 'fuck me' and dumped takeaway pizza on a glitter-specked table. She set Tilda up in front of the TV, the girl chatting animatedly as Frankie fetched her pizza and glasses of water. A feeling he was an intruder on rare bonding time.

He got started on the pizza. More pink: ham and pineapple, the fruit stained a dull rose by the meat. Why hadn't he tuned in to the discussion about what to order?

Frankie turned the TV up, loud enough for him to catch its muffled blare, and joined him at the table. She grabbed a slice of pizza and began picking off the pineapple. 'I didn't thank you properly before. For Tilda, the ambulance.'

He shook his head. 'How's Maggie?'

A shadow crossed her face. 'Induced coma. There's swelling on her brain.'

He looked at Tilda. She was watching a cartoon but casting little glances their way, as though not wanting to be taken by surprise again. 'Shouldn't you tell her what's happening?'

'Why?'

'To, you know, prepare her for the worst.'

Frankie flicked a chunk of pineapple into the box. 'You're an expert at preparing for the worst. You find it adds much to your quality of life?'

'The length of it, maybe.'

'You're thirty-two, jury's still out.' She sat back. 'I'm stuffed and I have to take Tilda to her great-aunt in woop woop tomorrow. Explain what's happened before I flake out.'

He went through everything he knew so far: the anonymous hacker and Transis, Maggie's text about Rhys Delaney.

Frankie was shaking her head before he'd finished. 'Don't know any of them. Why are you so freaked out about this? You said the other feds aren't interested in you. Just ignore Imogen Blain and get on with your life.'

Once, he would have told her. Laid his heart open and celebrated with her, mourned with her.

'Just tell me what you know,' he said. 'How's Maggie involved?'

She took a bite of pizza, took her time chewing it. 'The docs belong to her. She put them in a deposit box and gave me the key for safekeeping – the one you found back in Jan. Long story short, I tried to sell them to pay some debts, but the damn things are incomplete. And, for your safety and mine, that's all I can tell you.'

The good thing about hanging around Frankie was the positive light it cast on his own failings as a sibling.

Odds were, Frankie was still holding on to the documents in the hopes of selling them. She might have moved them to her own deposit box but she was unlikely to have risked taking them out of the bank. Which meant the key should be nearby – in her backpack or pocket, in the car. Or he was completely wrong, and she'd hidden the docs wherever she'd been living.

'You got any leads on the guy who shot you?' he asked. 'He could be Maggie's attacker.'

'I'm betting he is, but no. He'll just be muscle anyway. Big bloke, like a weightlifter.' She began de-pineappling another slice, then lowered it. 'You know, I've changed my mind, you've got a real problem. That guy's either connected to Imogen, or following the same leads as her. Either way, he might come after you if he thinks you're involved.'

He stared at her: she was right. Not just Imogen after him, but an unknown man with a gun. No way to protect yourself from something like that, no way to protect your friends, your family. Breathless, chest tight.

Frankie was still talking, saying something about dirt.

'Sorry, what?' he asked.

'You need to flip it,' she said slowly. 'Go after Imogen. There'll be dirt on her somewhere. Do a deal with the hacker.'

'I tried. He's not the sharing type.'

'Well it's that, or sit there trying to work out how to get the docs from me.'

Her ability to read his mind would have got her burned at the stake a few centuries ago. A waste of time trying to deny his intentions – just had to be thankful some flicker of remorse had kept her talking. He stood and went fetch Maggie's laptop from his car.

When he got back, Frankie was watching cartoons with Tilda. An arm around the girl's shoulders, heads close: a domestic scene he sometimes allowed himself to imagine but had never thought Frankie might. A breaking news banner scrolled across the bottom of the screen: the arrest of a family-values politician for sex crimes. Something involving an octopus? Frankie snatched the remote from Tilda and changed channels. Financial news, and the arrest of a hot young developer, John Jacklin, for dodgy real estate deals. No octopuses involved. Tilda settled in to watch, possibly taking notes.

Caleb found a spot in front of the cherub-free fridge and opened the messageboard Sammi had set up. Not a lot he could offer the hacker, but money might do the trick.

—I'll pay for info on Transis

Frankie wandered into the kitchen as he pressed send. Apart from her usual Doc Martens, she'd really embraced the new look, right down to the woven friendship bracelets.

'The mic's live,' he told her.

She backed away to the opposite counter and mouthed, 'What's the plan?'

He knocked his fist against his neck, the sign for 'greed'.

'What?'

He slowly fingerspelled the word: only five letters so there was a chance she'd get it.

'Grade?' she asked.

'Yeah,' he said out loud. 'I'm hoping he responds well to external examination.'

The Guy Fawkes avatar flashed onto the screen, along with a message.

—*u really deaf?*

That was the question? Not how much or why?

—Yes

—*u lipread video?*

—Not live, you have to type. How much do you want for the info?

—*job not $ got a video with shit sound. tell me what maggies saying and I'll tell u everything*

A link appeared at the bottom of the page.

# 11.

Caleb shut the laptop. Frankie was looking at him, eyebrows raised.

'He wants me to lip-read a video,' he said. 'Maggie.'

A video of Maggie talking to a colleague, or of an argument that led to a large man smashing her head into the floor? Frankie looked as though she was going through the same thought process: tensed, her eyes on the laptop. Happy to steal from her sister but obviously deeply worried about her.

A sibling relationship even more complex than his with Anton. Ant, his little brother. The worry never went away, an ache like an abscess. Ant was in email contact these days, slow to answer Caleb's messages, quicker to answer Kat's. His bank withdrawals showed he was travelling up the east coast, but that was it. No phone number, no visits, no video calls – which meant he was either getting clean or diving to the depths of his heroin addiction. One day Caleb might forgive himself for dragging Ant into a case and fucking up his life. He hoped not.

Frankie straightened from the bench. 'I'll put Tilda to bed.' She stopped halfway across the kitchen. 'Make sure the sound's off. The speaker icon.'

Good tip. He waited until she'd taken Tilda into one of the bedrooms, then moved to the glittery table. The video was webcam footage, Maggie dressed for a party, hair up, silver glinting at her ears, typing one-handed as she spoke on the phone. Steady speech but nothing instantly readable except for a clear 'No'. Or maybe it was 'know'. Fucking homonyms, should be banned.

A few seconds in, she stiffened, mouth opening. An impenetrable tangle of words spilled from her lips, then she lowered the phone, eyes wide. The screen went blank.

He started as the table vibrated beneath his hand, Frankie tapping to get his attention. He closed the laptop.

'Tilda wants to say goodnight,' she said.

Not entirely sure how to take that. 'Why?'

'What am I, Dr Spock?' She nodded at the computer. 'What is it?'

'Maggie on the phone. Have a listen, see if you can get anything.' He stood and went to the bedroom.

The bedside light was on, casting a gentle glow across the room. Tilda was lying with the puce bedspread pulled to her chin, her home-cut fringe sticking up in tufts. The price tag was still on the collar of her pyjamas. She sat up, hands clasped neatly in her lap. 'Thank you for looking after me today.'

'It was a pleasure.'

There was a stiffness to her, as though the worries of the day had wrapped steel bands around her. Handed from person to person and picking up on everyone's tension, no idea where her mother was. If she was his child he'd tell her a story, then lie beside her so she could drift easily to sleep.

'Would you like a bedtime story?'

She considered it, then shook her head.

'OK.' An oddly deflated feeling. 'Goodnight.' He signed his favourite version of the word, the double-handed thumbs-up that turned into the setting sun, and was rewarded with one of her blossoming smiles. A glimpse of the child from the photo at Maggie's, laughing with her father. She signed 'goodnight' and lay down, still smiling.

Frankie looked up from the screen as he came in. 'She OK?'

'Worried, but stoic.' He hesitated. 'Was she close to Petronin?' Instant regret: stupid to have revealed his underbelly to Frankie.

She gave him a long look. 'You did Tilda and the universe a favour by killing Petronin. She might have a few fond memories of the guy, but he was a violent piece of shit. Even Maggie was celebrating.' She stood. 'Can't hear a thing on this, there's a party going on. Doof-doof music.' She flopped onto the couch and went to kick off her boots, then gave up and lay back with them on, seemed to go straight to sleep.

He sat and played the tape at half-speed. It took a few repeats but the first section unfolded as he got a feel for Maggie's speech patterns, remarkably similar to Frankie's.

*'It's safe. I'm the only one who knows.'*

A good start, but the next part was harder. Much harder. Words tumbling and skidding, with no gaps to shape them. He slowed the tape to quarter speed, then eighth, gradually untangling the threads.

*'No! Don't tell anyone about —— Please.'*

A missing two-syllable word that had to be a name. Start with the obvious ones – not Martin or Amon or Tilda or Frankie. Damn it, names were the worst: infinite combinations of vowels and consonants, half of them looking like something else. Hard enough in real life, but almost impossible with no depth to the image. There was a strong chance he wasn't going to get it.

A memory surfaced: his father repeating a sentence over and over, waiting for him to understand. The daily drills. He'd forgotten about them. The meaningless shapes of what had once been sound, the disappointment in his father's face, the gut-twisting tension. They'd started when he was five, soon after the meningitis, gone on for years. Funny not to have remembered something that had loomed so large at the time.

He turned to Frankie, still lying with her eyes closed, Doc Martens propped on the arm of the couch.

'You awake?'

She sat up, bleary-eyed. 'Not really.'

He told her what he had, and what he didn't have.

'A name?' She winced. 'The one thing you're truly shit at.'

A bit harsh: he was shit at other things, too. 'It starts with a vowel or open consonant. Something like Shona. Maggie ever mention a name like that?'

'No, but she wouldn't. She doesn't trust me enough.' A grimace. 'Always was the smart one.' She sat back and went to kick off her boots, turned the action into an unconvincing stretch. The second time she'd done that

Her boots.

The only clothing she hadn't ditched in her Earth Mother makeover. Safe and unremarkable: the perfect place to hide a safety deposit key.

An easing in his chest. A way out. No jail, no gunman, just give Imogen the key and get on with his life. It'd take a bit of managing with Tilda here, but her presence would make things safer, too. If he brought Imogen to the motel, Frankie would hand over the key without a fight: she wouldn't risk the girl being hurt or alarmed. But he'd better confiscate Imogen's taser, just in case.

He stood. 'I'll try again tomorrow. When are you leaving? It'd be good to run any possible names by you.'

'Late check-out's twelve. I'll give you till then.' She came to lock the door behind him, paused before closing it, some emotion clouding her eyes. A moment to recognise it as sorrow. 'I'm sorry, Cal. I know you're only in this because of my fuck-ups.'

He stood motionless as she closed the door. Fuck.

A brisk walk around the corner to his car, but no large men were lurking in the shadows. He'd parked outside a busy convenience store: good cover for his presence if Imogen really was tracking his phone. He wasn't going to give her anything until she'd agreed to a few demands. Doors locked, he unwrapped the phone from its foil envelope and put it in the dash holder. Kat first – catch her before bed. She crashed early these days.

The video icon flashed for a long time. He was about to give up when Kat appeared, the image wobbling as she propped the phone on the coffee table and curled up on the couch; in her slop-around-home clothes of leggings and an oversized T-shirt, the dark blue one she'd pinched from him years ago, a little faded now. A deep, deep need to be there beside her.

He flicked on the light so she could see his hands. 'I didn't wake you, did I?'

'At nine-thirty? Please. I don't go to bed until at least nine-forty.' She peered at the screen, her smile dipping. 'Why are you in your car? Has something happened?'

'Yeah, I found Frankie. It's over.'

She briefly closed her eyes. 'God, what a relief. How'd you find her?'

'Long story.' Their hiatus meant they'd been avoiding evening visits, but it didn't have to stay that way. He could be on that couch in fifteen minutes, in her bed, in her arms. 'I could come over, if you like. Tell you in person.'

'Yeah, that'd be nice.' She hesitated. 'But I should warn you, I've got company.'

Probably one of her older sisters. Kat's family had always been frequent visitors, but since the pregnancy her sisters had been on a roster. Always wise to know what he was getting into. He liked all three women, but his status as potential not-ex-husband for

Kat was currently under very vocal review. 'Multiple sisters, or just one?'

'Just Georgie.' She hesitated, then added, 'Plus Jarrah.'

Aware his smile had turned into a grimace, but unable to control it. Jarrah sitting across the table from Kat, being relaxed and charming and definitely thinking about the heat of her soft body. Disturbingly easy to imagine them as a couple: the shared passions and backgrounds, the joys of a relationship unburdened by sorrow. If Caleb asked, Kat would tell him about her feelings for the man. Which he must never, never do.

'You've got a full house,' he said. 'How about Friday? I'll cook.'

'You're on.' She crossed her arms over her chest as though holding him to her: *I love you*. A kick to his heart every time; years thinking he'd never see her sign it again.

'Love you, too.'

He ended the call and stayed sitting, not quite able to take the next step. He owed Frankie nothing. She was a lying, manipulative criminal who'd hurt Kat to save herself.

Who'd risked everything to save him.

Had held him up in his lowest moment and coaxed him from his pain.

He banged his head against the seat, each thump a little harder. Do it. He grabbed the phone and typed.

—Docs are in a deposit box. Know where key is. Written confirmation you'll leave Frankie and me alone when you've got it

Imogen's reply came so quickly, she must have been holding her phone.

—*Where?*

—Confirmation we're out. Make it good in case I have to show it to the media or your bosses

The next text took a long time to arrive.

—*I, Senior Constable Imogen Blain of the Australian Federal Police, confirm that Caleb Zelic and Francesca Reynolds will have no further questions to answer from me upon receipt of the safety deposit key.*

The phone vibrated again.

–Address

—Have to take you there. Logistics involved

—*I'm not in Melb. Stop stalling or I'll talk to homicide*

How the hell could she not be in Melbourne? In the middle of some dodgy case, her colleague's face shot off, and she'd popped out of town. God, he just wanted this to be over.

—Not stalling, there's a child involved. Threats won't make me change my mind

Another long wait and the phone buzzed again.

—*Back early am. Will txt. DO NOT FUCK ME AROUND*

He turned off the phone. The delay was hard, but worked in his favour. Frankie probably wouldn't even argue with him and Imogen if Tilda was awake; a protectiveness to her with the girl he'd never seen before. And he was the arsehole who was going to use it against her.

# 12.

He kept his appointment at Alberto's, arriving gritty-eyed and shivering before dawn, regretting his choice of a light cotton jacket and jeans. Sleep had been slow to come despite the long run he'd done after leaving Frankie. He'd gone for another this morning. Slipping into old habits – have to watch that.

He grabbed the box of CCTV cameras from the back seat and headed through the grey light to the kitchen. He'd put his restless night to good use by looking through everything Alberto had sent about the sabotage: four misdelivered catering orders and the cancelled electricity account. Small acts that had packed a hefty financial punch, all done in the past month via Alberto's security-free computer system. As far as suspects went, it was anyone in the world with internet.

The kitchen was ablaze with light. Alberto and his grandson, Nick, were hard at work cooking arancini. A matched pair with their lean builds and darting movements, the only difference Nick's full head of wavy brown hair instead of Alberto's gleaming scalp. They signed as they dropped rice balls into the oil, eighteen-year-old Nick holding forth on his footy playing and likely promotion to the A-team, Alberto offering encouragement.

Caleb shifted the box under one arm and went in. The room was warm and smelled like deep-fried happiness. Nick gave him the usual smile and wave, but Alberto's genial expression dropped to reveal relief. Caleb dumped the box on the counter to free his hands. 'Another bad delivery?' Hard to see how: Sammi had already emailed to say she'd locked the system up tight.

'Nothing like that – the café. Go and see. My cousin's going to fix it today, but I can't bear looking it.'

That explained the closed kitchen hatch. The catering side of the business brought in the money, but the café was Alberto's pride and joy: a hub for the Deaf community and a place for friends and family to gather. An attack on it would be a blow to his heart.

Caleb went down the short corridor and switched on the lights. Age-softened bricks and a high arched ceiling, a casual array of armchairs, sofas and tables. The two large windows facing the street were a cobweb of crystals, their panes sagging into the room. Laminated glass. Breaking that had taken some force, smashing at it over and over until the film gave way and the glass split and fractured. Unease lapped his spine. Alberto was right, this was nothing like the previous events – this was an act of violence. The first act was rarely the last, rarely the worst.

He smoothed his expression and returned to the kitchen. Nick and Alberto were scooping arancini from the oil and laying them on wire coolers.

'Anyone see anything?' Caleb asked.

Alberto set down his ladle. 'No. The alarm went off around midnight, but no one was here when I arrived. The cops say they'll do a doorknock today, so maybe they're taking the sabotage seriously now.' His face showed no hope.

'You got that list for me?' Caleb asked. 'People with a possible grudge?'

'There's no one.'

Nick's head lifted sharply.

Caleb kept his eyes on Alberto. 'Keep thinking. I'll need to talk to your staff, too. When are they in?'

'Soon, but it won't be any of them.'

'Just to rule them out.'

'I'm not kidding myself. This place goes under, everyone's out of work. You know how hard it is for us in the job market.'

Not just the market, but often the jobs themselves. Caleb had hated every minute working at the insurance companies where he'd begun his investigative career. Constant battles about phones and group meetings, co-workers' irritated sighs. Agreeing to go into business with Frankie had been one of the easiest decisions of his life.

'Keep thinking,' he told Alberto, and went to set up the CCTV.

It was reasonably quick work, even stopping along the way to talk to the non-family staff members as they arrived. All three looked stunned at the vandalism. They gave alibis he'd be checking, but he couldn't see any of them being behind the incidents.

By the time he'd finished, the kitchen was busy with cooking and outraged conversation, Alberto making a good show of looking unconcerned. Nick was on clean-up duty, emptying the bins. Caleb said his goodbyes and gratefully took the bag of arancini Alberto handed him. He devoured them in the alley while he waited for Nick to appear with the rubbish. There was an earnestness to the teenager that reminded him of Ant – or what Ant used to be like.

Ant had been just north of Sydney when he'd last made a withdrawal from his rapidly dwindling bank account. A faint possibility he was heading for Queensland, the place of their one interstate holiday as kids. A great couple of weeks. Ant had befriended a stray dog on the first day and smuggled it into their shared tent against their father's orders; they'd spent the rest of the holiday denying everything as they clawed at their fleabites.

The kitchen door opened and Nick appeared, lugging three

plastic bags. A little start as he saw Caleb, then he heaved rubbish into the bin and wiped his hands on his pants. 'Hey. You need something?'

'Information. Who are you worried about?'

'What? No one.'

'I'll get it from the Deaf grapevine, so why don't you get in first with your version? Who's got a grudge against Alberto?'

Nick's eyes lowered. 'Dad.'

A man no one at Alberto's had ever mentioned. Which was unusual enough he should have noticed. Most topics were enthusiastically discussed by staff and customers alike: divorce, bad dates, bad haircuts.

'Why?' Caleb asked.

'Grandad thumped him in the cafe, told him to piss off.'

Caleb took that in. Despite Alberto's boxing background, he'd never given any hint of underlying violence. Then again, people could show very different masks when it suited them.

'What happened?'

'Dad was – He hit Mum sometimes. Grandad found out.'

'When was this?'

A shrug. 'About a year ago, I guess.' Affecting nonchalance, but the ache of the memory was held in his hunched shoulders.

'You got an address or phone number?'

'No.'

Which meant asking Alberto's daughter, Ilaria, a painfully shy woman who'd only recently started making direct eye contact with Caleb. Confronting enough to have that kind of conversation in spoken language, but sign stripped you bare; every thought and emotion exposed, with no chance of a discreetly averted gaze.

'Your mum's here afternoons, isn't she?'

'Don't talk to her about Dad!'

'I'll go easy. I promise.'

Nick gave him a look of undisguised misery and went quickly back inside, head bent.

Caleb headed for his car. Would a man wait a year to take revenge on someone? Revenge that would hurt his own family? People did far worse things to those they claimed to love, sometimes intentionally, sometimes out of sheer stupidity.

His phone buzzed as he was getting in the car: Imogen with her usual light touch.

—*Flinders st station 11. DO NOT FUCK WTH ME*

Three hours away. Frankie would be awake by now, probably scowling over her cereal while Tilda caught up on the latest financial news.

A strong impulse to go for another run to shake the heavy feeling in his chest. Possibly a cue to ring Henry Collins, his therapist. Definitely a cue. And one he would heed because he was a man who took responsibility for his mental wellbeing no matter how uncomfortable the process. Yep. Absolutely. No doubt about it at all.

He texted before he could reconsider.

—any chance of an extra session? Not urgent

The reply came almost immediately.

—*Vic Market in 20*

————————

The high, arching sheds of the Queen Victoria Market weren't too crowded yet – the restaurateurs finished with their shopping, tourists yet to come. Long rows of stalls were heaped with jewel-coloured fruit and vegetables; the mingled scents of pawpaw, mango, tomatoes. Henry Collins was sorting through a stack of rockmelons, lifting each one to his face and inhaling deeply before discarding it.

The Vic Market was a first, but he and Caleb had been meeting outdoors since their first stilted appointments in Henry's office four months ago. It worked surprisingly well despite the choreography needed to keep the communication flowing.

A melon appeared to have passed the sniff test. Henry placed it in his wicker basket and looked at Caleb. 'Tell me about the girl.'

'Is this professional behaviour, groping fruit while I reveal my angst?'

'As you're paying me a great deal of money for my professional services, I'd say by definition, yes. Tell me about the girl.'

'She's nine, seems bright. But it's got nothing to do with her, it's Frankie I'm feeling bad about.'

Henry pressed his nose to another rockmelon. The man had clearly been a labrador in a previous life: the same floppy gold hair and outward geniality, same ability to grip his prey in unyielding jaws. Caleb usually went home from their sessions feeling like his brain had been gently shaken loose. They'd been at it twenty minutes now and he already had a low-grade headache.

Henry rejected the rockmelon and headed for the tomatoes. A wash of warm colours from yellow to deep purple, each variety identified by a small wooden stake: Green Zebra, Black Krim, Shirley. That last one had to be named for somebody – *'Happy birthday, Shirley, this reminded me of you.'*

Shirley. He tested the shape in his mouth, pictured Maggie saying it. *'No! Don't tell anyone about Shirley. Please.'*

Henry was waiting with the basket slung over his arm. He'd gone for the Black Krims.

'Can you say "Shirley"?' Caleb asked him.

'Shirley.'

No, but maybe something like it. Shirner, Kirner, Turner?

'Say, "Don't tell anyone about Turner. Please."'

Henry obliged without comment, then turned to pay for his shopping. Almost, but not quite. Not that it mattered: Caleb had made his choice.

Henry faced him, smiling amiably. 'Finished with the intrigue? OK, tell me more about the girl.'

Not this again. 'There's nothing more to tell. I barely know her.'

'And yet you've spent the past twenty minutes avoiding saying her name and reverted to the combative behaviour you displayed in our early sessions.'

'So this *is* a session? Because it feels more like a grocery expedition.'

Henry stood with the loose-limbed patience of a teacher waiting for the Year Nine sex ed class to settle. Tedesco had promised the man was unshockable, and Henry had proved it by merely nodding when Caleb had finally revealed that he'd both killed a man and covered it up.

'Her name's Tilda,' Caleb said, 'I've been trying to pretend she doesn't exist, but she does and she's a sweet oddball. And seeing as her mother might be dying, I'm feeling like a bit of a prick for depriving her of her other parent.'

'There's a lot to un–'

'Please don't say unpack.'

'– unpack in that statement. Do you blame Tilda for her father's actions?'

'Of course not. It's not her fault he tried to kill me.'

'But somehow it's yours?'

So much pain because of him: brother lost, best mate murdered, Kat injured. A phrase slid into his head: 'He destroys both the blameless and the wicked.' Maybe a quote, maybe his brain presenting him with an inconvenient truth-bomb.

Henry's focus had shifted to something behind Caleb. 'Is it possible someone's following you?'

A few seconds to comprehend the words – fucking Imogen, she just couldn't wait. He didn't turn. 'Woman, mid-thirties?'

'No, a man. He's hiding behind a stall, keeps glancing at you.'

'Can you get a photo?'

Henry passed him the shopping basket and reached for his phone, lowered his hand. 'He took off.'

'Which way?'

'Towards the lane.'

Good Decisions didn't include following strange men down alleyways. People got hurt that way. Hit with iron bars and bundled into unmarked vans. An actual physical effort not to do it, leg muscles cramping.

'What'd he look like?' Caleb asked.

Henry beamed. 'You're not going to confront him?'

'No. Can you describe him?'

'He was wearing a blue cap. A baseball cap.'

'Big man? Muscly?'

'I didn't really get a good look. He was behind the stall.'

'Age?'

'Thirty?' A rising tone that instilled no confidence.

Possibly Frankie's shooter, possibly not, but almost certainly following Caleb to get to her. But how had the man known he was here?

'Did you tell anyone you were seeing me?' he asked Henry.

'No, Caleb, of course not.'

His phone. The bastard must have been tracking it. Listening to it, too – he'd run when Caleb had mentioned taking his photo. Which meant he'd heard the entire therapy session. For fuck's sake. Frankie had been right to be paranoid about the damn thing.

Frankie.

He'd used the phone near the motel last night. It wouldn't take long for the guy to check Caleb's movements and work out why his phone had been offline last night, see where he'd turned it on again. Start doorknocking.

Caleb shoved the shopping basket at Henry and ran.

# 13.

He left the car in a side street near the motel and climbed onto a dumpster to scale the back fence. A steep drop into the carpark behind the building. He landed hard on his feet, the shock jarring through him; wasn't getting over that again. Frankie's car was still there, along with five others.

Caleb took the stairs to Frankie's room at a run. No answer to his knock.

Frankie and Tilda lying hurt inside. Dying. Dead.

He hammered on the door, and it opened. Frankie scowled out at him. Back to her usual jeans and black T-shirt, her wet hair spiked. 'You want to knock a bit harder? I don't think all the neighbours heard you.'

He tried to catch his breath. 'You have to get out. A man was following me. Blue baseball cap, no other description. Don't know if he's your shooter, but I used my phone near here.'

Colour drained from her face. 'He here?'

'Don't know, but the rear carpark was clear a few seconds ago.'

'Check out the front. I'll take Tilda to the car.' She was already closing the door.

He took the service path along the side of the motel, then edged open the high wooden gate that led onto the street. A narrow, tree-lined road, autumn leaves banked against the parked cars. Nothing moving, but something snagged in his brain.

He scanned the street without trying to focus. There – a silver Holden parked a few houses down, no leaves against its tyres. A person just distinguishable in the driver's seat. Rounded head, maybe a baseball cap. Caleb backed away.

When he reached the motel carpark, Frankie had the engine running, hands on the wheel. She lowered the window as he approached. Tilda stared wide-eyed from the back seat. Dressed in crisp new jeans and a blue jumper two sizes too large. He gave her a smile she didn't return.

'One guy,' he told Frankie. 'Silver Holden, thirty to the right.'

She sat still, her eyes moving rapidly as she ran through possible escape plans. Hopefully she'd come up with something he hadn't. 'I'll draw him away in the car,' she finally said. 'You wait here with Tilda.'

And be responsible for Tilda? 'No. You stay, I'll drive.'

'He's after me. She'll be safer with you.' She held his eyes. 'Please, Cal.'

Shit, she was right. 'OK. Go.'

She said something to Tilda that had the girl scrambling from the car and coming to stand by his side. 'Fifteen minutes,' Frankie told him. 'Petrol station on Victoria.' She accelerated away.

He took Tilda to wait in the service path; sitting with their backs to the wall, the gate to the street firmly bolted. No cherubs or rosy-pink flamingos here, just raw bricks and pine palings, the cold leaching from the concrete into his jeans.

Acid bit his stomach. Frankie was a fast driver but it'd be difficult to shake someone in these tight streets. And even Henry Collins would find it hard to absolve Caleb if Tilda lost another family member because of him.

She shifted next to him, pulling her knees to her chin and hugging her legs, a pink tinge to her eyes as though she was trying not to cry.

'You OK?' he asked.

'I'm a bit worried.'

God; undone by honesty.

'It's all right, no one's going to hurt you. Or Frankie,' he added quickly as her mouth began to tremble. 'A man just wants something she's got. We'll go and meet her in a few minutes.'

It was a vague reassurance, but some of the strain left her face. 'Is he friends with the man Mum was cross with?'

He kept still. 'Not sure. Who was your mum cross with?'

'I'm not supposed to talk about her work.'

'So he works with her?'

Her mouth snapped shut, Frankie's genes showing clearly in her jutting jaw. OK, his usual interrogation techniques weren't going to work. Beginning with him using the word 'interrogation'.

But a game might, with the bonus of distracting her. 'Do you want to play a game while we wait?'

A small nod.

'How about Spy? You ask three questions about a real person, and the other player has to answer truthfully. Whoever discovers the most interesting thing, wins.'

'I haven't played that before.'

'I'll go first, so you can see how it's done. Have you ever heard of someone with a name like Turner or Kirner?'

Deep sympathy crossed her face. 'That's not a very good question.'

'I guess not. You've got a good chance of winning this. So, have you?'

'No.' She held up a forefinger to mark off his question.

'What's the most interesting thing you know about the man your mum was cross with? Just about him,' he said as she frowned, 'not about her work.'

A second finger joined her first one. 'He died.'

Right. That *was* interesting. Could she be talking about Martin Amon?

'When –' He stopped as she began to uncurl a third finger. 'This is just to clarify. It's still the second question.'

She mouthed 'clarify' and tucked her finger back in her fist.

'When did he die?'

She thought, then said, 'Friday.'

Not Amon then, but only a few days before the federal cop's death. 'OK,' he said, 'last question – what's his name?'

'I don't know. My turn.' Her eyes widened in anticipation. 'Can I see your hearing aids?'

He hesitated before smoothing back his hair. She leaned in, her face inches from his head. A feeling she was about to pull out a screwdriver and have a good poke around.

She finally sat back. 'Can you hear anything without them?'

'Not unless it's really loud.'

'How many –?' She paused. 'This is just to clarify.'

He held back a smile. 'Sure.'

'How many decibels?'

'About a hundred and ten.'

'Like a jackhammer?'

A remarkably accurate estimate. 'Yes. How do you know about decibels?'

'I read a lot.'

He bet she did; all those hours in the library after school. 'You've got one more question, but I think you've won anyway.'

'Does it take a really long time to make a sign name for someone?'

Nicely done: reminding him of his promise but not hassling him about it.

'Sometimes,' he said. 'But I'm pretty sure I'll come up with one for you soon.' He stood. 'I'll check the street. If it's clear, we'll go to Frankie.'

There was no sign of the silver Holden, no men, with or without baseball caps. He watched for a full minute then beckoned to Tilda. 'Let's go.'

The plane trees were russet against a deep blue sky, sunlight pushing back the morning chill. An unexpected touch as Tilda slipped her hand into his: warm and a little sticky. He looked down, but she was concentrating on the footpath, making sure she stepped on every leaf in her way. A flicker of something surprisingly like hope: if a career criminal like Maggie could raise a child like Tilda, he had to be able to make a halfway decent job of it.

Movement to his left. Someone lunging from behind a garden fence.

Caleb pushed Tilda out of the way as a stream of liquid fire hit his face. Eyes and mouth burning, lungs welded shut. Down on his knees, clawing at his skin. Small hands gripped his arm. Tilda. Slipping, wrenched away. He threw himself forward and grabbed a thin limb. Holding on tight, eyelids fused. More spray. Air and face igniting. On all fours, coughing and retching. A high sound ripped the edges of his hearing. He cracked open his eyes: fractured colour and light, someone moving towards the road, a car.

Get to them. Go. Crawling across concrete and grass, breath scouring his throat. At the car. Hands out, touching a hub cap, door, handle. Fumbling for it, lifting. A lurch and it tore from his hand. Falling forward. Onto the road.

Gone.

# 14.

He found his way to the petrol station, stumbling, eyes streaming, through the streets. Frankie ran to him as soon as he rounded the corner, looking past him, her face a white blur. She grabbed his arm, speaking quickly, shaking him.

'She's gone,' he said through thick lips. 'I'm sorry. I'm so sorry.'

———

He washed his face in the servo's bathroom. Hearing aids out, tears and muck oozing from his eyes. Frankie came in and out of the room, checking her messages on the shop's payphone, then reappearing to ask more questions. She finally paused next to him, shifting restlessly while she waited for him to look at her.

He wiped his eyes on his T-shirt and blinked rapidly. 'What?'

'Still no message. Why haven't they called?'

'It's too soon.'

The kidnappers would want her to sit with her fears first, live through each and every imagined horror. From what he'd been able to glean, she'd managed to throw the tail at the first set of lights. The guy must have doubled back almost immediately and lain in wait for him and Tilda. Or, even more likely, there'd been more than one person, the car just a decoy. Caleb had been oblivious. Just wandered past, congratulating himself for having managed to keep a child safe and relatively happy for ten minutes.

'You going to call the cops?' he asked Frankie.

'No, they'll … and …'

He wiped his eyes again. They were beginning to clear, but tears still fogged his vision. 'Sorry, what?'

'No cops,' she signed. 'People give paper.'

He tried to work it out. 'When the kidnappers call you'll give them the documents?'

She nodded. 'You definitely wouldn't recognise the guy?'

They'd been through this several times. Neither of them had got close enough for an ID, but Frankie seemed unwilling to accept it.

'No,' he said. 'I just caught the movement. Maybe a hoodie or balaclava.'

She was shifting from foot to foot, her eyes locked on him: desperate to know something, but too afraid to ask.

'He didn't hurt her,' Caleb said. 'He won't. He obviously had orders not to kill me – used pepper spray to get me down, didn't knife me when I held on to her.' He didn't say the rest, that the kidnappers probably didn't want the attention a dead body would bring. That he was pretty sure Tilda had been screaming.

Frankie went to say more, then left the bathroom without speaking.

He retrieved his aids from the top of the hand dryer and wiped them carefully with toilet paper: if the spray had ruined their circuitry, he'd be in trouble. They were new ones, top-dollar bluetooth models that were slightly better at eliminating background noise than his previous pair but even more delicate. He put them in and clapped; heard the distant *pop*. Tilda would have followed his actions with interest, asked about the relative benefits of bluetooth sensitivity over old-school robustness.

He should have held on to her.

He should have moved faster.

He should have accepted his fate and not involved Frankie.

When he finally left the bathroom, the servo was empty. Small and over-lit, with shelves of brightly coloured junk food. A cashier appeared from behind a closed door and stood watching. Caleb nodded to him, but the man didn't move. Understandable – he must have looked pretty dubious when he'd staggered inside. Was still looking pretty dubious according to the bathroom's fly-specked mirror.

Frankie was at the back of the room, sitting at the lone plastic table by the self-serve coffee machine, a notepad, pens and coins laid out in neat rows. Trying to wrest some form of control from her panic.

She started speaking as soon as he sat. '... calls...to my...'

He squinted. 'Sorry what?'

Her mouth tightened with annoyance at having to repeat herself. An expression he'd seen almost daily since he was five. Never before on Frankie's face.

'Just a bit slower,' he said. 'It's still blurry.'

'I've got Maggie's calls and emails forwarded to me. What haven't I thought of?'

'Nothing. We just have to wait.'

She clenched her hands in her lap to stop them shaking, but her leg was still jiggling. He went to touch her, then stopped; Frankie wasn't a tactile person, made even less so by stress.

'Any update on Maggie?' he asked.

'Unchanged.'

Was it better or worse that Maggie didn't know?

'It's money laundering,' Frankie said.

'What?'

'This. Maggie's laundering money. The docs are her financial records. Or part of them – she keeps everything separate, lots of checks and balances.'

Not surprising Frankie had kept that information from him. Or that she'd tried to sell the documents. Information like that would fetch a nice bit of cash from the right buyers: those who wanted it kept secret, and those who wanted to expose it. Blackmail, kickbacks, the possibility of following the trail to steal the money.

'She keeps hardcopies?' he asked.

'Yeah. Went offline a while back because the feds were sniffing around. But then she had a break-in, things moved, like the house had been searched. She freaked out, got everything into a deposit box that day.' Frankie's expression fractured. 'She gave me the key because she didn't want it around Tilda.'

She stood and returned to the payphone. A quick call, no words spoken, the lack of information obvious in her rigid stance. Her answering service again: no message from the kidnappers. She stayed standing when she'd hung up, looking around the servo as though searching for inspiration. 'OK,' she said, 'I need a good place for the exchange. What d'you reckon – a park? Is there one near here?'

'It's OK,' he said slowly. 'They'll ring and we'll do what they say. We'll have her back soon.'

Her face was skull-like. 'OK? I worked these cases, I saw the fucking fallout. Do you know how often kidnap victims are killed during a handover? Before a handover? Most are dead within hours.'

Oh God, what had he done?

He stood. 'Then we go to the cops. They can do door-to-doors, check traffic cameras.'

'We can't. Maggie works with some seriously dodgy people, some of them in law enforcement. We go to the cops, the kidnappers'll hear about it. Jesus, for all we know your mate Imogen is behind it.'

Imogen. He had to tell Frankie.

He took a slow breath. 'I told Imogen I knew where you were. That I could get the key. I know it's in one of your boots.'

She jerked back. 'What?'

'Imogen wouldn't have taken Tilda,' he said quickly. 'She knew I was going to help her – we're meant to be meeting at eleven.'

Her cheeks flushed. 'And what about her mates? What about the leaking fucking sieve that's the police force? What about every crim in Melbourne who wants a piece of Maggie's business? All Imogen had to do was mention it to the wrong person and they would've come sprinting to my door. And you.' Her mouth twisted. 'You fucking opened it and let them in.'

# 15.

He waited across the road from the servo. Standing outside a fried-chicken shop, face stinging, eyeballs rolled in ash, watching the petrol station's digital clock. Fourteen minutes. One more and he'd go back in. A growing fear they shouldn't be waiting for a phone call, that they needed to take control of the situation and hunt for Tilda. Hard to see Frankie letting him help, every spitting word of her anger deserved, but he had to find a way. Couldn't live with a child's death on his hands. Anything would be better than that: going to prison, leaving his own child fatherless. And Kat would agree.

*'Most are dead within hours.'*

The clock numbers flicked over: 10.30.

She'd been gone fifty-one minutes.

He waited for a break in the traffic and jogged quickly across the road.

The small servo was crowded. People queuing to pay for petrol, teenage boys browsing the snacks, jostling and calling out to each other. Frankie was barging through them towards the door. She pulled up short when she saw him.

A surge of hope. 'They called?'

'No, I'm going to look for her.' She pushed past him and walked outside.

He ran after her, following as she strode around the corner towards her car. 'Let me help,' he said. 'We work well together, you know that. We'll have more chance of finding her if we do it together.'

She was pulling out her keys, walking to the driver's side.

'You can trust me,' he said. 'I couldn't live with myself if she – I don't care about Imogen, or going to jail. Just let me help get Tilda back. Please.'

Frankie opened the door and looked at him, her face hard. This was it. She was going to tell him to piss off, then get in her car and drive away.

'You're fuck-all use to me if you get arrested,' she said. 'Spin Imogen some story to keep her away.'

———————

He retrieved his phone from his car and brought it back to Frankie's, along with the discarded silver foil and Maggie's laptop. As he climbed in, Frankie's eyes went to the computer. 'What's that for?'

'We'll need it to contact Guy Fawkes if I work out the video.' He shook his head as she went to protest. 'It's not about getting Imogen off my back, it's about information.'

He texted Imogen, saying Frankie had left but he was on her tail. It wouldn't win the cop over, but it should put her on hold for a few hours at least.

'OK to keep the phone?' he asked Frankie, not quite holding his breath.

'Despite your fuckhead behaviour with it, yes. It'd be good to have it. Just keep it wrapped and only use it on the move.'

His breathing eased. Gone were the days he'd go hours without checking messages. Texts were forwarded to his email now, and his phone always near him. At night, he hooked it up to his vibrating alarm so Kat's texts would wake him.

Frankie grabbed her bag from the back seat. Being active seemed to have calmed her a little, but her movements still had a jerky quality; fumbling with the zips on the backpack, fingers slipping. She eventually tugged a camera from an inside pocket and shoved it at him. An expensive piece of equipment, with multiple settings and a large touchscreen to view photos.

'What's this for?' he asked.

'Maggie's records. Didn't want to upload them.' She pulled a packet of chewing gum from the ashtray and fished out a small memory card.

He inserted the card and swiped through a few photos, then went back to the beginning and zoomed in on each one. A show of trust, letting him see them. Pages of spreadsheets. No names, but a row of recurring digits down the left-hand side that had to be client numbers. Around thirty of them. Transactions showed dates and amounts: money going in and money going out. Lots of zeros after the dollar signs. He did some quick mental calculations, stopped when he got to ten million.

He looked at Frankie. 'This would make a lot of people very nervous.'

'Yeah, so don't go spreading it around you've seen it. Tilda's safer if no one on that list knows we've got it. So are we. We hand the originals to the kidnappers and pretend none of it ever happened, OK?'

No argument from him; the thought of thirty well-connected criminals knowing he'd seen their dirty laundry wasn't a comfortable one.

'Sure,' he said. 'What now?'

'Odds are, the same people behind the kidnapping sent the shooter after me. Killed Amon. And if they know about these records, it's either a client on that list or someone connected to them. But I've got no idea how to ID anyone.' She paused. 'Any bright ideas welcome.'

He examined the first page. She was right – those account numbers couldn't be turned into names without more information. Smart move on Maggie's part. And an explanation as to why she'd risked entrusting Frankie with the key.

'Any chance of us finding a master list?'

'No. It's probably in another damn vault.'

So approach it from a different angle. Laundering that much money would involve a lot of employees. People to pass cash through casinos and small businesses; bookkeepers to create false invoices; lawyers to fudge records.

Lawyers.

The Rhys Delaney mentioned in Maggie's texts was a lawyer.

—*Rhys Delaney on for today*

A man with no police record who might have been meeting with Maggie the day she was attacked.

Frankie was watching him, not moving. 'You've got something?'

'Possible employee.'

# 16.

Rhys Delany's office was a couple of blocks back from the bay in Williamstown. A bit of whimsy in the brick turrets and porthole-like windows, but everything else was businesslike. The doors opened directly on to a reception area carpeted in reassuring grey, a hallway of offices tucked to either side, discreet open-plan desks to the rear. The receptionist nodded hello from behind a high timber counter and continued her phone conversation: a serious exchange that involved a lot of frowning and consulting of her computer. Frankie gave it ten seconds, then went to the far end of the waiting area and unwrapped the phone; the second time she'd checked messages in the past twenty minutes.

The receptionist hung up and faced him. According to the plaque on the desk she was Mrs Marion Gillis: Office Manager. A fierce-looking woman around Frankie's age, with a blunt fringe and heavy-rimmed glasses. The wall calendar featuring a basket of ribboned kittens had to belong to a coworker. She gave Caleb a smile with no trace of warmth. 'Can I help you?'

'I hope so. My name's Caleb Zelic. My partner and I are after Rhys Delaney.'

'Do you want ...?' Her words were lost as she turned to the computer.

'Sorry, what?'

'Do you want...?' And back to the screen.

Did he want what? A coffee? A unicorn? People who looked at him when they spoke?

'Sorry, could you look at me when you speak? I'm deaf. I'm lip-reading.'

She spun back to him, mouth open. 'Oh, I'm so sorry. You poor thing, how terrible.'

Shit, a mourner. A very loud mourner. Her lamentations had drawn the attention of everyone in the room, including Frankie. His fault: he'd let himself be fooled by a stern facade, instead of taking into account the much greater significance of the kittens. He spoke softly in an effort to lower her volume. 'We're hoping to see Delaney now. Is he in?'

'You speak very well, you know. A little quietly, but just like a normal person.'

A meteor, a weapon, something to end this now. 'Is Delaney free?'

'I'll ask.' She picked up the phone and punched in the numbers. 'It must be so hard for you. Do you know about cochlear implants? My neighbour's cousin's son got –'

Caleb looked away until she'd lowered the receiver.

'You're in luck,' she said. 'Down the hallway to the last office. Do you need help?' She glanced at Frankie, who was coming towards them. 'Or is that your carer?'

He headed off at a semi-jog. Frankie caught up to him outside Delaney's office and went in without comment. Could always rely on her lack of sympathy, thank God.

Delaney was a damp-looking man with a bland face and a shirt two or three shades away from its original white. His handshake proved his sogginess. 'Please do sit. How can I help?' An easy read except for that sweaty upper lip. A temptation to grab a tissue and blot it.

Frankie shifted her chair so Caleb could see them both clearly. 'We're after information.'

She handed Delaney a business card. One of their old ones, their names on the front, along with the words 'fraud investigations'. Also with the word 'partners'. She'd been carrying that around a long time.

'Fraud?' Delaney swallowed. 'I don't understand. Are you police officers?'

'We work closely with the police,' Frankie pulled a notebook from her pocket and flipped to a new page. 'Tell me about Maggie Reynolds. How do you know her?'

Delaney's shoulders loosened, as though he'd been bracing himself for a different question. 'I'm sorry, I'm not familiar with that name. Can I help you with something else? Conveyancing? A contract?'

'Mr Delaney.' Frankie waited until the man's eyes met hers. 'We know.'

Delaney's gaze flicked to a timber-framed photo on his desk, angled to display a wife and young family. 'Nothing happened.'

'Explain what "nothing" means,' Caleb said. 'And maybe we won't have to talk to your boss.' He nodded at the photo. 'Or your wife.'

'Nothing. Really. Just, a woman approached me at a party last week. We talked, that's all.'

Maggie?

'What was her name?'

'Kw ... vo.'

Zero chance Caleb was going to get that. Frankie wrote something and tilted the pad for him to see: *Quinn Devereaux*.

'Describe her,' he told Delaney.

'Beautiful, really beautiful, with long black hair. Petite.'

Not a great description, but definitely not Maggie: she had the same rangy build as Frankie.

'Tell us everything,' Caleb said. 'What, when, where.'

'It was a fundraising ball for a charity. Game Goers. I do pro bono work for them.' He paused to see if he'd impressed them, went on quickly. 'Quinn just came up, started talking. After a while she suggested we go to her room for a drink. It wasn't until we were there that I realised she was a, you know.'

'Prostitute,' Frankie said.

Delaney looked hurt. 'Criminal. She wanted to know if I could set up shell companies to, um, filter money through.'

'Filter?' Frankie said. 'Is that a polite term for launder?'

'I didn't do it. I left once I realised what she was after. Never saw her again.'

—*Rhys Delaney on for today*

The message had been sent by someone with the initial D. Could be Devereaux.

Caleb leaned forward. 'We've seen the phone records. We know you met with Quinn yesterday.'

'No.' Delaney's tongue touched his moist upper lip, a darting movement like a small pink lizard. 'I mean, yes, we were meant to meet, but she rang and cancelled at the last minute.'

'Show me the call log.'

Delaney scrolled through his phone and thrust it at Caleb. Only one call between the pair, from Quinn to Delaney at noon yesterday. The lawyer had included Quinn's profile photo: a woman in her early thirties, with elvish features and long dark hair. Familiar in a distant way. The TV news, some scandal involving a public figure, the suggestion of favours traded for sex. A taint to the memory: a face Caleb associated with bad news.

He sent himself her number then looked through Delaney's photos. A man who used a profile picture for a woman he'd only just met had definitely kept the original shot. More than one, in this case: five clear photos of Quinn wearing a slinky midnight-blue dress, champagne glass in hand. Definitely familiar.

And the memory slotted into place – the hospital waiting room and the looping repeats of a news channel. It had been the second miscarriage; the dragging loss, the fear that this was their future.

Frankie was staring at him, obviously wondering why he was taking so long to check a few calls. He passed her the phone.

'Is Quinn OK?' Delaney asked as Frankie flicked through the photos. 'She's not hurt or anything, is she?'

A deviation from the expected script.

'Why do you ask?' Caleb said.

'She sounded sort of scared. And her phone keeps ringing out.' Delaney kept talking without waiting for an answer. 'You're not going to tell anyone, are you? My wife's just had a baby. I mean, I didn't actually do anything but this could kill my career.'

A strange desire to stomp on the man. Without answering him, Caleb stood and followed Frankie to the door, turned back as he reached it. 'Does the name Kirner mean anything to you? Or something similar?'

Delaney's face grew even damper as he tried to come up with an answer that would make them leave. 'I don't think so.'

Frankie waited until they were a few steps away before speaking. 'Just a mark. Quinn's the one we need. Did I notice a glimmer of recognition when you saw her?'

'Yeah, she was involved in a sex scandal a few years ago. A politician or judge. Someone with a great name, Lovecock maybe. Remember that?'

'No, but bless your somewhat creepy memory for faces. I don't suppose you can remember her surname, too? I'm betting it's not Devereaux.'

'No.' He looked around the corner into the reception area: Mrs Gillis was on the phone again. He speed-walked past her, pretended he couldn't see her waving.

# 17.

Outside, the sky was still clear, but a brisk wind was coming up from the bay, bringing with it the sting of salt and the smell of fish and chips. A few pedestrians were heading down the hill towards the beach-side shopping strip, chins tucked into their collars, foreheads leading.

Frankie tried Quinn's number as they got in the car and shook her head. 'Ringing out. We'll have to get her name from the news reports and track down her address.'

He checked messages as he rewrapped the phone. Nothing from Kat, three from Imogen.

—*What's happening?*

—*What's happening?*

—*What's happening?*

She was nothing if not consistent.

He texted back.

—Driving. Got a lead. Might be a while

A thought rose to the surface as Frankie started the engine. She wouldn't have registered the car in her name, but Imogen could use other ways to find it.

'You give the motel your car rego?' he asked.

'Jesus. How'd I not think of that?' Her forefinger tapped a rapid beat on the wheel. 'OK, I've got a mate near here who can help. We'll be able to use his computer, too.' She pulled onto the road without looking, and a horn sounded, loud enough for him to hear. A jolt as she slammed on the brakes. 'Any other basic safety measures I've forgotten?' she asked, waiting for a large red truck to pass.

He gave his seatbelt a surreptitious tug. 'No.'

Frankie managed a U-turn without T-boning anyone and headed away from the water, tapped his arm after a couple of blocks. 'Who's the person you asked Delaney about? Kirner?'

'Maggie's video. I'm trying out names.'

'How the hell d'you get from Shona to Kirner? They don't sound anything alike.'

'Look, not sound.'

She touched a hand to her lips, tried the words. 'Jesus, no wonder you're so shit at names. Is that why you kept calling me Spiky when we first met?'

He looked at her. 'No.'

---

Frankie's mate ran a used-car dealership in an industrial estate on the city's edge. A small, rubbish-strewn lot hunkered in the shadow of the West Gate Bridge. There was a heaviness to the high curving span from this vantage point, the claustrophobic sensation of tonnes of concrete and steel pressing down. Impossible not to think of the bridge's history, the half-built structure's sudden collapse, the thirty-five workers crushed to death beneath its weight. Frankie glanced up at it and shivered as they headed into the yard. The vehicles were all three or four years old, with the suspiciously glossy hue of recent paint jobs.

A man appeared from the prefab office and stood on its step: stringy hair, body, tie. He sighed heavily when he saw Frankie.

'Close friend?' Caleb asked.

'Nicked him a few times.' She thought about it. 'Didn't nick him a few times. He'll lend us something without any paperwork.'

Caleb had missed Frankie's loyal network of ex-coppers and ex-cons, bored public servants and IT workers. His band of go-to people was growing steadily but would never rival hers.

The dealer watched them approach, probing his gums with a forefinger. Frankie stopped a little further from him than Caleb usually liked. He went to move closer, stepped quickly back as he caught a whiff of stale breath and body.

'Ferret, my man,' Frankie said. 'This is a mate of mine, now a mate of yours. He'd like to use your computer while I decide which of your completely legal cars you'd like to lend us.'

Ferret investigated his mouth a bit more, then removed his hand. 'Yeahorright.'

Caleb left Frankie to kick tyres and braved Ferret's office. The man wasn't a hoarder, at least; only a desk and computer, along with a dozen mouldering takeaway containers. Caleb blew the crumbs from the keyboard and typed using as few fingers as possible. New reports on the sex scandal referred to Quinn as 'high class escort, Quinn Renbarger'. A slight disappointment that the judge's name was Lovelay not Lovecock. No charges had been laid, but the judge had been photographed going into a hotel with Quinn soon after he'd dismissed charges against an illegal-brothel owner. An attractive, if disparate, couple: Quinn with her fine good looks and forthright stare, Angus Lovelay twenty years older but fit and tanned, turning a besotted gaze towards her.

None of the usual sites came up with contact information for either Quinn Renbarger or Quinn Devereaux, but a May Renbarger lived outside Burton, a small town two hours north-west of Melbourne. On the electoral roll there for the past thirty-two years. Likely a relative, with that unusual surname, but also an unknown quantity. If he and Frankie drove out there, they risked wasting valuable time. If they rang May, they risked alerting Quinn.

The office lights flashed. Frankie, clutching an off-brand Tupperware container and jiggling a set of keys. 'Got her?'

'No, but a possible rel, right age for her mum. Two-hour drive.'

'Shit.' The keys jiggled faster. 'Guess we should go?' An upwards inflection instead of her usual even tone – had he ever caught indecision in her voice before?

He stood. 'Yeah.'

There was no sign of Ferret outside, but Frankie led the way towards a bulky black Ford Territory, ducking her head against the wind.

Caleb gestured to her plastic container. 'Ferret give you lunch?'

It took her a long time to answer. 'A gun.'

He stopped walking. Frankie never carried a gun; hated them. 'What the fuck?'

She faced him. 'I know how to handle one.'

'That's not my problem, and you know it. If you go waving a gun around, people are going to start shooting.'

'Feel free to bail.' She stood still, a glimpse of Tilda in the set of her mouth. Behind her, the long line of the West Gate Freeway was feeding trucks into the city.

Make Good Decisions.

Tilda had been gone two and a half hours. One hundred and fifty minutes.

He held his hand out for the keys. 'I'm driving.'

# 18.

He parked behind a battered ute and got out. A bare dirt yard and greying weatherboard, a musty tinge to the air. Two rows of metal cages ran down the driveway, head height and filled with birds – turkeys, geese, ducks, chickens – the concrete floors layered with shit and matted straw. The house next to them was sagging, its veranda supported on one side by a broom propped on three bricks. Smoke leaked from the chimney's crumbling mortar.

'Christ,' Frankie said. 'A long way from drinking champagne and rooting judges to here.'

'A lot further from here to champagne and judges.'

She gave him a look. 'Quite the philosopher, aren't you?'

She'd fidgeted the entire journey, adjusting the air vents and winding down her window, unwrapping the phone every half-hour to check messages. He'd stopped telling her it was too early to hear from the kidnappers.

A woman opened the door to Frankie's knock. Somewhere between forty and seventy, no hint of Quinn in her sunken cheeks and eyes. The odours of the house seeped out: damp walls and green firewood, ancient meals. The kind of poverty that ran through families like a dominant gene. His father used to speak of houses like this as a warning: work hard, or all my toil will have come to nothing.

'Mrs Renbarger?' Caleb said.

'Who's asking?'

'We're not journos.' He held out a business card.

She didn't look at it. 'Didn't ask what you weren't.'

'We're looking for Quinn. We're friends of her employer.'

May Renbarger went to close the door, and Frankie stuck out her foot. A short impasse, then they both looked at something behind him.

Quinn was coming from the cages towards them, shovel in hand, dark hair tied in a loose bun. No other car on the property: she'd either got a lift or hitchhiked. She called something, and May retreated inside, shutting the door.

Frankie moved down the steps, setting herself up to lead the questioning. That wasn't going to work – Frankie could make people reveal secrets they'd hidden from themselves, but she was too on edge to interview anyone.

He joined her in the yard. 'I'll lead.'

'I'll fill you in later if you're too tired to follow both of us.'

'I'm fine, you're not. Let me do it.'

A look of jaw-clenched mutiny. 'She's my niece, not yours.'

'Exactly.'

Frankie held his stare, then took a half-step back.

Quinn stopped just out of reach, hand tight on the shovel. The ethereal good looks from Delaney's photos but none of the welcoming expression; dark eyes narrowed, head thrust slightly forward. A silk shirt showed beneath her ancient oilskin, a long streak of bird shit down her tailored black pants. She flushed as she caught his glance, raised her chin. 'What do you want?' Even speech, despite her obvious tension.

'We're here about Maggie. I'm Caleb. This is Maggie's sister, Frankie.'

'Never heard her mention a sister.' She laughed at Frankie's scowl and loosened her grip on the shovel. 'Oh yeah, I can see it now.'

Caleb tried unsuccessfully not to smile. 'What are you doing here, Quinn?'

'Reckon that's my question.'

Fair point, circle back. 'Someone kidnapped Maggie's daughter this morning. We're trying to find her.'

Her mouth hung open. 'Tilda? You're kidding.'

'You know Tilda?'

'Sure, everyone does. Weird kid. Sweet, though. Who took her?'

*Everyone.* His hopes of narrowing the pool of suspects vanished. Beside him, Frankie's head lowered.

'We don't know. We're hoping you can help.'

'Fuck, I don't know anything about it. I've been here since last night. Ask Mum.'

Which meant she'd left Melbourne only hours after Maggie was attacked. No change of clothes, no car, no phone. To a house she'd obviously worked very hard to get away from.

'You heard Maggie was hurt?' Caleb asked.

'Yeah. Rang her house and a cop picked up. And I don't know anything about that either.'

Frankie shifted, but he kept his eyes on Quinn. 'Why'd you cancel your date with Rhys Delaney?'

'Who?'

'Your honeytrap. The man who took quite a few photos of you at a party last week.'

Quinn's breathing hitched. She covered it with a cough, gave him a heavy-lidded smile. 'I know a lot of men, some of them like taking photos. Sorry I can't help. You can see yourselves off.' She was turning away.

He caught Frankie's eye and signed, 'Do it, then go.'

'You'd better go fix your makeup,' Frankie told Quinn. 'I'll be ringing my good mate Bobby James from *The Daily Dirt* when we leave. He'll make out you've spilled secrets on all of Maggie's clients, whether you've fucked them or not. It'll make great TV.'

Quinn had frozen in place, fear hollowing her face.

'Let's go,' Frankie told him and strode towards the car.

He went to follow.

Quinn dropped the shovel and grabbed his arm. 'You can't let her. Please. They'll kill me.'

'It's her niece. She's desperate.'

Car exhaust blew towards him, mingling with the rank scent of the birds. Frankie had timed it perfectly to send Quinn into panic.

'Jesus, all right.' Quinn released him. 'Just tell her to stop gunning the engine, will you? It'll freak Mum out.'

He gestured at Frankie, who turned off the engine.

Quinn reached into her back pocket for a packet of cigarettes. Her hand wasn't shaking, but it took her a few attempts to get one going. 'Two years off the damn things and I'm sucking them down like I never stopped.' She took a long drag and blew the smoke away from him. Still oscillating between trying to brash it out and charm him. Did she ever relax her guard?

'Who are you scared of?' he asked. 'Delaney?'

'That mope? He'd only be dangerous if you had a sweat allergy.'

'Then what happened at the party?'

'Nothing.'

'Quinn, you jumped when I mentioned it.'

'Well yeah, that'd be the big bloke who was following me there.' She spoke quickly, as though desperate to get all the words out now she'd decided to talk. 'Thought he was just a standard creep, then yesterday, Maggie rang. Must've been just before she was hurt. She was scared, never heard her like that before, said someone was cleaning house and I should get out of town.'

He stood still. There was a chance that didn't mean what he thought it did. 'What did she mean by "cleaning house"?'

'That someone's getting rid of evidence – and people. I was in the city when she called, so I went home to get my stuff. My flat's right on the tramline, you know, just before the stop. And as we're going past I see the same guy from the party. He's in my place, coming out of the dunny. Needless to say I shat myself. I stayed on the tram and jumped on the bus here.' She looked at the cages, her mouth creasing as though she'd tasted something bitter. 'Dunno what I was thinking.'

'What'd he look like?'

'Blond, I think. Big, like muscly big. Bit taller than you, maybe six three.'

Possibly Frankie's shooter again. Good to know, but it didn't get them very far.

'Does Maggie know someone called Kirner? Or a name like it.'

'Dunno, Maggie's not much of a sharer.' She looked towards their car. 'Must be nice working with the friendly sister.'

Fuck. No names, no leads, just a two-hour drive to find out someone had been after Maggie and her employees.

'What else can you tell me?'

'That's it. The full friggen extent of my knowledge.' A hard suck on the cigarette, cheeks drawing in. 'Do you think Tilda'll be OK? Did that big bloke take her?'

*'Most are dead within hours.'*

'I don't know.'

'Jesus. Tell me when you know something, yeah? I might sleep again. You reckon he'll come here? How'd you find me?'

'I'm good with faces, recognised you from Delaney's photos.'

'Recognised me? How?'

'The sex scandal with Lovelay.'

She flinched as though struck. A glimpse of unguarded emotion, no bravado or charm, just pain. 'Don't call it that. It was a relationship, not a scandal.'

'Sorry, didn't realise.'

'You and everyone else. Angus was the best thing that ever

happened to me, a real sweetheart. But the world took one look at me and decided it had to be dirty.' Her gaze travelled across the yard and came to rest on the listless house. 'Should've known better – the past bloody sticks to you, doesn't it?'

# 19.

Frankie backed out of the driveway in a spray of gravel, startling the birds so they bashed around their metal cages. She straightened the car and headed towards the town centre, going too fast for the dirt road. The vehicle had a lot more grunt than Frankie should be in charge of right now – or any time. She glanced at him. 'Talk.'

No, she was going to ask questions if he spoke now. Trying to lip-read Frankie while she drove was a white-knuckle ride at the best of times; in her current mood it'd be terrifying.

'Wait until you park,' he said.

She turned to him; a bend coming up, large red gums lining the road. 'Now.'

He clutched the edge of his seat. 'OK. Just, look at the road, will you.' He waited until she was facing forward and went through the conversation, trying to remove Quinn's fear from the retelling. He'd left his number with her, but why would she use it? Even if she decided she knew more, Quinn had no reason to trust him.

'Cleaning house?' Frankie said when he'd finished, eyes bleak.

'The muscle man's a good link,' he said quickly. 'The party was black-tie, so there'll be photos. If you spot him we can do a reverse image search.'

'I can't ID him.'

'You probably remember more than you think. When you see –'

'It was dark, all I got was his shape, then he started shooting.'

Damn. They just couldn't catch a break.

She took the corner into Burton's main street without slowing down, scattering a flock of pigeons. A pockmarked sign declared the place a Tidy Town finalist, population 520. Both statements seemed historic. Ten or twelve weatherboard shops, a two-storey pub, a few parked cars. The only people out were three teenage boys lounging by a milk bar that advertised smokes, cup-of-cinos and internet. Frankie pulled abruptly into the kerb beside them.

Caleb eased his grip on the seat. 'Coffee?'

'Phone. Service keeps dropping out.' She climbed from the car, the boys watching with bland interest as she headed for a weathered public phone.

Caleb's eye went to the newspaper banners on the shopfront. A photo of a slickly dressed young man in handcuffs, the headline 'Jacklin Pleads Innocent'. John Jacklin, the almost-definitely guilty property developer Tilda and Frankie had been watching on the news. The stirrings of an idea: a small-business owner standing in the way of a major development would irritate a lot of people. Be interesting to see if anyone had recently bought out Alberto's neighbours.

Caleb sat up as Frankie slammed down the phone and strode towards the shop. The boys moved from her path as though repelled. He slid quickly from the car and caught up to her inside the door. A large space with a few rows of badly stocked shelves, and a bain-marie with sweating chips and pies. Down the back, a hulking grey computer sat next to the plastic-covered magazines.

Frankie headed straight for the counter. The shop owner was watching TV with the kind of focus that suggested he had a lot riding on the three o'clock at Caulfield. An impressive brow and gut, thin lips. He glanced at her and returned to the races. 'Food's what you see. You want soy milk or vegan crap, you're outta luck.'

'Picked us for tourists,' Frankie said. 'Smart man. Your pay-phone's dead.'

'Not mine.'

'Good to clear that up. Your computer work? Got internet?'

He didn't look at her. 'Whaddaya reckon? Be a bit of a dickhead havin' it if it didn't.'

She tilted her head. 'So does it?'

Caleb stepped in front of her. 'We'll take an hour.'

Frankie went straight to her emails: a handful of unread messages, including audio files from her answering service; nothing with Tilda's name in the subject line. She listened to each one for a few seconds before moving on. When she'd gone through them all she turned to him, the tendons in her neck tight cords. 'Something's wrong. They should have contacted me by now.'

Five hours. Was this how it was going to be? Never knowing what had happened, just hoping a little less each day, heart shrivelling in his chest?

'There's no rule book.' He nodded towards the computer. 'Check the party photos. We can make a shortlist of anyone who fits muscle man's description, show them to Quinn. What'd Delaney say the name of the charity was?'

'Game Goers. Football players for mental health.'

No wonder the solicitor had been keen to go. He'd probably spent the entire night flitting between the footy players, Quinn, and the WAGs.

Frankie found the charity's website and clicked through the photos: a lot of white teeth and fake tan, a lot of blond men who looked like weightlifters. 'Jesus,' she said. 'Like one of those nightmares where everyone looks the same.'

'Check for Quinn, see if he's in the background.'

The ball had been held in a large room with columns of smoked black glass and gold fittings. People in sequinned dresses and sleek tuxedos smiled for the camera. Delaney and Quinn appeared a few times in the background, but the photographers had been focused on the celebrities, not damp-looking solicitors.

Frankie sat back. 'It's pointless. He's just muscle, anyway. We need to find out who Imogen was investigating with Transis.'

'Got any mates in the feds?'

'No, but we need the stuff that's left out of official reports, anyway. Who they bribed and who they let go, informants.' She screwed up her face. 'You need to meet with Imogen.'

'We can't trust her.'

'No. We'll text when we're nearly there, give her short notice. A shopping centre, maybe. Highpoint's on the way back.'

'I mean, we can't trust her answers. We've got no idea what she's involved in.'

'We can judge the quality of the information once we've got it.' She stood. 'I'll get coffees.'

'Make sure he doesn't spit in them.' Caleb did a quick check of his messages. Returned emails confirming the three staff members' alibis. And a redirected text from Kat, the usual heart flutter of fear/happiness as he opened it.

—*Hope you're OK after all the stress. Working on something interesting. Might show you Fri xx*

Kat on a creative roll was something special. She'd been on a pretty sustained one for the past few months, despite her fears. Or maybe because of them. Before he'd met her, he hadn't known it was possible to turn pain into beauty. He hesitated: tell her about Tilda? No, not yet. Let her be unburdened by his troubles for a while. He sent a quick reply and stood.

Frankie was already coming towards him with the coffees. Behind the counter, the shopkeeper's face was flushed dark red. Frankie shoved a cup into Caleb's hand, was halfway out the door before he'd moved.

He caught up to her outside. 'What'd you do?'

'Asked for almond milk.'

---

On the way back he kept to the speed limit, mindful of the gun tucked in Frankie's backpack, the very deep need not to end up in police custody today. She was checking messages every fifteen minutes now, a twist of tension every time she unwrapped the phone, never releasing. As he stopped at the shopping centre turn-off, she turned to him, the last rays of the sun casting an orange glow across her face. 'I'm coming in.'

'That's a bad idea – Imogen'll want the docs if she sees you.'

'I'll leave the gun in the car.'

Jesus; she'd considered taking it? 'What if she whips out the taser? Tries to arrest you?'

'I run, you hit her.'

A feeling she wasn't joking.

She was still looking at him, some involved thought process going on behind her furrowed brow. 'If I happen to go under a bus at some stage, the bank's around the corner from Maggie's. Box number's on the key.'

Unearned trust, unwarranted. No idea how to respond to it.

She pointed out the window. 'Lights.'

He accelerated and took the turn into the underground carpark, left behind a sky the colour of tarnished brass.

# 20.

They chose one of the few stores in the shopping complex with no CCTV. Eastern Dreams sold cheap silver jewellery and expensive healing crystals. Caleb and Frankie were the only potential customers, but the listless sales assistant had barely glanced at them, possibly stunned by the sandalwood incense.

Only a few minutes left of the thirty-minute window they'd given Imogen.

In the back corner Frankie was going through a shelf of crystals, picking each one up and putting it down, glancing towards the front door every ten seconds. She studied a chunk of quartz. 'Like being back in Mallacoota. If that shop assistant comes at me with the tarot cards, I'm out of here.'

So that's where she'd been hiding out the past few months. Hard to imagine Frankie in the feel-good coastal village, but it explained the Earth Mother clothes she'd been wearing.

'Mallacoota?' he said. 'Is that why your chakras are so well aligned?'

She faced him, still holding the quartz. 'How are your chakras these days?'

He stepped back. 'They don't respond well to violence.'

'Serious question. How's the head? Last time I saw you, it was pretty fucked.'

Heat rose up the back of his neck. 'Good.'

'So no more little freak-outs or –'

He turned to examine a lumpen clay pot Kat would have winced at. A thump to his upper arm, closed fist, knuckles to the bone. 'Ow.' He rubbed his bicep. 'You right?'

'Don't pull the look-away act on me. I'm not asking for fun, I need to know if you're going to lose your shit in the middle of a tense moment. So tell me, on a scale of one to ten – one being you having a little lie-down in the middle of a bushfire – how would you rate your desire to live?'

He loosened his jaw. 'Ten.'

Her expression did a good job of conveying disbelief. 'That's a pretty amazing turnaround. What brought that on?'

Hours of excruciating therapy, medication, retraining neural pathways. Hope.

'Kat's pregnant.'

A smile wiped the hardness from her face. 'Cal. Mate. That's the best fucking news. Congratulations.' Her smile dimmed as she no doubt remembered the last two times, and exactly how little use he'd been to her afterwards. She opened her mouth to speak, but he was saved by Imogen appearing at the front entrance.

'She's here,' he told Frankie.

The fed was dressed in a nondescript blue shirt and black slacks, hair pulled neatly back. She faltered when she saw Frankie, then headed straight for them, ignoring the sales assistant's lethargic greeting. Hands safely away from her pockets and any secreted stun guns.

Jasmine perfume tangled with the incense as she reached them. 'Well, don't you two look cosy together.'

A little stand-off as she tried to position herself against a corner wall, but Caleb and Frankie stood their ground. She glanced over her shoulder at the door, then looked at Frankie. 'Where are Maggie's records?'

'We need your help first. Tell us about Transis. Who were you investigating?'

'Now, or I arrest your mate here for murder and come up with a nice charge for you.'

Caleb spoke before Frankie could fire back. 'Maggie's in hospital with head injuries. Someone assaulted her yesterday.' A nod of acknowledgement from Imogen. So she knew. Not surprising she'd been keeping tabs on Maggie.

'Someone kidnapped her daughter this morning,' he went on. 'Tilda. We're trying to find her. We think it's connected to Amon's murder.'

Imogen's eyes went to the front entrance, tracking a passing shopper. 'You should contact your local police if you're concerned about the safety of a minor.'

Jesus, what did he have to do to get through to her? He tried to find the right words, words that would make her care. 'She's nine. She's been gone eight hours.' He caught Frankie's flinch, but kept going. 'It's not just Amon, someone else is dead, too.'

Imogen's head whipped towards him. 'Who?'

'I don't know his name, but he died last Friday.' And Caleb might just leave out the part about Maggie being angry with the dead man.

Imogen was staring at him. 'How do you know about that?'

'You know who I'm talking about?'

'How –?' She broke off as the saleswoman drifted towards them. Blonde dreads and rough hemp pants and singlet.

Caleb's skin itched sympathetically.

'... sale on all jewellery items.'

'We're right, thanks,' Caleb said.

'Thirty per cent off everything in the top case, twenty for the bottom.'

Imogen and Frankie turned and spoke simultaneously. 'Fuck off.'

The pair of them probably would have got on well under different circumstances.

Imogen waited until the shop assistant had hurried back to the counter, then spoke. 'What do you know about Jordan's death?'

A name – that was a good start.

'How's Jordan connected?' he asked.

'Stop. Messing. Me. Around. People are dying, and we could all be next.'

*People*. A sick feeling she wasn't just talking about Martin Amon and Jordan. 'Who else is dead?'

She was on the balls of her feet, a feverish shine to her eyes. About to do something: run, attack, scream.

'We called you,' he said slowly. 'We wouldn't have done that if we were involved in their deaths.'

Her jaw worked. 'Give me your phones.'

'We haven't got any.'

'Show me. Turn around, hands against the wall.'

A great way for Imogen to stun them and grab the key. He caught Frankie's eye, communicating in a glance – *Run?* She shook her head and they both faced the wall. The cop gave them a brisk pat-down, Frankie first, then him; the least sensual thing he'd done with a woman, including the time he'd had his wisdom teeth out.

There was something in Imogen's hand when he turned around. A flash of panic – but it was an oversized phone, decorated with silver and purple stars, nothing like the stun gun. Or anything he would have expected her to own.

Frankie squinted at it. 'You're not worried about someone listening on that? Or tracking it?'

'No. Bought it ten minutes ago from a street kid.' She opened an online photo album and thrust the phone at them. 'This is what you're up against.'

He took it from her.

A man sitting in an armchair. Blood, a spongy mess where the top of his head should be. His brown rabbit-like goatee clearly visible. The federal cop who'd interviewed Caleb in the farm office.

Against all instinct he swiped to the next photo: another suburban house, people in white cotton overalls, numbered markers on a polished wooden floor, the slumped form of Beardless visible in the background.

Caleb lowered the phone, mouth dry. Worse than he'd thought. Much worse. Amon was bad enough, but people who would hunt down and kill three cops wouldn't hesitate to murder a child. Tilda shot or bludgeoned, her bright eyes dulled.

It took him a couple of attempts to speak. 'Feds,' he told Frankie. 'They interviewed me after I found Amon.'

She sagged against a display case, a hand to her mouth.

'The Transis team,' Imogen said. 'I'm the only one left.' Fear in her eyes, but something else, too, something he'd seen in the mirror eight hours ago, pepper spray still burning his eyes – guilt.

'Was Jordan a cop, too?' he asked.

'Informant. He approached me last week with information that led to an arrest. A couple of days later he took a dive off an overpass. Suicide or accident, according to the coroner.' She looked at Frankie. 'I wonder what your sister would say.'

Frankie's face was still ashen but she returned the cop's stare. 'If she wasn't in ICU, probably that she was hurt by the same person who killed Jordan. We've got a possible description of her attacker – tall, fair-haired, looks like a weightlifter.'

No spark of interest in the cop's face.

'You know him?' Caleb asked.

'Tell me what you know about Jordan's death.'

'Maggie's daughter mentioned him – no details, just that he'd died. Now tell us about Transis.'

'The documents first.'

Another stand-off, but one they weren't going to win. Frankie finally spoke. 'The Commonwealth in Malvern. Under my name.'

'And the key?'

'The kidnappers took it.'

Impressive, really, what a good liar she was. Nice move dangling that prize in front of Imogen, too: the cop couldn't get into a deposit box without a warrant or key, but it'd keep her off their backs while she tried.

'How the hell am I supposed to get into it, then?'

'Use your charm,' Frankie said. 'Your turn – tell us about Transis. What were you investigating? *Who* were you investigating?'

Imogen headed for the rear exit, her pace just under a run.

'Wait,' he called, 'what's Jordan's surname?'

She didn't look back.

Frankie turned to him, a little colour returning to her cheeks. 'Any chance the name "Jordan" fits the video?'

# 21.

He watched the video while Frankie drove, cupping the screen to shade it from the passing streetlights. A strong suspicion her eyes were on him more than the road. 'Jordan' slotted neatly into the gap between Maggie's words, but didn't quite feel right. Some tiny synching problem that snagged like a fine thread. Or he could just be tired after the pepper spray and lip-reading strangers, the ratcheting tightness as each hour passed.

He closed the laptop and said, 'Maybe.'

Frankie switched on the internal light. 'How likely?'

'Maybe.' He peered past his reflection at the road: a freeway, almost in the city. 'Where are we going?'

'To ask Tedesco to look into Jordan. The cops' deaths, too.' She glanced at the road; not quite long enough. 'You'd better text, we're almost at his house.'

'How do you know where Tedesco lives?'

Her eyes slid to him. 'I know everything.'

Sometimes that was very easy to believe. He pulled the phone from the glove box. Tedesco probably wouldn't be able to – or want to – help, but it was worth a try. Whoever Jordan was, his death was at the centre of things.

'We should talk to Fawkes in person, too,' he said.

'Who?'

'The hacker.'

'He won't want to meet.'

Caleb went to speak but stopped. The computer wasn't connected to wi-fi, and Sammi had seemed pretty sure closing the lid would make it safe – still, smarter not to risk it. He switched to sign. 'I'm hoping his paranoia will help.'

'His what?'

He fingerspelled the word, Frankie glancing between the road and his hands, mouthing each letter, but getting them all wrong.

Her face wrinkled in doubt. 'Banana?'

One of these days he'd teach her how to fingerspell properly, but not while doing a hundred on a freeway.

'Paranoia,' he said out loud.

He texted Tedesco, then set up a hotspot and opened the messageboard on the laptop.

—Need to meet in person. Got news

He only had to wait a few seconds for the reply.

—?

—About the video

—?

—In person. Someone might be monitoring email

A long wait, then a new message appeared.

—*show yourself + drivers licence*

Did he really want to offer up his ID to a man connected with a hacktivist collective?

Frankie was craning to see the screen, the car drifting towards the semitrailer in the next lane. 'Eyes front,' he said, pulling out his licence. 'He wants me to ID myself.'

'Don't. He won't meet you – he's just playing games.'

Caleb uncovered the camera, gave the hacker a good look at him, then his licence. A message appeared.

—*check back 90 mins for address*

Interesting Fawkes hadn't asked his location. Not at all

concerned that Caleb might be in a different state or country.

—Email. I'm dumping the computer

No need to give his contact details; the hacker was probably trawling through his life as they spoke.

He turned off the laptop and lifted it. 'Bit of noise,' he told Frankie, and smashed it against the dashboard. A fair bit of hammering before it cracked open. He tore out its guts, dropped the pieces in the footwell. No reason at all to be thinking of the words 'barn' and 'door'.

Frankie shook her head. 'I can't believe you just doxed yourself. You do know how Anonymous works? That they dump information online for kicks?'

'With a political agenda.' He thought about it. 'Usually.'

———

They parked on a side street opposite Tedesco's suggested meeting place, a 7-Eleven a few kays from the detective's house. While waiting, they risked using the phone to look into the cops' deaths. It didn't take long to find the news reports. Both men had been killed the day after Martin Amon: Beardless in Melbourne, Rabbit-face in Canberra. No mention of their names or the fact they were police officers, no link drawn between them and Amon.

'You think the journos were warned off?' he asked.

'More likely they don't know. The brass'll be shitting themselves, trying to work out what happened. Or trying to cover it up.' She thought for a moment. 'What's your take on Imogen – bent, or just scared?'

'Hard to tell.'

'Come on. You've got a little meter running the entire time you talk to someone, assessing their every blink and twitch. Give me the readout.'

'She's genuinely scared and has a very low threshold for breaking rules. Further analysis will require more input.'

A figure rounded the corner of the 7-Eleven: Tedesco, wearing gym clothes and jogging slowly, cheeks puffing as though cooling down after a hard run. The kale diet was pretty standard, but exercise was new.

Frankie turned to Caleb. 'Maybe you should talk to him alone.'

He nodded. It hadn't occurred to him she'd come. Tedesco had only seen the aftermath of her betrayal, not the years of friendship or the risks she'd taken for him. Putting the pair of them together would be like connecting two live wires.

Frankie grabbed his arm as he went to leave. 'Don't mention Tilda.'

'It's our best shot. He won't endanger her.'

'Not intentionally, but can you guarantee he won't involve the cops?'

The only thing Caleb could guarantee was that the detective would do what he thought right.

'OK,' he said. 'I'll keep her out of it.'

Tedesco was waiting under a streetlight, bent over, bracing his hands on his thighs. He straightened as Caleb approached, trying to pretend he wasn't gasping; flushed despite the cool evening, his face slicked with sweat. No recent birthdays or health scares, months on from any possible New Year resolutions. Which left only one likely scenario.

'Dating someone new?' Caleb asked.

A full three seconds before Tedesco answered. 'The exact nature of the relationship is yet to be determined.'

Caleb hesitated. He was almost certain they were discussing a he, not a she, but the subject hadn't been broached in the twelve months they'd known each other. Plenty of reasons why a homicide cop might want to keep that side of his life private.

Particularly one who'd got off to a rocky start by killing a bent cop.

'Does the person of interest have a name?' Caleb asked.

'Several.' Tedesco wiped his forehead on his sleeve. 'So, what's the emergency? Need me to look into another cop? Assistant commissioner, maybe?'

'Not quite – some murders.'

The detective's faint smile evaporated as Caleb told him what he needed. 'Jesus, Cal. Dead cops. Does it involve Imogen Blain?'

'Yes.'

'Then you should probably know she's been on stress leave since last week. Was asked to take it, if I'm reading it correctly.'

Which meant Imogen wouldn't have access to all her usual sources. Shit.

'OK, thanks. Can you help? I wouldn't ask if it wasn't important.'

'I'll try,' Tedesco said slowly. 'But I wouldn't get your hopes up. My mate's not in the same department as Transis, I doubt he'll be able to find anything. Or that he'd tell me if he did.'

Caleb had known it was a long shot; its probable failure shouldn't leave him feeling this sick. 'Thanks. Appreciate it.'

Tedesco was studying him. 'Looking a bit rough around the edges. You sleeping?' He still did this every now and then: a little assessment carried out with the efficiency of the farm boy he'd once been, scrutinising the stock for soundness of body and brain. Excruciating, but oddly comforting.

'Yeah, just a stressful couple of days.'

'No flashbacks?'

'No.'

'Panic attacks?'

OK, now it was just excruciating. 'You want a report from the shrink?'

'Nah, I get the group email.' Tedesco gave what looked like a back-cracking stretch. 'I'll let you know about the feds.' He went to go, then turned back, an unusually awkward bob of his head. 'The person of interest is generally known as Luke.'

Caleb returned to the car, a positive expression plastered on his face. Frankie was clutching the phone, her skin stripped of colour. An email open on the screen, the message, *NO POLICE*. A video link at the bottom.

The air left his lungs. Proof Tilda was alive, or proof she was dead.

Frankie's lips barely moved. 'I can't look.'

'Wait here.' He slipped the phone from her grasp and walked a little way down the road, out of her line of sight. A few slow inhalations before pressing play.

Tilda crossed-legged on a couch, eyes huge in a wan face, hair wild. She spoke directly to the camera, looked up as though at the person holding it. The picture went black.

Tilda alive.

Alive and unharmed, not locked in a cellar, not buried in a shallow bush grave. A weight lifted from his chest, allowing him to breathe properly for the first time all day. Not safe, not by a long way, but a proof-of-life video meant the kidnappers were serious about an exchange.

He jogged back to the car.

'It's OK,' he said as soon as he opened the door. 'She's all right.'

After Frankie watched the video, she sat with her eyes closed, shivering. He turned on the heating. An urge to talk to Kat. To be with her and hold her and tell her all his fears and terrors. She'd probably be working late on her new sculpture. Loose-limbed and happy, thinking only about the task at hand. He'd have to tell her about Tilda tomorrow, whatever the news.

He checked the video: nothing distinguishing in the background, just Tilda confused on a brown couch, a wood-panelled wall behind her. The email drew a blank too. Sent through one of the major servers; no way of pinpointing its origin. He forwarded it to Sammi, asking her look into it, but didn't hold out much hope.

Frankie opened her eyes. 'They didn't make any demands.'

No, they were softening her up, giving her a glimpse of what could be, letting her imagine what might. The next message would come soon, and it'd be threatening.

'They're getting organised. Took her without any planning. What did she say?'

'Time and date. Filmed it about an hour ago.'

The phone vibrated: Sammi.

—*No info. $50 added to your bill*

She was fast, at least.

He explained the message to Frankie, who scrubbed a hand through her hair, making it as untamed as Tilda's. She was still shaking. 'Fuck. What do we do now?'

'Wait for Fawkes' email.' He kept talking as she shook her head. 'Nothing else we can do.' No leads, no ideas. Just waiting for the kidnappers to contact them. Trying not to think about slaughtered policemen and a dead man called Jordan, the risk each minute brought.

'Yeah, OK,' Frankie said. 'But we can't sit here with the phone on. We need an internet café – somewhere with coffee.'

She needed food, not coffee, something with lots of calming carbohydrates. Both of them did, probably: neither of them had eaten all day.

'I know somewhere close.'

# 22.

Alberto's café was open for business, new windows gleaming. A room full of colour and movement: lamps on each table and strands of fairy lights looped along the brick walls, a dozen customers signing animatedly. Not a bad turn-out for the usually slow Thursday night; the community turning up to support Alberto after the vandalism. And to catch up on the news.

Frankie stopped in the doorway, taking in Nick's greeting from behind the coffee machine and a few waved hellos from the customers. Caleb had given her the basics of the sabotage job, but hadn't said anything about the café or his connection to Alberto. And right now he had no idea why he'd risked exposing it to her. She gave him an unfathomable look and headed for a table in the back corner.

Nick approached, his usually bright smile missing a few watts.

'More problems?' Caleb asked. There hadn't been any messages from Alberto.

'No – I mean, Grandad just told me to cancel the marquee. The one for the fiftieth. He said there's no point if the business is … I've never seen him like this before.'

'I know. I'm working on it.' Not very well, not with any results. He turned to Frankie. 'Point to what you want on the blackboard or ask me to translate. Nick doesn't speak or lip-read.'

'Why not?'

'Same reason you don't sign.'

'I sign.' She proved it by laboriously signing to Nick, 'Want coffee white, food hot.'

Nick gave her an encouraging smile and replied slowly. 'Sure. Do you mean spicy hot?'

'Yes, hot.'

An odd request from a woman whose tastes usually ran to salt and cholesterol. She'd probably meant to sign 'please' but accidentally touched her fingers to her lips instead of her chin.

'This one, then.' Nick pointed to the penne all'arrabbiata on the blackboard and received a thumbs-up from Frankie.

'You don't want that,' Caleb told her. He'd tried Alberto's version of the chilli-infused Calabrian dish once and would rather be pepper-sprayed than eat it again.

Frankie gave him narrow-eyed look. 'You really mansplaining my order?'

'Deafsplaining. You asked for –'

'I know what I asked for.'

He gave Nick his order, got a puzzled look at his request for a glass of milk as well as his usual long black.

Frankie sat back as the young man left. 'So how long you been doing this?'

'What?'

'Being with your people.'

Were they his people? 'A few months.'

'And you're doing a job for them? Brave man, pissing in your own backyard. So what's your theory – greed, fear or revenge?'

The unholy trinity of criminal motivation.

'Possibly dodgy developers. And there's an ex-son-in-law who might hold a grudge. Although he's been out of the picture a while.'

'People can simmer for a long time if they've got a real fire in their belly.' She looked around the room. 'They might be better off just selling if the business is damaged.'

'Alberto won't sell. This is one of the few Deaf-friendly workplaces around.'

'They'll cope in other jobs. You did.'

'Cope' was the right word. He hadn't realised how enjoyable work could be until he went into partnership with Frankie. Hard to know why she'd asked him and not a fellow cop: they'd been a good team the handful of times their paths had crossed in his days as an investigator and hers as a cop, but he'd come with no connections and limited experience. Not to mention a few communication issues. Was it because she thought he'd be easy to manipulate?

He wavered, then asked the question. 'Why'd you ask me to go into business?'

Her expression didn't change. 'Your sunny nature.'

Nick's mother, Ilaria, was coming from the kitchen bearing two large plates and a glass of milk. A fine-boned woman with the same wavy brown hair as Nick, but only flashes of his brightness. Always in muted greys and browns, her clothes a couple of sizes too large. Strange to see her in the café instead of the kitchen.

Her eyes skimmed their faces as she set down the food. 'Nick'll be over with the coffees in a minute.' A gentle signer: small movements, close to her body. She glanced around the room and adjusted the already straight table lamp.

Caleb hesitated; they couldn't have a private conversation in a room full of signers. 'Want me to come outside?'

A wry smile. 'Guess there isn't much point. It's not like everyone doesn't already know my business.' She stood a little straighter. 'Nick said you're looking for Tony. I'd rather you didn't.'

'Alberto told you about the trouble with the business?'

'Of course.'

'You think your ex-husband could do something like that?'

'No, he's too impatient. You won't talk to him, will you?' Direct eye contact now, her fingers plucking at her apron.

Couldn't say yes, shouldn't say no. 'I'll speak to you first if I have to.'

She gave him a short nod and left, tension radiating from her like phosphorous.

Frankie watched her go, then picked up a fork. 'You were the best raw talent I'd seen, and I could stand being in the same room as you.' She stabbed a piece of penne. 'Most of the time.'

A moment to work out she was answering his question about their partnership. Jesus, a compliment. No idea what to say in reply, so he just pushed the milk across the table as she ate her first mouthful. There'd be a second or two before her brain caught up to her mouth, then the entire five stages of grief.

She stopped chewing, eyes widening. 'Christ.'

At the bargaining stage.

'Hot,' he said, twisting his hand away from his lips. 'Please.' He brought his hand from his chin. 'Good not to get the two confused.'

She grabbed the milk and gulped it down. 'You could have warned me.'

He managed to eat half his meal before Frankie claimed it, then went to find Alberto. The cook was in his cramped office behind the kitchen, pecking one-handed at the computer. He looked up as Caleb toggled the lights. 'That was fast, I only just texted'

'Something else happen?'

'In a way. Come and look.'

Alberto switched on the outside lights and led him to the narrow gap between the building and side fence, one of the few places not covered by the cameras Caleb had installed. He lifted an upended rubbish tin, revealing a jerry can and handful of rags. Petrol wafted into the air. A raw wooden fence beneath low-hanging eaves. If that caught alight the building's ceiling would be down before the fire brigade got there.

Alberto replaced the bin. 'No idea how long it's been there. I found it half an hour ago when I was stacking boxes by the fence.'

Had the arsonist had a change of heart or just been interrupted? Too much to hope it was an empty warning.

'Check your insurance,' Caleb said. 'Make sure it covers fire. Water damage too. Everything.'

Alberto patted the air. 'It's all right, Nick gave me the lecture last week. I upped the insurance, got top cover on everything.'

That was going to raise a few red flags if he ended up making a claim.

'Make sure everything's well documented. You go to the cops yet?'

'Had to use the NRS, couldn't get an interpreter. They say they'll come and look.'

A relayed phone call wasn't going to cut it; the operator wouldn't have voiced any of the fear behind Alberto's typed words. It might take the cops days to respond to a calm message about a can of petrol.

'Give it a couple of hours, then go to the cop shop,' he told Alberto. 'Use a pen and paper if you have to.' He stopped to get his thoughts in order. 'Is anyone pressuring you to sell? Developers or neighbours?'

Alberto shook his head.

Damn. It was looking more and more like the danger was coming from within. 'Tell me about Nick's father.'

A flush crept up the cook's face. 'It's not Tony.'

'You like him?'

Alberto's mouth folded. 'The man's an arsehole. A hearie. Tried to keep Ilaria and the boy away from us, barely bothered to learn sign. I should have known sooner what he was ...' He rubbed a hand across his face. 'I don't want Nick knowing, but I pay his dad to stay away. The business goes down, the bastard doesn't get any money. He's a problem gambler, needs it.'

'Got an address?'

'He's overseas. Thailand.'

'You sure?'

'I paid for the ticket. One way.'

Maybe the man had stayed put, maybe he hadn't, but if the cops didn't take Alberto seriously now, he'd need more help than Caleb could currently give. Broken windows were bad enough, but arson could be fatal.

'I'm too distracted,' Caleb told him. 'It's not safe. If the cops give you the run-around, you need to get someone else on the job.'

Alberto was motionless, the overhead lights casting his eyes into shadow. 'Please don't make me expose my family to a stranger.' He turned and went back inside before Caleb had a chance to respond.

# 23.

Caleb fetched Alberto's ladder and moved one of the cameras to cover the side fence. Rearranging lifeboats. Anyone determined to burn down the building would do it whether or not there were cameras. The only hope was that the arsonist really had changed their mind.

Frankie came outside as he was packing everything away. She held up the phone. 'There's an email from Fawkes.'

A short message containing a lot of information.

*—harold holt pool in 45. just you. do laps in slow lane get head wet*

'What d'you reckon?' Frankie asked. 'Conspiracy nut?'

Good question. Holt's death in 1967 was a favourite of the conspiracy theorists. The then prime minister had gone for a swim in rough seas off Portsea and never returned. Most people accepted he'd drowned, but some held out he'd been taken by a foreign government. Everyone agreed that naming a pool after him was in very dark humour.

'Probably just careful,' Caleb said. 'Bad acoustics for a directional mic, and I can't wear a wire.' Or hearing aids. Which meant trying to follow an unfamiliar speaker with no intonation to guide him. An accent or lisp could stop him, a mumbler or fast-talker.

Frankie was frowning, apparently coming to the same conclusions. 'I'll go.'

'No, it'll spook him. I'll change the location.' He typed a quick reply.

—Can't do pool. Need hearing aids

The message came instantly.

—*39 mins*

————————

They made it with three minutes to spare. Caleb bought bathers and changed in record time, headed out to the large undercover pool. A soaring glass ceiling reflected the rippling water against the night sky. Nearly closing time, but the under-fifteen squad were still ploughing up and down the pool, teammates cheering them on; audible even without his aids. More than 110 decibels, then – he'd have to tell Tilda. Hopefully tonight; please God tonight. The kidnappers couldn't want to keep her till tomorrow, surely. To guard and feed an upset nine-year-old, risk Frankie going to the police, an inquisitive neighbour. There'd be another video any minute now, the handover soon after. Had to be.

He dove in and got going in a steady freestyle, pausing at each end. Five laps, six, seven; increasingly worried Frankie would lose patience and come in. It had taken most of the journey to convince her not to act as back-up, and he wasn't sure his arguments had stuck.

A shadow moved across the bottom of the pool as someone slipped into the lane ahead of him. He swam to the end, caught hold of the ledge. A man in his early twenties, with shaded goggles and a black swimming cap pulled low on his forehead. Long face and nose, thin limbs twitching with energy. Kat would sketch him in sharp vertical lines.

'I'm Caleb.'

'No shit. Why are you interested in Transis?'

No accent or chewing gum, just the rounded vowels of a private school boy. A prayer of thanks to the gods of lip-reading. Now to speak without auditory feedback; it'd be a short conversation if he accidentally started yelling.

'I'm looking for a child who's been kidnapped,' he told Fawkes. 'I think it's connected to the taskforce.'

'What kid?'

'Maggie Reynolds' daughter.'

Fawkes grabbed the edge of the pool, hauling himself out.

Caleb caught his arm. 'I'm not working for Maggie, I'm just looking for her daughter. Her name's Tilda. She's nine.'

The young man glanced at a passing lifeguard and dropped into the water.

Caleb kept hold of his wrist. 'Tell me what you know, and I'll tell you what Maggie's saying on the video. Start with Imogen Blain. What do you know about her?'

'Never heard of her.'

His arm had relaxed slightly in Caleb's grip, but his gaze was darting around the pool, from the walls to the swim squad at the far end of the room.

'It's a pool,' Caleb said. 'Can't be bugged.'

'Everything can be bugged.'

'Then mouth the words, I can't hear you anyway.'

Fawkes frowned. 'Like. This?'

'Yes. Tell me about Maggie – what's your interest in her?'

'Staying alive.'

'She threatened you?'

'Not her – her clients. I did some work for the feds a few months back. For Transis. To, you know, get myself out of some trouble. I was ... and ... I ... they ...'

'Slow down. What kind of work was it?'

'Hunting down dirty money. A thread traced back to Maggie. Nothing major, but interesting, so I told them. And then ... he ... they ...'

'Slower.'

Fawkes' mouth folded petulantly. 'It's really. Hard. Talking. Like. This.'

An urge to laugh. 'Yeah, must be difficult. What happened when you told them about Maggie?'

'They shut Transis down. Then this big bloke came to my house and told me to hand over my hard drives and forget everything ... smashed up ... scared ... my mum ... Bastard.' Spit flecked the corners of his mouth, the fear fresh even months later. Outrage, too, as though hurt his good work hadn't been appreciated.

'If that all happened months ago, why are you worried now?'

'Because some informant went and got one of Maggie's clients arrested last week. Another one found out and decided they didn't want to be next. Killed the informant and most of fucking Transis.' Fawkes wrenched his arm from Caleb's grasp. 'Now tell me about the video or I'm out of here.'

Fawkes had timed his move for the lifeguard's return patrol, apparently deciding the woman's attention could play in his favour.

When she'd gone, Caleb said, 'I'm missing the name, but Maggie's saying, "It's safe. I'm the only one who knows. No. Don't tell anyone about blank. Please." The name's something like Turner or Kirner.'

'You don't know?' Fawkes was tightening his grip on the ledge.

Reveal he had access to Maggie's records, or let a possible ally leave? The young man was heaving himself up.

'I've seen Maggie records,' Caleb said quickly. 'She IDs clients by a string of numbers. If I get you a copy, could you work out their names?'

Fawkes edged closer. 'What sort of strings? Sequential? Different lengths?'

'Random, all nine digits.'

'Won't be a code, then. She's probably just written the names in the back of a book.' He paused, head bobbing. 'Maggie's no genius – I'd be able to trace her clients through the transactions.'

She might not be a genius, but she was smart enough to have protected herself from hackers, Frankie and the feds.

'How? They'll all be run through intermediaries.'

'I'm fucking good, I'd work it out. You got the records here? Can you give them to me now?'

No, Fawkes was too keen – the all-consuming focus of a zealot showed in his thrusting head. A vision of him posting the names online, the kidnappers panicking and killing Tilda. Slow it down, but keep the channels open. 'Not yet. I'll contact you. What's the best way?'

The hacker's face slackened with disappointment. 'Reply to that email, I guess. Be good for another twenty-four hours.' Apparently holding out little hope of Caleb's success.

'Better than that,' Caleb said. 'A phone number, a name.'

'Mate, with all the questions you're asking, I reckon they'll be coming for you next. I don't want my name, number or DNA anywhere near you.' He pulled himself from the pool.

'Wait. Maggie's client, the one who got arrested – what's his name?'

Fawkes looked back with a shrug. 'Think he's a builder. That's what Maggie called him.' He walked quickly away, his thin back hunched as he disappeared into the change rooms.

# 24.

Frankie was sitting in the passenger seat, hands in her lap, head back, but nothing relaxed about her. She'd parked as far from a streetlamp as possible.

She sat up as he climbed in, pressing the light switch so it would stay on. 'Anything?'

'Nothing clear, but he reckons he could work Maggie's clients from her records.'

Alarm in her face. 'Christ no. He posts them online, Tilda's dead.'

'It's OK, I agree. He –'

She held up a hand. 'Move from here first, I checked the phone a couple of times.'

He pulled out the keys but didn't start the engine. Frankie was shameless in her snooping, but there was a chance she wouldn't have read a text from Kat. 'Anything for me?'

'Yeah, someone called Henry Collins is pretty keen to see you.' Her gaze travelled across his face. 'Or are you worried about Kat?'

No reason to deny it. 'Yes.'

'I'd tell you.' She hesitated, then asked, 'How's it going?'

'On schedule.' Just like the last two pregnancies, the abruptness of their loss still shocking.

Frankie's forehead creased as she examined him. 'And how are you doing?'

'As expected.'

A terrible moment thinking she'd say something sympathetic, but she just gently punched his arm.

He drove as he told her about his chat with Fawkes, no real destination in mind, just that they needed to stay somewhere central while they worked out what to do. When he'd finished, Frankie swivelled to face him. 'It's not that easy to shut down a taskforce. That's someone with a direct ear to very senior cops.'

The same not-particularly-comfortable thought had occurred to him. He switched on the windscreen wipers as rain beaded the glass. The freeway was busy for this time of night, a steady stream of trucks, cars and motorbikes all heading for the city, nothing on the outbound side. Had he missed a warning? Eastern suburbs being evacuated due to some toxic spill?

Frankie waved to catch his eye.

He didn't turn. 'Could we table this for later? Like when we can talk without dying?'

She faced forward. Ten seconds of stillness before she started fiddling with the air vents. A quick adjustment of the louvres, the nozzle direction. And now she was switching through radio stations, muddy sounds filling his ears.

He merged left to use the emergency lane as a buffer. 'OK, go.'

She flicked off the radio. 'The bit about the builder doesn't make sense. It's cash-based. He wouldn't need Maggie – could do his own laundering.'

'Maybe he was making too much. Did a job for a chippie last month, and he was making way more than me.' So much more it had briefly made Caleb regret not taking up his father's long ago invitation to join him in the building business.

'No,' Frankie said, 'we're talking big money, can't be a builder. You must have misread the word.'

'I didn't.'

'How do you know?'

'Because I've been doing it for thirty fucking years, Frankie. I know when I've misread something.'

'Yeah? Well you're misreading the room right now.' She swung back to the road.

The rain was heavier now, laying a film of oily water across the asphalt. He eased off the accelerator and nudged the wipers higher. Frankie was probably right about the builder. Laundering would chew up thirty or forty per cent of the profits – you'd need serious money for it to be worth it. So maybe they weren't looking for a small-business owner, but a developer. In the motel, Tilda had watched the TV report about the developer's arrest with keen interest. The only time she'd been distracted enough to stop watching him and Frankie. As though she knew the man, or had heard his name. John Jacklin. Who'd just today pled innocent to fraud charges.

'I might know who he is.' He explained about Jacklin, and Tilda's rapt attention. 'Timing's right – he was arrested last week. Find his address, he should be on bail.'

'Yeah, OK.' She began unwrapping the phone.

Not quite the enthusiasm he'd expected. 'Problem?'

'He won't know anything. Maggie keeps everything separate. Didn't even like foods touching when she was a kid – had to give her a lunchbox with compartments until she was seven.' Irritation more than fond remembrance in her expression.

How had seven-year-old Frankie approached eating? With a flick-knife? Strange to think of her as a doting older sibling. He used to make Ant's lunches sometimes. Back in the days when Ant had followed him around, copying his every action, both of them daring each other on in pissing contests and offensive jokes.

'You made Maggie's lunches?'

She glanced up from the phone. 'I made everything.'

Something more than doting, then: necessity. In all the years they'd worked together he'd gleaned only the most basic information about her background. Left home at seventeen, possibly already on the piss. A childhood on the distant fringes of Melbourne with a mother she never mentioned and a cop father who'd died suddenly when Frankie was thirteen. Possibly why she'd become a cop herself, stuck with it despite the obvious personality clash. Be interesting to see what she'd say if he suggested it.

Frankie turned to him, and he flinched. A sudden fear she really could read his mind. 'Yes? What?' he said quickly.

'Jacklin's in remand,' she said and returned to her research.

No bail for a first-time offence?

The rain abruptly dumped down, veiling the world in white. The car ahead slowed in panic. Caleb pumped the brakes, windscreen wipers on full, peering at the prisms of tail-lights ahead of him.

Frankie tapped his arm.

'Wait. I'll take the next off-ramp.'

She tapped harder, fingers jabbing.

His stomach dropped. 'Tilda?'

'Maggie's awake.'

---

The hospital's rear doors were locked for the night, a sign directing people to the front entrance. Nine-forty: too late for visitors. Too late for bad news. How to tell a mother her chid was gone?

He followed Frankie around the corner, neither of them speaking. The rain had stopped, the glistening streets nearly empty, only a white-coated doctor furtively smoking up ahead; he glanced in their direction and stepped a little further into a service alley.

Caleb looked at Frankie. 'Will they let you see Maggie this late?'

'They'd better.'

He wouldn't want to be the nurse who told her to come back in the morning.

'Will Maggie talk to us?' he asked.

She was a little slower to answer this time. 'Getting in the door might be tricky if she's ditched my guard for hers.'

'I can stay outside.'

'I meant for me – she was pretty pissed off about the key. But she'll listen when she knows it's about Turnip.'

*Turnip.* That's right – Frankie had called Tilda that when she'd first greeted the girl at his office.

He kept his tone even. 'Does Maggie call her Turnip, too?'

Her face softened. 'Yeah. It started because of the Swedish name. You know, swede, turnip, but she really looked like one when she was a baby. This big white forehead and wispy hair.' She smiled. 'Still does.'

*Turner. Please.*

*Turnip. Please*

He pictured Maggie's frightened face in the video, her words butting up against each other. *'No. Don't tell anyone about Turnip. Please.'*

It slotted perfectly into place. So the person Maggie had been speaking to knew Tilda could ID Jacklin, maybe even other aspects of Maggie's work. The kidnappers? No, the timing was wrong – Tilda had been taken days after that tape was made.

But less than an hour after Caleb had tested possible names in public. Standing with Henry Collins by the tomato stall, saying each word slowly and clearly, all while the man in the blue baseball cap listened in.

His blood turned to ice. Frankie had never been the target: the kidnappers had recognised Tilda's nickname and gone after her.

'Maggie's video,' he said to Frankie. 'The name.'

She shook her head, her gaze going to the service alley a couple of metres away, the doctor taking the last few puffs of his illicit cigarette. He had the Hollywood good looks and highlighted hair of a plastic surgeon, but the build of a heavyweight boxer; easily capable of tearing Caleb apart when Frankie started yelling at him. Yes, wait until they were alone before admitting what he'd done.

They were level with the man when it clicked – muscle-bound, with fair hair.

'Run!' Caleb yelled to Frankie.

He was grabbed, shoved forwards, head slamming into the wall.

A shockwave of pain.

And somehow sitting. The ground sliding in front of his eyes, blood dripping onto the concrete. Hollywood dragged him into the alley and yanked down his jacket to bind his arms.

Frankie in front of them, hands raised, face hollowed and white. High brick walls and stained ground, lights flickering at the edges of his vision. Something hard against his temple. A gun. The same gun that had killed all those cops? Big gun, blow a big hole in him.

A distant rumble: Hollywood speaking. Be still and let Frankie negotiate. She was already talking, her eyes darting between Hollywood's face and the gun. '... give you the key. Just tell me where Tilda is first.'

The barrel smacked his temple, dull ripples through his skull. More rumbling from Hollywood.

Frankie stepped back, mouth opening. 'No, don't!'

A flash. Something dragged over his head – a plastic bag. Twisted shut, a forearm pinning it. Panic clawed through him. Trying to wrench away, the bag sucking against his mouth. Break it, chew it. Body jerking, chest staving inwards. Frankie's blurred figure coming closer, coming to rip the bag from him. No – giving something to Hollywood, moving away again. Ribs crushed. Plastic melding to face, nose, tongue.

And released.

Lying by Hollywood's polished shoes, drawing in shuddering breaths. Frankie beside him on her knees, head bowed.

Hollywood was examining a silver key, gun trained on Caleb. A chiselled symmetry to his face, eyebrows neatly shaped. Beneath his lab coat, a tailored suit and white shirt, grey silk tie, only his scarred and ridged knuckles giving a glimpse of his inner violence. He slipped the key into his breast pocket and pulled out a phone. Texting someone. No hurry; waiting at the beautician's to freshen up his tan.

He finally lowered the phone and turned to go.

'Wait,' Caleb said. 'Tilda. Where's Tilda?'

Hollywood glanced back, looking slightly puzzled that Caleb was speaking to him. 'Haven't found her yet.'

# 25.

He scavenged a limp tea bag and sugar sachets from the motel's meagre stocks and made Frankie tea. They were only a few blocks from the hospital, but neither of them had had the energy to go any further. The only room left in the place, a one-bed unit with bare brick walls and overhead lights that shimmered when he turned his head. Why hadn't Hollywood killed them? Would have been the work of seconds. Hadn't been squeamishness, that was for sure.

He carried the tea to the couch, pain netting his skull. Not concussed, but not far off it. He sat next to Frankie, handed her the tea. 'You ring the hospital?'

'What?'

'The hospital.' He pointed to the wall-mounted phone by the kitchen.

'Oh. Yeah. Wasn't them.'

'Maggie's not awake?'

'No. Maybe tomorrow. Depends on the –' She touched her head. 'There's still swelling.' She raised the tea to her mouth, lowered it. 'He hasn't got Turnip. I don't understand. How can it not be him?'

No way of breaking the news gently. 'I think someone took her because of the video. Maggie's talking about her, calling her Turnip.'

Frankie's eyes went blank. 'What?'

He went through it slowly, told her about testing the names aloud, the kidnapper listening in. 'I'm sorry. I should have been more careful.'

'It was Turnip? Maggie was saying –' She drew in a sharp breath. 'They wanted Turnip, not the docs?'

'It's good,' he said quickly. 'They just want information from her, or maybe to keep it from someone else. If they wanted her dead, they would have done it already.' Aware he was trying to reassure himself as much as her, that he hadn't voiced the other, greater horror.

Frankie was shaking her head. 'There's a chance the kidnappers won't kill her, but that guy, whoever he's working for – they will. They'll find her and kill her.'

*'Haven't found her yet.'*

'No,' he said. 'We'll get her first.' The words were dry husks in his mouth.

Frankie stood abruptly and went to the bedroom, turning her face as she closed the door. Her backpack was in there. She'd be getting out her kit and unrolling it, reaching for the needle and oblivion. He'd always judged her for that. But to forget everything. To forget the long and bloodied history of his mistakes; that, he could understand.

A hint of sound, a raw wail that ripped through him. He went to turn off his aids, then lowered his hand and stood.

Frankie was sitting against the wall, knees drawn to her chest. No booze or needles, nothing but naked grief on her face as she wept. Choosing to feel the unbearable without dulling the pain. A memory: eighteen years old, a few weeks after his mother died. His father bowed over the kitchen sink, shoulders heaving. He'd never seen his father cry before, hadn't known what to do with such unfamiliar grief. Still didn't.

He sat beside Frankie and laid a tentative hand on her arm. She buried her face in his shoulder. Arms around her, holding her tight, his body shuddering with her sobs.

# 26.

Awake. A figure leaning over him, shaking his shoulder. Kat bleeding, needing an ambulance. He shot upright. Not Kat: Frankie. On a couch in the bare-brick motel. He dropped his head into his hands and tried to remember how to breathe. A blaze of light as Frankie switched on a lamp. He raised his head.

'Come on,' she said. 'Wake up.'

'I'm awake.' A strong possibility he'd never sleep again. It had been a deep and strangely dreamless sleep while it lasted, the kind usually reserved for the drugged or guilt-free. He checked the clock: 5.12 a.m.

'Tilda?' he asked quickly.

'No. I got ... Jacklin ... morning.'

'What?'

'I got onto ... mate in remand ... Jacklin ... morning.'

'Um.' He put the words together, had a stab at their meaning. 'You called a mate in remand and we can see Jacklin this morning?'

'Yes.'

Nice to know he wasn't the only person she'd woken in the middle of the night. A glimpse of her rumpled bed through the bedroom door, a laptop on the pillow. A laptop?

'Where'd the computer come from?'

'Junkie ... thirty bucks. Jacklin's ...'

'Wait. Let me put my aids in.' His brain too, hopefully – he could usually read Frankie without them.

He eased himself up, head and body protesting. A bit of a shuffle as he crossed the room. Frankie tailed him, talking as he grabbed his phone from the bed and went into the bathroom. He shut the door in her face, locked it to be on the safe side.

A grim image in the mirror: bloodshot eyes and a dark two-day beard, a puffy bruise on his forehead, blood crusted where the skin had split. He cleaned the worst of it, then unwrapped the phone. Kat had the motel's number, but he couldn't quite shake the feeling of that waking dream. Nineteen weeks today, a milestone they'd never quite reached before. Only five more and they'd reach the phrase 'possibly viable'.

The phone lit up: eight texts. Eight texts in the middle of the night. Oh God.

He swiped through them without reading the contents. Tedesco and Alberto; nothing from Kat. He lowered himself onto the toilet and closed his eyes. Two different futures lived in the space of seconds. When he'd got his pulse back under a hundred, he read the texts. Tedesco's first.

—*I was unable to gain any official information about the informant or police officers. Please exercise extreme caution. Work under the assumption all the deaths are suspicious and linked.*

Tedesco had helpfully attached copies of the relevant news reports: nothing they hadn't already found. Shit. There just didn't seem to be a way into any of it. Caleb sent his thanks and opened Alberto's message.

—*Police come see. Help not.*

The stress was palpable in each terse sentence. English was Alberto's second language, one he preferred not to use, but his grammar was usually a lot clearer. Difficult to know what to do next. Before going to bed, Caleb had sent a spray of emails enquiring about Ilaria's ex, paying the motel clerk a hefty bribe for the use of the office computer. Not that he held out much hope – even if he found Tony, it'd be hard to prove he was involved without catching him in the act. *If* he was involved. According to Sammi's security report, whoever had accessed Alberto's ordering system had done it from within Australia.

Caleb rewrapped the phone and put his aids in, caught a faint, rhythmic thudding: Frankie either moving furniture or banging on the bathroom door. He opened it and she shoved a takeaway cup at him. 'Took you long enough.'

He examined the drink as he headed for the couch. Murky grey liquid with a boggy odour, a little like a swamp at midmorning. Drink it or send it for analysis? 'What is it?'

'Some superfood shit from a yoga place, the only shop open. They swear it's got caffeine.'

He tried it. Flavours that should never be combined: milk and something plant-like, with overtones of dirt. He picked a fleck of green from his lips. Broccoli. He was drinking a broccoli latte. Or not drinking it, as the case was.

He set the cup on the coffee table. 'OK, why the sudden enthusiasm for Jacklin? You said he wouldn't know anything about Maggie's work.'

She perched next to him on the couch. 'That's when I thought he was a client. He's not, he's an employee. And not casual-hire like Quinn – someone in the know.' She grabbed the laptop from the table. 'Had a poke around. Jacklin set up his company with Daddy's money a decade ago. It limped along for ages, then suddenly became very successful two years ago. Inexplicably successful.'

'We already know he was laundering money.'

'You have to have money to launder it. It's coming from other people. Look.' She flicked through a dizzying series of tabs. 'He's charged with faking invoices and employees, land sales. It's got to be fifteen, twenty mil.'

She was right, that was a lot more money than a not-very-successful developer could have generated on his own – the land sales alone would be. But she hadn't woken him at five a.m. to talk about money laundering.

'So you want to snoop around his apartment before we talk to him?'

'Thought you'd never ask.' She passed him the laptop, page open to an image of a towering metal and glass apartment block. 'He's one of three on the top floor.'

'The cops will've gone through everything.'

'We're not looking to convict the guy, just for connections. He's single, so the place'll be empty. And my lock picking's pretty good these days.' She paused. 'Though we should probably bring a pry bar just in case.'

He zoomed in on the photo. Sheer glass walls and a security desk, external cameras. Lots of cameras. No idea why Hollywood had let him and Frankie go last night, but it wouldn't happen a second time. If they were found sniffing around Jacklin, they'd be dead. And all for an apartment that had been gone over by the cops.

'Too many cameras,' he said.

'Cameras are fine. Security won't stop us if we look like we belong.'

'It's not security I'm worried about.'

'Christ. A few months ago you were poking sticks at bikies, daring them to gut you. Now you're having vapours over a bit of B and E. When did you get so fucking soft?'

Nineteen weeks ago.

No idea what his expression showed, but the fierceness left her face. 'Maybe I should go alone,' she said slowly. 'One person's less noticeable than two.'

*'Haven't found her yet.'* How could you live with yourself, knowing what you hadn't done? Knowing what you had.

He got to his feet. 'We haven't got a pry bar. You'll have to kick it in, if you can't open it.'

———

John Jacklin lived in the Docklands, a shiny new suburb built on the ruins of the old city wharfs. A place of expensive landscaping and patron-less shops, all overlooked by a sluggishly turning observation wheel. Not many people around at this hour; possibly blown away by the icy blasts whipping through the wind-tunnel streets. They'd been waiting fifteen minutes for someone to trigger the apartment building's carpark doors, and Caleb's hands had gone numb. His cotton shirt and jacket weren't going to cut it today. At some stage he'd have to go back to his flat for a change of clothes; a toothbrush and handful of headache pills, too.

'It's taking too long,' he said. 'Let's do the courier trick.'

'As my mum used to say, "It won't work, so don't bother."'

That was twice now she'd volunteered information about her family; unprecedented behaviour. He chanced a question. 'Any uplifting sayings from your father?'

'Nothing as uplifting as your father's. How'd it go? "If your best isn't good enough, try harder"?'

Why did he tell her these things?

'It was supposed to be encouraging,' he said.

'Encouraging? Jesus. No wonder you're such an over-achiever and your brother's such a fuck-up.'

Hardly an over-achiever: a tenuous marriage, a one-man business and a therapist.

Frankie straightened as a Range Rover swung around the corner and into the driveway.

A hairy-knuckled hand appeared from the driver's window, waved a card at a sensor. The roller doors lifted. When the car was through, they ran inside. The driver was already striding towards the lift. Another wave of the security pass, and the doors opened. Caleb headed for them, loose jog, neighbourly smile, nothing to alarm the locals. The driver managed to avoid seeing him as the doors closed in his face.

Frankie reached his side. 'Servant's entrance for you, mate.'

He nodded towards the card reader. 'That'd be the stairs.'

Her smile faded.

It took Frankie an impressive forty seconds to pick the stairwell lock, but she pulled up short in front of the electronic one on Jacklin's apartment. 'Ah, shit.' She was flushed from the eighteen-flight climb, but not seriously out of breath. A strong suspicion she'd had a little lie-down while he'd waited for her on the top landing.

'It's fine,' he said, unwrapping his phone.

The building was all style over substance, and the fancy-looking biometric lock was exactly what he'd expected. He found a close-up photo of Jacklin – studio shot with high resolution and good lighting, the young man's trademark smirk – and held it up to the scanner. The lock flashed green.

He rewrapped the phone. 'There you go, no need for lock picks.'

'No need for smug pricks, either.' She swung the door open to reveal a darkened room. Deep and wide, with a wall of glass at the far end overlooking the bay, dawn bleeding into the murky horizon.

On a console to the left, a small red light was winking.

Caleb put out a hand to stop Frankie entering. 'How long before the cops get here?'

'Twenty, thirty. Bit less if we want to play it safe.'

'We're out of here in ten.' He flipped on the lights, and Jacklin's flat lit up like a luxury morgue; black floor and white walls, stainless-steel fittings. No knick-knacks on the few shelves. Damn. They weren't going to find anything here except hospital-strength disinfectant.

'Worth a try,' Frankie said, not looking convinced.

'You take the bedrooms and ensuite, I'll do the study and bathroom. Look for Maggie's client list, too.'

'She wouldn't have given that to an underling.'

'Worth a try.'

The study had the same forensic ambience as the rest of the flat, along with a layer of chaos: desk drawers upended, spilling papers and pens across the floor. No computer, but a gaping wall safe and filing cabinet. Not the work of the police – someone had done a rapid and thorough clear-out. Caleb ran his hands along the walls and floor, checking for a second safe; no loose panels or carpet. No secret compartments in the desk, the sheets of paper all blank. Into the bathroom. Nothing except matt black tiles and a worrying quantity of nozzles. A room designed for very clean people. Or very dirty ones.

Frankie was in the grim kitchen, upending drawers. 'Nothing,' she said. 'Place has been turned over.'

'Yeah.' He checked the microwave clock: they'd been inside ten minutes. 'Time's up.'

'Living room first. Two minutes.'

He hesitated, then followed her. Not much to search: a black leather couch and sculptural chairs, a lone wall cabinet. The only decorations were an artistically mounted moose head on one wall, and an electric guitar and shovel on another. He felt along the floors and furniture while Frankie hunted through the cabinet. The moose head gave him the evil eye as he looked behind it; a small plaque on its mount read 'Ontario'. So Jacklin was a hunter. What was the shovel a memento of, a good day in the garden? No, breaking ground for the Connoy Hotel. He checked the scrawled signature on the guitar: a Telecaster once owned by Keith Richards. A man of simple tastes.

He turned to Frankie. 'Time to go.'

'Hang on, I'll just do the –'

He walked out.

She caught up to him at the stairwell door. They took the stairs at a fair clip and slipped out of the garage in the wake of a cream Mercedes. A police car was pulling up in front of the building as they strode past.

'See,' Frankie said. 'Plenty of time.'

# 27.

They arrived at the remand centre half an hour before visiting hours. A modern building on the outskirts of town that looked like a regional art gallery. Large stone urns instead of bollards at the entrance, filled with swaying native grasses. Not quite the glamorous surroundings Jacklin was used to, but almost hospitable if you ignored the razor wire and cameras.

'Classy,' Frankie said as they walked up the path. 'You reckon they'd let me live here?'

Spoken like someone who didn't own a redbrick Edwardian in Brunswick. So she'd sold her house – that must have been a wrench after twenty years. Smart, though, if she had debts; the place would have gone for a packet.

'Sold your house?'

'Wasn't mine to sell.' She headed through the automatic doors.

The centre was less welcoming inside, with metal detectors and bullet-proof glass, double security doors. A sign by the front desk warned of firearm and drug scanning. Frankie had made a show of stowing the gun in the boot, but he hadn't thought to remind her about drugs. She was pretty distracted, could easily have forgotten a stray baggie of smack. Risk her anger, or risk her getting arrested? Hard decision. As they approached the counter, he tapped her arm and pointed discreetly to the sign.

She turned a stony face towards him. 'Do I look like a fuckwit?'

He waited a beat. 'Rhetorical?'

He retreated at her glare, leaving her to deal with the first wave of bureaucracy.

It took forty minutes to go through the paperwork and scans, but they were finally shown into a cafeteria-like room, metal tables bolted to the floor, floating stools emerging from their central poles like strange white lily pads. A lot of people already seated, prisoners in olive-green overalls, visitors in jeans and tracksuits. The familiar smell of close-held bodies, sweat and anxiety. The old stress rose unexpectedly in him. Ant had only been nineteen when he'd done a stint for possession; six endless months, every visit leaving Ant only slightly less distraught, Caleb shattered.

Frankie led the way to an empty table near the internal door where the prisoners appeared. Some of the frenzied energy had left her, but she was still on edge, shifting on the stool and rubbing her hands on her jeans, eyes never leaving the door. A strong temptation to ask more about her living arrangements. She'd been in the same house for two decades; not just unusual in Melbourne's vicious rental market – extraordinary. That kind of long-term lease only happened between relatives. Which had to mean Maggie.

She spoke without looking at him. 'I can feel you thinking from here. Just ask the damn question.'

'What exactly is the deal between you and Maggie?'

Her eyes met his. 'She gives me the odd job and occasionally lets me mind Tilda. That exact enough for you?'

*Lets* her mind Tilda: a lot of history held in that one small word. Maggie was the one with all the power in their relationship, and Frankie resented them both for it. Glimpses of his own sibling fuck-ups there. He'd done more to harm Ant than just dragging him into a case; he'd been too controlling, too judgemental. Never giving him money or encouragement, greeting every happy period with distrust.

A cold worm of an idea burrowed into his brain. Was that how his own kids would come to see him? A father incapable of giving love without criticism? It'd be an apple straight from the Zelic family tree.

Frankie straightened. 'That him?'

A prisoner was standing in the doorway, looking around the room. Fine brown hair and a dimpled chin, the kind of superficial handsomeness that didn't stand up well to stress or olive-green overalls. Caleb raised his hand. Jacklin looked at him but didn't move, face wrinkled in doubt.

A fellow prisoner was trying to get past. One hand on Jacklin's shoulder, shoving hard. Repeated movements, as though punching his back. No, not punching – stabbing.

Caleb rose from his seat.

Jacklin staggered forward and dropped to his knees, the whites of his eyes showing. Blood spilled from his gaping mouth. People standing, running, lights flashing. Guards sprinted to the door and tackled the assailant. A spattered trail of blood as one of them kicked the attacker's shiv aside.

Jacklin toppled slowly forward and lay unmoving, his head angled as though still watching the room, eyes unblinking.

# 28.

Caleb drove to his flat, the need for a warm place and clothes overriding the faint worry someone might be waiting there. A small, boxy place with aluminium windows and sheet concrete walls. Charmless, but looking a lot better than when Frankie had helped him move after his split with Kat. He'd finally got rid of the last tenants' garish colour scheme a few months ago, replaced it with off-white walls and flat-pack furniture. Solid and liveable, but instantly disposable if Kat didn't want any of it in their new home.

A singed smell rose in the air as he turned on the heater; the dust of a long summer burning away. Frankie was clutching her backpack to her chest on an armchair, an unnatural stillness to her now the manic energy was gone. Her lack of sleep was showing in her dull skin and puffy eyes. His own eyes were aching, pain radiating from the bruise on his forehead, compressing his skull.

Neither of them had mentioned Jacklin's murder on the way here; no need to put fears into words.

The police had taken a while to release them – just forms and questions, not suspicion. A hastily constructed story of wanting to ask Jacklin about a mutual friend had smoothed over any queries. But it wouldn't take long for their names to flash alarms somewhere, to someone.

'Have a nap while I change,' he told Frankie. 'Couch isn't bad.'

She nodded, but didn't move.

He washed down a handful of painkillers in the bathroom,

then showered and changed into jeans and a warm jacket, didn't bother shaving. A few minutes to clean his aids and put in new batteries. They weren't beeping their low-power warning yet, but the bluetooth chewed through the batteries and he couldn't risk them going dead in a tense moment. Better not to imagine what that tense moment might involve. Who it might involve.

Twenty-six hours now, the weight of each minute crushing his thoughts.

Frankie was at the dining-room table when he finally joined her, belongings spread across it, including the black-market laptop and Tupperware-enclosed gun. Strange to think his life once didn't include things like that.

She started talking before she'd looked up. '... works for Maggie.'

Years since he'd had to tell her not to do that. 'Say that again.'

'Maggie only works on recommendations. There'll probably be a link between Jacklin and the killer somewhere – a business one.'

'You think Jacklin worked with Hollywood's boss?'

She paused. 'Hollywood? That's really what you're calling him?'

'If the name fits, Spiky.'

The slightest of smiles. If we search Jacklin's work history we'll find Hollywood's boss. 'We can narrow it down to people with serious connections. Discreet, though, so we can ignore anyone who flashes their cash.' She faltered. 'What do you think?'

That it was a very weak thread to pull. 'Great idea.'

He worked solidly for half an hour, getting bare-bones information on a handful of Jacklin's business partners, before realising the pain in his stomach was hunger. A quick forage in the kitchen unearthed some of Alberto's minestrone; a few days old but with enough garlic to fight any food-borne pathogens. He poured it into two bowls and chucked them in the microwave for a few minutes, checked his phone while he waited.

A text from Imogen.

—*CALL IMMEDIATELY*

Damn. The bank had only been open a few hours; he'd hoped chasing the safety deposit box would occupy her all day. She'd either worked out the documents had been taken, or run into Hollywood. An interesting meeting to imagine. He rewrapped the phone without answering.

The microwave darkened. He checked the result: cold soup, hot bowls. How was that possible? He shoved them back in.

There had to be a quicker way of sifting through Jacklin's associates. The list already ran to an entire page, and Caleb hadn't started the man's largest project, the Connoy Hotel. The seed of an idea: Jacklin's morgue aesthetic didn't run to knick-knacks, but he'd kept the shovel from the Connoy's ground-breaking. Was he particularly proud of the project, or was there something more to it? A souvenir of his entry into the shiny world of money laundering? Jacklin was a bit of a show pony; it'd be in character to display something he wanted to talk about but couldn't.

The microwave darkened again: somewhat warmer soup, much hotter bowls. His hands in tea towels, he carried the bowls to the dining room. Frankie nodded her thanks and kept working, typing one-handed as she spooned in the occasional mouthful. Caleb skimmed a newspaper article on the Connoy while he ate. Not much detail, but a few photos: parquetry floors and columns of smoked black glass, gold-leaf fittings. Familiar. The ballroom where the moist solicitor Delaney had fallen for the honeytrap charms of Quinn. A man goes to a fundraising party in a hotel: not exactly a smoking gun. And Delaney wasn't the kind of well-connected person they were looking for. But he might be a link to one.

'I might have something,' he told Frankie.

Hope lit her face. 'What?'

'There's a chance Jacklin and Rhys Delaney knew each other.' Her expression dampened as he explained about the hotel. 'I know Delaney's not exactly influential, but he could be connected to the boss.'

'Yeah.' Frankie visibly rallied and turned to the keyboard.

He went to sit beside her as she searched. Jacklin and Delaney didn't appear in any photos together and weren't connected on social media. No common schools or clubs or universities; no mention of them attending the same conferences.

Frankie sat back, shoulders slumped. 'Could be a coincidence. The Connoy's big, half of Melbourne's probably been through its doors.'

True. And a building the size of the Connoy had to have involved a lot of lawyers.

'Try the legal angle,' he said. 'Delaney's a business lawyer. "Conveyancing" was one of the first words out of his mouth.'

She typed quickly, turned to him, grinning. Delaney had done the conveyancing for the Connoy. At last, a tiny fingerhold to start climbing.

'Ring first?' he asked. 'He might be with clients.'

'Fuck no, we need to catch him by surprise.' She slid the gun from the container and tucked it into her backpack, headed for the door.

---

The kitten-loving office manager was coming up the street as they reached Delaney's office, a tray of sandwiches in her arms. Lunchtime. Hadn't thought of that; it'd be hard keeping Frankie calmly occupied if Delaney had nipped out for a bite.

Mrs Gillis bypassed the severe look and went straight to a

broad smile when she saw him. A gusting wind was coming from the bay, but her blunt grey fringe didn't move. 'Caleb, isn't it?'

'Good memory.'

'You're hard to forget. I've been telling everyone about you.'

For fuck's sake.

Mrs Gillis turned to Frankie. 'Isn't he clever? It must be so wonderful working with him.'

'Constantly have to pinch myself.' Frankie's eyes went to the sandwiches. 'D'you know if Delaney's out for lunch?'

'Oh, I'm afraid he's not in today.'

An unexpected blow that left them both speechless. He recovered first. 'Was that sudden? We were supposed to see him.'

'Well yes. I think it's his wife.' Her mouth snapped shut as she realised she'd crossed the line into gossip. 'Do come in if you'd like me to reschedule.' She hurried up the steps.

Frankie waited until she'd gone and said, 'Dead or skipped town?' Fury at either prospect.

'Or a genuinely sick wife.'

She flicked her hand. 'We need a list of his top clients. He can't have too many, he's mid-level at best.'

'You want to talk to his wife?'

'Yeah, but not for this. I'll bet Mrs Gillis can magic up that kind of info in seconds.'

'Good idea.'

She made a hurry-up motion. 'So go on then, ask her.'

And get pity-slimed again? 'No way. You do it.'

'She's not going to tell me. You're the one she's mooning over. Lay it on thick, too – she won't give it up easily.'

Fuck. Just seriously fuck. 'Wait here, will you? I don't want any witnesses.'

She smirked. 'Should I be organising a clean-up team?'

He went inside.

Mrs Gillis beamed like a grandmother receiving a macaroni necklace. 'You'd like to reschedule?'

'Not yet. I'm hoping you can help me with something else first.'

'Of course.'

'It's a bit delicate, but I'm supposed to be helping Delaney on a job, some work he's putting my way. Would you be able to give me a list of his five major clients?'

'Oh.' She sat back. 'No, I don't think so.'

Do it do it do it. He took a breath. 'I've got all the company info, of course, it's just the personal contacts I need. He told me yesterday, but Frankie was on a call instead of taking notes, so ...' An urge to claw out his tongue and set it on fire.

'Oh.' Her face crumpled. 'You couldn't understand him, you poor thing. I'm sure my boss will be across it all.' She reached for the phone.

'No,' he said quickly. 'It doesn't really instill confidence. Not everyone's as understanding as you. If you could just, um ...' He looked at the computer.

She shot a glance at the corner office and turned to her keyboard. A flurry of fast typing, then a page spat from the printer by her desk. She quickly folded it, handed it to him. 'I hope it helps.'

'Thanks,' he said. 'Really appreciate it.'

'No, thank *you*. You really are an inspiration.'

He gave her something like a smile and fled.

Outside, the air was cool against his cheeks. Frankie was in the middle of the footpath, feet wide as though ready to stride into battle. 'Got it?'

'What I could.' He unfolded the page. Mrs Gillis had dragged the contact information from different sources and dumped them all in one document. A mess of names and phone numbers in different fonts – but a familiar organisation among them all: the charity, Game Goers. Host of the ball at the Connoy Hotel and recipient of Delaney's boasted pro bono work.

Frankie tapped the paper. 'A charity would be a great way to launder money. Maybe Delaney's dirtier than we thought.'

Game Goers certainly had a lot of influential people as patrons, all conveniently listed by Mrs Gillis. A dozen or so names printed in tiny letters. He ran his finger along them, stopped on the third one: Judge Angus Lovelay.

Lovelay, the man who'd once been involved in a sex scandal with Quinn. Suspected of dismissing a court case in return for sexual favours.

# 29.

They went to a brightly festooned ice-cream parlour opposite the foreshore park. A bit too close to the local police station for comfort, but it had free wi-fi and a waitress happy to leave them alone. The cold change had kept most of the tourists away, and the shop was empty apart from a middle-aged woman with badly dyed hair and a baggy tracksuit. She'd been here when they'd arrived and was watching them work as she slowly ate an ice-cream, calling out the occasional question about their research. If she asked too many more, there was a good chance Frankie would brain her with the laptop.

None of their contacts had found a current address for Lovelay, and Quinn and her mother weren't answering the phone. Their own research had proved a dead end, too. There were a lot of older photos of the judge at society events, usually with his tawny-haired wife and son by his side, but those appearances had stopped after the scandal. Lovelay had quietly divorced and retired, his ex-wife dying of a stroke two months later. From everything to nothing in an instant; how did a man survive that? No career, no family, no reputation, just looking at yourself every morning in the mirror, knowing it was all your fault.

'No one's that invisible without trying,' Frankie said. 'Particularly someone who used to be a social darling. Lovelay has to –' She looked behind him, scowling.

The ice-cream eater must be back at the questions.

'Focus,' he said. 'Lovelay has to be what?'

'Hollywood's boss.'

A huge assumption, but Lovelay did fit the description: a well-connected person with ties to Maggie. Odds were, if he wasn't the boss, he'd know who was.

'OK,' Caleb said, 'let's say he is. What are we going to do if we track him down? He's hardly going to confess.'

'Jesus Christ.'

He blinked, then realised her anger was directed at ice-cream woman, not him. The coffee had been a mistake; Frankie was wound so tight it was making his teeth ache. 'Do we need to move shops?' he asked. 'Because the whole split-attention thing is kind of unsettling.'

She placed her hands flat on the tabletop, made an obvious attempt to focus. Her leg was jiggling the table. 'What do you suggest we do, then?'

'Take everything to Imogen. She might be on leave, but there's a chance she knows a back way into a few databases.'

'Yeah.' Frankie nodded, kept nodding, possibly unaware of it. 'OK, let's do it.' She heaved her backpack onto the table and handed him the phone.

As he unwrapped it, the woman appeared at their table. 'What are youse guys doin'?'

Frankie's eyes were thin slits. 'Planning a murder.'

Believable. Completely believable.

The woman backed away to her table and Frankie turned her attention to him again. 'Come on, text. Thirty minutes, same place as last time.'

Frankie hyped up, in an enclosed space with Imogen. No, they needed somewhere outside with good sightlines and no chance of getting jumped. The foreshore park, maybe. Or even better, the pier.

'How about a nice walk on the pier instead?'

---

The yachts in the marina were lifting on a choppy swell, their masts ticking a presto beat. Across the bay, the city towers glinted against a leaden sky. Nobody on the foreshore now, just a lone man fishing from the retaining wall, rainproof jacket zipped to the neck. No threat – he'd been here the past hour. Caleb glanced in his bucket as they passed: two small fish gaped desperately, their eyes dull silver coins.

Frankie came to a halt halfway down the wooden pier, where a stubby arm branched out towards the nearby dock. Caleb stood next to her, eyeing the gap across the water to the dock, the sheer drop at the other side. He'd had a vague thought it might be possible to jump or swim the distance, but it was too far, the water too rough. If they were wrong about Imogen and she turned up with Hollywood, he'd have to run interference. Give Frankie the best chance of getting away; give Tilda the best chance.

'If Hollywood shows, you run,' he said.

Understanding in her eyes; gratitude. 'Thanks.'

On the far side of the park, Imogen's black sedan was coming past the shops.

He nodded towards it. 'She's here.'

Imogen turned into the street that led to the pier and parked illegally at the end. Only her visible in the car. No other vehicles slowing on the main street; no one loitering in the park. Relief rinsed some of the tightness from his muscles. Imogen gave the area a slow scan as she headed down the path towards them. The same business attire as yesterday, with a long black coat; a woman who paid attention to the weather forecast.

Frankie hoisted her backpack onto her shoulder. 'Maybe you should lead.'

'OK.'

They'd spent the past half-hour discussing strategies, Frankie getting more indecisive as the minutes passed.

Imogen was on the pier now, limping slightly as though her shoes were rubbing. No, not her shoes – a weight in her coat pocket, banging against her leg with each step. A handbag slung across her shoulder, so probably not her purse. Unease stirred.

Frankie tapped his arm.

'Hang on,' he said.

Impossible to make out the shape, but too heavy for her taser or phone. The wind plastered the coat against her leg, revealing a hard edge.

A gun.

# 30.

'Right pocket,' he told Frankie. 'Something heavy, maybe a gun.'

Frankie stiffened. 'Shouldn't have one. Not if she's on leave.'

She shouldn't be carrying it in her pocket instead of a holster, either. Imogen might be happy to break rules, but a gun would be awkward to reach there and hard to draw; only someone who wanted an element of surprise would carry a weapon like that.

Frankie let her backpack drop to her wrist, holding it partly behind her. 'Gun's in the front pocket. Move beside me and pull it out.'

The fed was thirty or forty steps away, couldn't miss him pulling out a gun.

'She'll shoot.' Any cop would, let alone one who was primed and ready to go.

Frankie spoke evenly, eyes on Imogen. 'Come on. If she's come to kill us we're dead without it, and so is Tilda.'

Twenty steps away.

He shifted, blocking Frankie's right arm from the fed's view. Hand behind him, feeling for the pocket. He peeled open the zip and slipped his hand inside. Cold metal: the barrel of the gun. He gripped it.

Ten.

'You alone?' he called to Imogen as he eased it from the backpack.

'Yes.'

Eight.

Too close, had to distract her. 'That guy in the park isn't with you?'

She didn't turn. 'No.'

Six.

Frankie swung the backpack out and dropped it at her feet, Imogen's eyes following the movement. Caleb shoved the gun down the back of Frankie's jeans. Heart thumping, trying to breathe slowly.

Imogen stopped a few arm-lengths away, eyes on him. 'A word with you alone.' Separate and conquer – how stupid did she think he was?

'I don't think so. We've got a possible name for the guy behind the murders.'

She stilled. 'Who?'

If she was bent, she'd go for the gun. He shifted onto the balls of his feet. A good chance he could tackle her before she fired.

'A judge,' he said. 'Help us, and I'll tell you his name.'

No movement, no tensing of her fingers. He risked looking at her face and caught the end of her sentence. '... evidence?'

'There will be. He's linked to a charity we think Maggie's been laundering money through.'

Was that disappointment in her eyes, or relief? 'We need to speak alone,' she said again.

'Here's good.'

She widened her stance, glancing from Frankie to him. 'Frankie set you up. She put me onto you.'

Clever: finding the crack in their relationship, prying it open. But why?

Beside him, Frankie was speaking quickly.

He kept his focus on Imogen. 'Really? She kidnap her own niece, too?'

'No. I don't know what happened there, but she's trying to sell

Maggie's records. She dragged you into this because she thought you could get intel from me.' Imogen's hand moved towards her pocket.

He went to run, but Frankie had the gun out. Wide stance, aiming at the fed's chest. Imogen was motionless.

By the retaining wall, the fisherman was scrambling away, abandoning rod and bucket. Shit. The police station was just around the corner; the cops would be here in minutes.

Frankie was gesturing for Imogen to kneel, but the fed stayed standing. 'Think about it, Caleb. I'm a fed, I don't know anything about local homicides. Someone sent me an email saying you knew where Frankie was. Gave me everything I needed to pressure you into contacting her – Petronin's name, photos, dates, witness statement.'

His chest eased. For all her faults, Frankie wouldn't have risked ruining his life on the off-chance the cop would feed him information.

'Kneel,' he told Imogen. 'Slowly.'

'I traced the email, Caleb. It was sent from Mallacoota. The same town where I found the supposed witness. He said Frankie paid him to make the statement.'

Mallacoota. The town where Frankie had been hiding out. *Like being back in Mallacoota. If that shop assistant comes at me with the tarot cards, I'm out of here.*

A slam of sound, splinters flying as a bullet notched the boards. Imogen dropped to her knees.

'Coat off!' Frankie yelled. 'Now.'

Imogen hesitantly obeyed, threw the coat to one side. It skidded across the boards and caught on the end of a plank.

Frankie waved at him, her eyes and gun trained on Imogen. '...fucking with your head, Cal. We mustn't have wrapped the phone properly. She was listening, heard me say I'd been in Mallacoota.'

Yes. Yes, that made sense.

Except Frankie had told him about Mallacoota in the crystal shop. His phone had been locked in the car.

Caught between falling and impact. 'I didn't have my phone then.'

Frankie's face was bloodless. She was shaking her head, but not in denial.

God, it was true. He'd never forgive her, never forgive himself. He moved backwards until he was standing next to Imogen, blocking Frankie's way. 'You really set me up? For money?'

'No, I just –' Frankie's expression broke. 'I needed your help, couldn't risk you saying no. I owe money, Cal. A lot of money.'

'And Tilda? Did you let them take her?'

'No! I don't know who's got her. So let me get past so I can find her. I'll explain everything later, I promise.'

'Explain it now.'

Her gaze darted over his shoulder. 'The cops are coming. Let me go, let me help Tilda. Please.'

He didn't move.

She swung the gun towards him, hand trembling. 'Cal, please. I don't want to hurt you.'

Frankie aiming a gun at him, finger on the trigger.

Tears spilled from her eyes and ran down her cheeks. 'Please don't make me hurt you, Cal. Please.'

Enough. He stepped towards her. Frankie's finger whitened on the trigger.

He threw himself sideways.

A thud, heat plucking his arm.

Up against the edge of the pier, on one knee. Jesus, she'd shot at him. She'd really done it.

She started towards the shore, then skidded to a stop. Sprinted back the other way, down the stairs to the outcropped arm of the pier. Imogen scrambled for her jacket on the jetty's edge.

He got to his feet, slowly walked to the top of the steps.

Frankie was at the end of the boards, looking at the sheer drop into the water. In the corner of his eye, a flash of red and blue lights. 'It's over,' he said.

She spun around, her back to the water, gun low by her side. Face stark, panic in her eyes. The wind was snatching at her hair, sending it into wild spikes. Her gaze shifted to something behind him. Imogen, trying to get past, to pull him away.

Frankie raised her gun. Aiming it at the fed. At him.

Too close to miss; the width of a room, a lifetime, a lie.

Imogen stopped pulling and raised her arms, gun gripped in both hands. An awkward lean as she aimed around him.

He stepped aside.

A bang.

Frankie jolted then staggered, red blossoming on her chest. She crumpled, the gun dropping from her hand into the water.

Motionless.

Frankie lay sprawled. The smell of seaweed and salt, the sharp tang of blood.

Imogen was still aiming the gun, chest heaving. A glimpse of uniformed men on the pier beyond her. She bent to put her weapon down and turned cautiously towards the cops, hands raised.

Frankie hadn't moved.

Down the stairs towards her. One foot, then the other, along the pier to her side. She was looking at him, eyes already dulling. Palms open to the wind-ripped sky, her blood seeping into the greying boards. Broken. Dying.

Not a friend, an enemy.

One last stuttering breath, and the light left her eyes.

He turned away.

# 31.

Shivering. Sitting in the gutter that faced the pier, blue and red lights pulsing all around. Lots of uniformed cops now, but no white cotton jumpsuits yet, no plain-clothes detectives. A crowd had gathered on the opposite side of the street, phones out, people pushing to get a better view. The constable beside him straightened as Imogen reappeared; a short conversation had the young man hurrying back to his colleagues.

Imogen squatted in front of Caleb. Flecks of brown in her hazel eyes – never noticed that before. She was talking to him, something about Tilda.

'What?'

Her lips thinned. 'Don't. Mention. The. Girl. To. The. Detectives.'

'Why?'

'Because we can't trust anyone. Just say I was meeting with Frankie, and you don't know why.'

He nodded.

'Show ... arm.'

'What?'

'Your arm. Show them.'

He followed her finger. His jacket sleeve was ripped, the skin beneath it angry red. A burn, the heat of the bullet kissing him. The bullet Frankie had fired.

'I'll text ... caught up ...tomorrow.'

He nodded again. Out on the bay, a wave slammed into the

**183**

pier, sending spray into the air. Frankie would be cold lying out there. No, not anymore. Not Frankie anymore.

A hand in front of his face, Imogen snapping her fingers. 'For fuck's sake, concentrate. Go through it – why were you here?'

Anything to make her go away: his savings, his kidneys. 'Frankie was meeting you. Don't know why.'

'Why did I shoot her?'

'She had a gun. Tried to kill me. Kill us.' Shuddering now, teeth chattering.

'Good. Stick to that … alive…' She paused. '… judge's name?'

His brain cranked slowly into gear. No – bad idea to give her Lovelay's name with all these cops around. With Imogen about to be interrogated. She was speaking again; he looked away, to the police tape fluttering at the entrance to the pier, to Frankie's abandoned backpack, the lonely mound of her body.

*'She had a gun. Tried to kill me.'*

It was true: Frankie had pointed a gun at him and pulled the trigger.

But he'd killed her instead. He'd stepped away and killed her.

# 32.

It was dark by the time Caleb finished giving his statement at the police station. Tedesco was waiting for him in the foyer, perched on a too-small plastic chair but completely at home. An uncomfortable decision to call him as character witness, but the homicide cops had gone in hard once they'd connected Caleb to Jacklin's and Amon's murders.

Tedesco stood. Neat slacks and polished shoes, an ironed shirt: date clothes.

'Sorry,' Caleb said. 'I've dragged you away from something.'

'Don't be a dickhead.' Tedesco jerked his head towards the door. 'I'll drive you home.'

───────────

The flat was cold. Tedesco switched on all the lights and headed for the kitchen, turning on the heater as he went. Frankie's bowl was still on the table, soup half-eaten. Dizzy. Standing on a thin crust of earth, deep caverns below. He'd seen a TV show about that as a kid – sinkholes. Must have been young, around Tilda's age. Haunted by it for months, the idea solid ground could open up to swallow cars, houses, whole lives.

A tap on his shoulder: Tedesco passed him a bottle of Boag's. Good idea, a toast to the dead. Should have stopped on the way to buy a bottle of Johnnie Red, Frankie's favourite off-the-wagon drink.

'Thanks.' He took the beer to the couch and skolled half it. Beyond tired, sharp blades digging into his skull. Should take some painkillers before it got worse, take the little emergency pills from Henry while he was at it. Guaranteed numbing calmness he'd only surrendered to a couple of times. Better still, he could sit here and feel every fucking thing he deserved to feel.

Tedesco was leaning back in an armchair, nursing a barely touched beer. A sense he was tamping down a very strong urge to find out more than his colleagues had told him.

'Frankie put Imogen Blain onto me,' Caleb told him.

Tedesco's expression didn't alter, but it took him a good twenty seconds to speak. 'Why?'

'She's in debt.' He stopped, tried again. '*Was* in debt. She wanted to sell Maggie's business records, thought Imogen had some missing info.'

A rare fuck-up on Frankie's part: he'd barely got anything out of the fed. The rest had been well planned, though. Pushing him into panic mode with that witness statement, faking her reluctance to stay. Had she even hesitated before dragging him into it?

Yes. That first night at the motel she'd apologised, maybe even felt remorse. *I'm sorry, Cal. I know you're only in this because of my fuck-ups.* But she'd done it, anyway.

Tedesco was staring at him, probably waiting for an answer.

'Sorry, what?'

'Why you?' Tedesco asked. 'It's not like you're close to Blain.'

'Guess I had an easy pressure point and a history with Imogen.'

A history with Frankie, too. Deal with it later, just focus on helping Tilda. Couldn't do it by himself, that much was clear. He looked at Tedesco. 'I need help.'

The detective lowered his head in acknowledgment. 'I'll stick around. You want me to ring Kat? Or Henry Collins?'

No idea how to deflect kindness like that. 'No. I mean, I'm right. But I need to know who Transis were investigating. Can you –?'

'Cal, mate. Leave it. I know it was complicated with Frankie, but give yourself a moment to grieve. You were close for years.'

'It's not about me, it's Frankie's niece, Tilda. Someone's taken her.'

Tedesco's face became blank. 'A child? When?'

'Yesterday morning. They sent a proof-of-life video last night.'

'What the hell are you thinking? Report it.'

'It's too dangerous.'

Tedesco set his bottle down. 'I'll take you to the station right now, help smooth things over if that's what you're worried about.'

'I don't give a shit about me. It's Tilda.' He sketched the events of the past two days, trying hard to get things in the right order, having to backtrack.

Before he'd finished, Tedesco was shaking his head. 'I'm not comfortable with this – you have to report it.' He stood. 'I'll go if you won't.'

Caleb shot to his feet. 'You can't! These people have got feelers everywhere. If the cops work out where she is, she'll be dead before the rescue team's got their boots on. Just give me one more day. Please. I've got leads. Twenty-four hours.'

Tedesco ran a hand over his bristled scalp. 'I need to think. This isn't – I need to think.' He walked out, his undrunk beer on the table.

---

Caleb went to Kat's. Around the back way and over her neighbour's fence, into the small courtyard behind her terrace. Pot plants and ferns, a few discarded sculptures; a reflection of all the places they'd shared in their seven years of marriage. Kat was framed by the kitchen window. Sitting at the table with her oldest sister, Georgie, chatting, laughing.

The back steps were pine boards, each of them warped and loose. Easy to slip on the way down, break a leg, a neck, a pelvis. Madness – who'd choose a soft wood for outside stairs? The back door opened, and Kat's short curls were haloed by the hall light, laughter still trailing from her. She switched on the outside light. 'It's safe to come in. I promise I'll protect you from Georgie.' Her smile fractured. 'What's wrong?'

He raised his hands to tell her. Couldn't form the signs.

She came down the stairs, stopping on the last one so her face was level with his, her eyes wide. 'Ant?'

Nothing as terrible as that, thank God. Not his brother, not even a sister, just a woman he'd never known.

'No. No, everything's OK.' His eyes were burning. 'It's OK.'

'Cal.' She touched his cheek. 'What's wrong?'

'Frankie's dead.'

She put her arms around him and held him while he wept.

# 33.

In the early hours he lurched awake, mouth dry, the sensation of falling. A high ceiling, sketches pinned to the walls: Kat's spare room. She was next to him, curled on top of the bedclothes in the T-shirt and shorts she wore as pyjamas. The weight of her arm across his chest. Holding him while she slept. No memory of her coming in to comfort him, but the shadow of the nightmare lay on him like a bruise. A new one this time: the pier and lowering sky, Frankie's fading eyes.

A car went by, headlights running across the walls and bed, the familiar planes of Kat's face. Smooth skin and dark lashes, the hint of smile lines at her eyes. A face he used to wake up to every day.

Last night they'd talked for hours in the kitchen, drinking cup after cup of sweetened tea while he'd tried to separate Frankie's lies from the truth. Horror in Kat's expression. Impossible to know how much of it was at Frankie's betrayal and how much Kat's fear for a young child. For his part in it all.

He eased the quilt from under her and pulled it across them both. She shifted sleepily against him. He held her warmth to him, staring into the darkened room, willing sleep to come.

------

Kat's side of the bed was cold when he woke up, but the tea on his bedside table was still hot. The burn mark from Frankie's bullet pulsed on his upper arm. A few inches to the right and – Had she meant to miss, or had he moved just in time?

He dressed in yesterday's clothes and put his aids in, checked the sketches on the wall. Preliminary drawings for a new work. Another white-bellied sea eagle; different from her usual style, but still undeniably fierce, undeniably hers. Plywood ribcage and legs, outspread wings. Kinetic and alive, as though it could take flight. Looked like she was playing around with moveable joints. If he was reading her scrawled numbers right, the sculpture would be nearly her height. No wonder she was excited.

As he went to find Kat, the thuds of a busy house vibrated beneath his bare feet. Georgie must have stayed the night, offspring in tow. By the time he'd got inside last night she'd disappeared, no doubt shooed away by Kat.

He didn't get further than the kitchen doorway. A large room with a wide central table, walls filled with Kat's pencilled doodles. No Kat here now, but all three of her sisters, along with assorted nieces and nephews. Six kids including Georgie's neighbour's son, all under twelve; eating toast and frying eggs, the twins stacking saucepans in the corner. A rising and falling jumble of voices. Hard to believe the place would be spotless when they left, and the fridge full.

Georgie was halfway through pouring the kettle. Dark hair pulled back in a serviceable ponytail, the same clear blue eyes as Kat's, not quite as forgiving. Just turned forty, moving comfortably into the role of community elder. People in the Bay had already begun calling her Aunty. She gave Caleb a long look. 'The prodigal is-he-or-isn't-he husband.'

So Kat hadn't told her the reason for his late-night visit, or the state he'd been in. Georgie might be terrifying, but she wasn't unkind.

'Hi, Georgie. School holidays?' Not yet, surely?

'Just Saturday. Come join the fun.'

Amelia and Helen had turned from the table. More blue eyes, more up-and-down looks. He was suddenly very aware of his three-day growth, bruised forehead, stale and ripped shirt – and the fact he was supposed to present as a good partner for their baby sister.

Georgie switched off a radio he hadn't realised had been on. 'Come and have breakfast. There's heaps.'

About to be quizzed. He wouldn't get away with pretending not to understand them: all three sisters knew how to make themselves clear. Very clear.

'I'm right, thanks. Where's Kat?'

'Dunno. So, how's it going? You good?' Georgie's gaze moved to the bruise on his forehead.

'She gone out?'

Amelia patted the empty seat next to her. 'Sit down, tell us how you've been doing.' Her cheek dimpled. 'What you've been doing.' The youngest of the three, she was usually his best ally, but he wasn't stupid: if Kat hadn't told them why he'd spent the night, he wasn't going to do it himself.

'She say when she'd be back?'

Georgie ditched any attempt at being subtle. Her hands went to her hips, a pose so habitual he'd made it her sign name. 'So you're staying over these days?'

He cleared his throat. 'Just last night.'

'You're not –?'

'– are you –?'

'– in with –?'

'– Katy?'

He held up a hand. 'One at a time, or nominate a spokeswoman.'

Georgie raised a finger, waited patiently while he decided whether to see it or not. How did they have the time to be sitting around Kat's kitchen any day of the week? All of them professionals, mothers, foster carers. Homes and workplaces three and a half hours away in Resurrection Bay. Defied the laws of time and physics.

'OK, go,' he told Georgie.

'Does Katy want you to move back in?'

'You'd have to ask her.'

'Do you want to?'

They leaned forward, unblinking. Important not to actually show the fear; tricky to pull off with people who'd known him half his life, but he could do it.

'That's between me and Kat.'

They laughed. Georgie carried the teapot to the table, still smiling. 'Katy's in the shower. Think she's hiding from us.' She paused. 'Or you.'

———

He found Kat's drill and tightened the screws on the back steps while he waited, keeping them safe till he could get to a hardware store. Kat would be shitty, but at least he'd be able to cross one thing off the nightmare list.

He was finishing the handrail when she appeared holding two steaming mugs. Barefoot, wearing jeans and a loose rust-red top, hair still wet despite the chill. Never seemed to feel the cold, ran even hotter in pregnancy. She came down the steps, disregarding their lack of structural integrity, handed him one of the mugs. Her toenails were painted red, yellow and black. 'The tiddas said you might be out here.' Speaking out loud, but she was the easiest person to read, in words and expression: worried and decisive. Once she'd put the tea down so she could sign, she'd tell him exactly what he should be doing and why.

'Did they use the word "hiding"?'

She smiled. 'They did, actually. Were they being particularly mean?'

'How would I know?' He sat next to her as she settled on the bottom step, bracing himself when her eyes went to the drill.

She set her cup down and signed, 'If you're in need of handyman therapy, you can tackle the mould in the bathroom next.'

A generous pass, coupled with a warning shot. He tried the tea – black with a hint of vanilla, nothing to be deduced from it.

'How you feeling?' she asked.

'Fine.' He stopped, made himself try again. 'Don't know. Numb. Sorry about the nightmare. Waking you.'

She shook her head. 'You still having them a lot?'

'First one in ages.' He caught her frown and said, 'Seriously. I'm solid. Well, scaffolded, I guess. I'll call Henry if I need to.' He thought through what to say next. Their reconciliation had nearly failed because he'd pushed a case too far; if Kat didn't want him to keep looking for Tilda, he was going to have a major problem.

She touched his knee to get his attention. 'You have to talk to Tedesco again.'

'What?'

'I know he's hard to budge, but you need help and you can trust him.'

'Yeah. I was going to try again this morning. So you're OK with me looking for Tilda?'

'God yes, how could you live with yourself? I can't stop thinking about her. She must be so scared.' Kat pulled a slip of paper from her pocket, handed it to him.

*C West, room 310*

'What's this?'

'Maggie's room number. I rang the hospital, she's awake.'

His blood congealed. Kat talking to people, Kat getting dragged into things; the horrors of the last time that had happened were written on her skin.

'Don't panic,' she said. 'I know the drill. Rang from a public phone, didn't use my name. The nurse said they're allowing ten-minute visits from family. Sounds like Maggie's pretty groggy, but it's worth a try. If she can tell you who's got Tilda, you'll be halfway to finding her.'

A churn of emotions, most of which he'd have to deal with later. Concentrate on making sure Kat didn't get drawn in any further. 'When are your sisters going back to the Bay?'

'Soon as they've finished hassling you.'

'It'd be good if you went with them. I'll be able to help Tilda a lot better if I'm not worried about you. I'll pick you up Thursday so you can be back for the ultrasound.' What arguments hadn't he touched on? 'It'd save your sisters from making the trip up here. They must be busy.'

'You can stop laying it on so thick, I'm already going.'

A catch there somewhere, had to be. 'Really?'

'I'm working with Jarrah. He's got a big studio down there.'

Caleb tried to keep the grimace from his face. 'The plywood bird?'

'Yeah.' Her face lifted. 'Jarrah's going to do the mechanical stuff. He's got a degree in engineering.'

Of course he did. A degree in engineering, a happy nature, a shit-eating grin.

Time to have the conversation. 'What's the story with you and Jarrah?'

Her eyes were on him, clear blue in the morning light. It took her a few moments to answer. 'Just colleagues these days.' So there'd been something, in the long months after their marriage imploded; divorce papers waiting, communication ceased, Kat recovering from two miscarriages and an uncommunicative fuckhead of a husband.

'Serious?' he asked. Did some part of him enjoy pain?

'Couple of months. Then you turned up again.'

Not sure how to take that, except to put it on the steadily growing deal-with-it-later pile. 'Couldn't resist my rugged good looks?'

A smile. 'Plus your modesty.' She picked up her tea and drank, gazing at the garden. Millimetres from him; too far.

# 34.

The carpark was a bare asphalt lot bordered by serviced apartments and a lone house ready for the wrecker's ball. No sign of Tedesco yet. The detective had got in first with a text suggesting they meet this morning. A similar request from Imogen, but with a lot less punctuation.

Caleb parked at the back of the lot. The wind had lifted, worrying at a sheet of loose roofing iron on the abandoned house. He'd showered and changed at his flat but still felt smudged around the edges. He'd gone to collect Frankie's car, too, checking that the memory card from her camera was still safely tucked in the ashtray. A strange moment, seeing her discarded takeaway cup in the footwell, her gnawed pen on the seat. As though she'd open the door any minute and scowl at him.

He closed his eyes, tried to do the breathing exercises from Henry.

On the pier, she'd begged him to let her get past. *'I'll explain everything later.'* There was nothing close to an explanation in any of the notebooks she'd left behind, just a record of her increasingly desperate search for Tilda. Whatever she'd had to tell him was lost. If there really had been anything.

A cold blast as the car door opened. He started upright, fists bunching.

Tedesco was getting settled in the passenger seat. 'Stand down, soldier.'

'Fuck.' Caleb pressed a hand to his chest. 'Might have to lie down.'

'Lesson learned, then. Sitting with your eyes closed and doors unlocked. And I thought you were smart.'

'Don't know what gave you that idea.'

The detective was in gym gear again, and what looked suspiciously like an exercise tracker on his wrist. With any luck he'd be perky and helpful after his morning work-out.

'You've got info on Transis?' Caleb asked.

'No. And I won't. This can't go on any longer. Alert the authorities.'

'I can't. Even Kat agrees I shouldn't.'

'Cal, what you and Kat are going through is rough, but this isn't the way to handle it.'

He stiffened. 'It's not about that. I'm trying to save Tilda.'

'Jesus Christ, will you snap out of it? We're talking about a child. They could kill her. They might have already killed her while you were dicking around trying to fix things with Frankie.'

'You think I don't know that? It's all I can fucking think about.'

Neither of them moved. The roofing iron was flapping wildly on the derelict house. A strong gust would send it slicing through the air. Tedesco turned his gaze from it to Caleb. 'This stops now. I'm reporting it.'

Dread settled over him like a damp cloth. 'You can't, Uri. These people are connected. They'll know if the cops find her. They'll get to her first.'

'Right now, you're her biggest threat.' The detective got out, didn't look back as he strode to his car.

---

Caleb arrived at the hospital strangely breathless after the two-block walk, took the lift instead of the stairs to the third floor. Ward C was a brightly lit space, single-bed rooms fanning out from a nurses' desk. Caleb headed slowly towards room 310. No idea how to tell Maggie about her daughter, about her sister.

A flash of blue as the duty nurse came to stand between him and the doorway. Bird-like, with sparrow-brown hair. The top of her head only came to his chin, but she looked ready to body-slam him onto the well-polished lino. '... hear me? I said you can't go in.' Neat little mouth and lips, tiny teeth.

'Ah no, sorry. I'm family. Maggie's nephew.'

She folded hollow-boned arms across her chest. 'I'm sorry, but she's had police and visitors all morning. She needs to rest.'

Police. It couldn't be about Tilda, not yet. Which meant they'd been here about the assault, and possibly Frankie's death. There was a chance homicide had managed to track her down. Be good to know exactly how much bad news he had to break.

'Why were the police here?' he asked.

'About the assault, of course. You'll have to come back tomorrow – she's exhausted.'

'I've got information about her daughter. She'll want to know.'

'Oh.' Her arms lowered. 'That's Tilda? Maggie's been quite distraught about her. She's somehow got it into her head the girl's missing.'

'Yes.' He edged around the nurse, towards the room. 'So I'll just talk to her quickly. Set her mind at ease.' Another step.

'Two minutes. I'll be timing you.'

He ducked past before she could change her mind. Maggie's room smelled of disinfectant, a still quality to the air. She was asleep, lying half-propped in bed, bandages around her head. Glimpses of Tilda in her thin face; of Frankie.

A man was sitting by her side. He stood, weight even in his feet. Alert eyes and short hair, the unsubtle bulge of a gun beneath his jacket: one of Frankie's hired guards. Probably ex-army, definitely professional.

Caleb ventured a bit closer, hoping Frankie had put his name on the 'non-threatening' list – and that Maggie hadn't removed it. 'I'm Caleb Zelic, Frankie's business partner.'

'Some ID if you don't mind please, sir.'

Caleb fished his licence from his wallet and passed it to him. The guard's posture eased slightly as he examined it. 'And if you could tell me the name of your first pet please, sir?'

A moment to regret both the name of the pet, and that he'd mentioned it to Frankie. 'Bunnykins.'

The slightest of quirks to the man's lips. 'Thank you, sir.' He returned Caleb's licence and leaned down to speak to Maggie. Her eyes opened. A hazy focus as she listened to the guard, but she nodded, and he went to wait outside the door. No obvious recognition as Caleb approached her; face open and vulnerable, nothing like the cool-headed criminal who'd once tried to kill him. Good. If she was that doped up, he might get some information out of her. 'Know you?' she asked. 'Feel I should know you.'

A jolt at the familiar rhythm of her speech, so like Frankie's despite the blurred edges.

'Yes, I'm Frankie's – I'm her friend.'

She lurched forward, words tumbling from her lips like in the video. 'Turnip. Has she got Turnip? ... Quinn said ... Turnip ... Frankie got her?'

So Quinn had been one of Maggie's visitors. Not a complete surprise – Quinn might have run back home when she was threatened, but she was smart and battle-scarred; she'd know it was safer to understand what she was up against.

'No,' he said, then stopped. Honesty wouldn't help either of them; Maggie was too confused, too distraught. 'Turnip's fine. Frankie's got her.'

'Oh. Oh good.' She settled back against the pillows. 'Loves Turnip. Only thing I can trust her with.'

'Who hurt you?'

'Can't remember, head's fuzzy.' She squinted at him, as though looking into a bright light. 'Do I know you?'

'I'm Frankie's friend. She needs your client list. To keep Turnip safe.'

'Can't have it. All her fault. Some dog found out she stole the records. Set the cops onto us.'

A moment thinking he'd misread her, then it clicked – she was talking about Imogen's informant, Jordan, the man Maggie had probably ordered killed. Better sidestep that part of the story. 'How did Jordan know Frankie had the records?'

'Don't know. Don't know him.'

'He didn't work for you?'

'No.'

Sudden clarity in her eyes. 'You're Caleb. Messed things up for my mates last year. You and Frankie working together again?'

Shit. Probably a matter of seconds before she remembered he'd killed her ex-husband.

'Just for a bit,' he said. 'She needs your client list. Where is it?'

'It's good you're working together. You're good for her. Fond of you.'

Unable to speak; his throat closed shut. He shook his head.

'True. Hated herself for fucking things up with you. Story of her life. Doesn't mean she doesn't care.' Her eyes were drifting, words thick in her mouth. 'Raised me, you know. Mum was hopeless. Drunk. Shouldn't've had kids.'

He swallowed. 'Frankie needs your client list.'

'Can't trust her with that. Tell me if she fucks you around again,

I'll pay. Should pay you for killing my ex, anyway. Saved me the hassle.' Her eyelids fluttered shut.

'Maggie.' He touched her arm, waited until she looked at him. 'What does Turnip know about your clients?'

Movement at his shoulder – the small nurse was there, tapping her watch. 'Time to leave.'

'Just a sec.' He turned to the bed. 'Maggie. What does Tilda know about your clients?'

Her lips barely moved. 'Nothing. Just a game.'

The nurse gestured to the door. The guard was there, sharp eyes on him.

Caleb got a little way past the nurses' desk before stopping. An entire conversation with Maggie, and all he'd discovered was that Jordan hadn't worked for her. No point hanging around waiting for her to wake up: even drugged and confused, she hadn't let anything important slip.

The small nurse was in front of him again. '... down?'

'Sorry, what?'

'You're a bit pale. Do you need to sit down? Or speak to someone? Visits like this can be upsetting for loved ones.' Not volunteering for the job, just going through a checklist.

'I'm fine. You mentioned before that Maggie had a lot of visitors this morning. Did you get any names? It'd be good to know who I still need to contact.'

A faint blush touched her cheeks. 'I may have overstated it somewhat, but the police were here a long time.'

'Of course. Anyone else?'

'Just her sister.'

A swooping sensation before he realised she couldn't be talking about Frankie. 'Quinn?' he asked.

'Yes. You must have just missed her.'

Quinn was a smoker; odds were she'd stop for a quick durrie

after a stressful visit. If he could find her, he could question her about Lovelay. 'Which way did she go?'

'I think towards the back entr–'

He took off, waving his thanks over his shoulder.

———

Quinn was sheltering in an alcove a few metres from the taxi rank, handbag slung across her chest. Onto her second cigarette, by the looks of it. Jeans and a navy hoodie, dark hair scraped into a loose bun. When she saw him, she stepped from the alcove, cigarette in front of her, ready to jab. A practised move. 'You following me?'

'I'm here for Maggie. Tilda's still missing.'

Her gaze darted to the hospital doors. Searching for someone?

'Frankie's not here,' he said.

'Yeah? You seemed pretty bloody tight the other day. You didn't tell me it was her fault all this happened. Maggie's going to kill her.'

'She's dead.' Much easier to say this time; just needed a bit of practice.

'What? When?' Her eyes were wide.

'Yesterday. A cop shot her.'

'Jesus. The pigs are involved?' She was tensed, getting ready to run.

'Federal cops. I think Rhys Delaney's gone, too. He didn't turn up to work.' He let her imagination fill in the missing pieces. 'There's a café inside. How about we tell each other what we know over coffee? Help each other out?' He did an obvious scan of the street. 'We're pretty exposed out here.'

She considered his words, flicked her cigarette onto the footpath. 'You'll have to buy. I'm skint.'

He bypassed the main cafeteria, leading her to the small café off the lobby, a low-ceilinged place with plastic tables and chairs. Quinn headed for the attached courtyard to light up, while he bought them coffee, added a couple of muffins; Quinn looked like she could use the carbs even more than him.

The plastic theme continued outside, with synthetic lawn and vases of fake flowers. No other customers – possibly scared away by the environmental toxins and Quinn's cigarette. She'd chosen the exact chair he would have: her back to the wall, an unimpeded view of the hospital foyer and café. Which meant her face was in shadow.

'Sorry,' he said, 'could you move to the other side? It's too dark there.'

Her words were unreadable, but her expression clearly said 'piss off'.

'I'm deaf. I need to see your mouth to lip-read.'

She laughed. Not the first time he'd had that reaction, but for some reason he hadn't expected it from Quinn. Always worse when he wasn't prepared for it.

She stood and moved into the light. 'Shit, and here I was thinking you fancied me, the way you kept staring at my mouth.' She plonked herself in a different seat. 'Never get the cute ones, always the slobs.' Turning up the charm again. Difficult to work out where performance began and ended with her.

He passed her the coffee as he sat. 'Thought you'd be halfway to Darwin by now.'

'Me, too. Then I remembered I don't have any money, skills or protection. I need Maggie to sort this out or I'm fucked.' She took a deep drag. 'So I guess I'm fucked.'

'You didn't get anything out of her?'

'Just about Frankie doing the dirty. Then I went and mentioned Tilda, and she flipped. Didn't realise she didn't know, or I would've kept my mouth shut. How'd she take the news about Frankie?'

'Wimped it. Didn't tell her.'

'Jesus, an honest man. Careful, or they'll kick you out of the club.' She blew a long stream of smoke at the No Smoking sign. Looked relaxing; maybe he should take it up. Something to do with his hands other than punching a wall.

*'Right now, you're her biggest threat.'* Tedesco would have made his statement by now, cops on the way to Maggie's bedside. Hard to see how the two of them could get past this. A friendship only a year old; ridiculous for its loss to make him feel this sick.

'You know who took Tilda yet?' Quinn asked. 'Was it that big bloke?'

'No, but he's after her. Probably working for one of Maggie's customers. Do you know where her client list is?'

'You kidding? I'm just the hired help. Not even that – I fuck the hired help.' Quinn was a lot sharper than she let on, a useful shield in her business, and one Maggie would have used.

'You do more than that,' he said.

'Sure. Sometimes I fuck for fun, too.' She gave him a raking look, but didn't seem to have her heart in it.

'Does that usually work as a distraction?' he asked, genuinely interested.

'I'm usually better at it. Off my game.' She sat back, eyeing him through the smoke haze while she decided if she could trust him.

He tried the muffin as he waited – blueberry and sawdust. When would he learn never to buy muffins? Almost be better off with banana bread.

'I'm a go-between,' Quinn finally said. 'Tell the workers what to do and when. Maggie keeps things tight, lots of buffers, airlocks, whatever. There's no way a client could have known Frankie stole the records.'

Frankie had talked about Maggie's tight security, too.

'What do you know about Rhys Delaney?' he asked.

'Not much. Maggie just asked me to keep him happy occasionally.'

*Keep* him happy, not make him happy. According to the solicitor, he'd only met Quinn once. 'How long has Delaney been working for Maggie?'

'No idea.'

A very literal take on his questions; he tried again. 'When did you first sleep with him?'

'Sleep with him?' She laughed. 'Aren't you friggen adorable? About a year ago, I guess. Maybe more.'

So Delaney had lied. Or Quinn was lying now – a distinct possibility if she was trying to distract him from her ex-lover, Judge Lovelay. There seemed to be real affection there.

'How well does Delaney know Maggie?'

She waved a hand. 'Airlocks etcetera, etcetera.'

He smiled, almost felt bad about the next question. 'What about Lovelay? He knows her pretty well, doesn't he? Introduced you to her.'

Quinn's thoughts played across her face as she considered lying, then realised her hesitation had given her away. 'Yeah, they're old mates.'

'I need to speak to him. You know his address?'

'Angus wouldn't have taken Tilda. He's a good bloke.'

'I'm not saying he did, but Maggie works on introductions, and Lovelay's a connector. He'll know more of her customers.'

'No. Sorry, but I'm not going to drag him into it. He did everything for me. Taught me things, introduced me to the right people. And he lost everything because of it – wife, kids, career. Doesn't deserve any more shit.'

Caleb doubted anyone in his life except Kat would protect him like that. Still, one person was good, particularly if that person was Kat.

'I won't drag him into anything, I just want to ask him some questions.'

She stood and stubbed her cigarette out on the plastic flowers. An acrid smell. 'I really hope Tilda's OK, but I'm out.'

'I'll find Lovelay,' he said. 'But before that I'll contact the fed who killed Frankie and tell her about your in-depth knowledge of Maggie's business.'

Her face hardened. 'Had you wrong. Thought you were one of the good ones, that you felt bad about Frankie threatening me. Turns out you're a bigger cunt than she is.'

He held her gaze. 'Now you know.'

# 35.

Lovelay's house was a grand two-storey mock-Georgian with a matching mock-Georgian garage, its sweeping lawn adorned by a marble statue of a woman – mock-Grecian. The kind of taste-vacuum that bemused Kat. She used to stop on their evening walks to examine similar places, the air of a doctor trying to understand a patient's benign but puzzling symptoms.

She'd be halfway to the Bay by now, probably caught up in a lively debate with her sisters. The entire family couldn't spend ten minutes together without trying to fix the world's wrongs. Car trips with them were like watching an un-captioned but engaging movie, usually with a healthy snack or two thrown in.

He knocked on Lovelay's door. Waited. Knocked again, pressed the doorbell for good measure. Nothing. Damn: like hitting a blank wall right after the starter's pistol.

OK, Delaney's house was only a fifteen-, twenty-minute drive from here. Speak to the man's wife, then try Lovelay again, break in if he had to. Caleb might not have Frankie's lock-picking skills but he knew how to smash a window.

---

No one answered Delaney's door.

Caleb peered through a gap in the living-room curtains. Scattered toys, old-style TV and lounge suite, a basket of unfolded washing. Nothing to be read from the scene, other than that a family with young children and modest spending habits lived here.

He tried the house opposite, a well-kept cottage with windows overlooking the Delaneys'. No answer. Shit damn fuck. He turned to check out the neighbouring houses: lights off, no cars. Too tired to keep doing this; he was going to make mistakes. More mistakes. You needed a partner for this kind of sustained work – even better, an assistant. No trust involved, just someone to drive while you napped, and call ahead to make sure people were home. Not cleave you apart, leave you holding the shards.

A tap on his back.

He lurched forward, caught himself before he went headfirst off the porch. In the doorway, an elderly woman was looking at him. Even smaller than the nurse at the hospital, with snappable bones, tiny feet in what had to be kids' shoes. 'Goodness, you're jumpy. You should take something for that.' Vowels so plummy she could make jam.

'Yeah. Do you know the Delaneys? I need to speak to a family member.'

'And you are?'

'Caleb. Caleb Zelic.' He handed her a business card, the one giving his title as 'security consultant'.

She studied it carefully. 'Couldn't you come up with a vaguer title?'

'Sure. I've got one that just says "consultant".'

A dry cough of a laugh. 'I'm afraid you just missed them. They left for Noosa thirty minutes ago.'

'Was that sudden?'

'I believe so.'

An impromptu subtropical holiday. Because Delaney was scared? Or because he was trying to mend his marriage after sleeping with Quinn?

The woman was watching him with bright black eyes, apparently eager for his next question.

'Do you know the family well?'

'I suppose that depends on your definition of well. June and I often chat, but we don't share our sexual exploits. I do hope you're not going to spoil her holiday. She's been so glum, but she was smiling away when she asked me to feed the cat. Do you think you could make that stop?'

He replayed her last sentence. 'Make what stop?'

'Your phone. It's chirping in the most annoying manner.'

Shit, he'd forgotten to turn it off after checking the map. 'Sorry, I don't know how to turn the sound off. Why has June been down?'

Her eyes went to the business card. 'What's this all about?'

'I'm following up a few things with Mr Delaney's work.'

'That's a very dull way of saying you believe he was on the take.'

That was sharp; maybe she could be his assistant. Or he could be hers.

'Would you be surprised if he was?'

'Yes. He's sulky but not sneaky. Then again, I'm no judge of character. I really don't understand what June sees in the man, and she adores him.'

'Has he spent an unusual amount of money lately?'

'Apart from the holiday, you mean? I really couldn't say.' Her hand went to the door. 'And I've probably slandered him enough. Best of luck with your consulting.' A brisk smile, and she closed the door.

He headed for the car, checked his messages as he got in. Alberto's daughter.

—*Dad's hurt. Someone beat him up*

# 36.

It wasn't quite sunset, but Alberto's house was ablaze with light, a lot of people visible through the net curtains. The place could have been built by Caleb's father: solid blond brick, all right angles and straight lines. The kind of house where you slept well at night, knowing the roof would stay on and the weather stay out. A much more abundant garden than anything Ivan Zelic would have planted, though – a mini-orchard of olives, lemons and apples, carefully pruned and mulched.

Nick answered the door, eyes red-rimmed and swollen. 'He's OK,' he signed before Caleb had a chance to ask. 'The doctor said nothing's broken.'

The nausea receded, but only a little. More than just bones could be broken in an assault.

Nick gestured him into the tiled entrance hall. Its wide double doors opened onto a living room filled with people: Ilaria, staff, customers. Everyone signing and eating, the mood somewhere between a funeral and a party. No Alberto darting among them, making sure everyone was fed and happy.

'Do you know what happened?' Caleb asked Nick.

'We were setting up, around six-thirty. Just me and Grandad.' Nick's hands jerked from one sign to the next with none of his usual grace. 'He went back to the car to get something, took ages. When I finally went to look, he was lying in the alley, kind of curled

213

up.' The teenager's lips pressed inwards as he tried not to cry. 'I was in the kitchen the whole time.'

Ilaria came through the living-room door towards them, eyes on her son. Dressed in her usual dull greys, but an intense focus Caleb had never seen before. She stopped in front of Nick. 'It would have been much worse for your grandad if you'd been hurt. He's thankful you weren't there.'

Tears rolled down the boy's face. 'It's Dad.'

Ilaria glanced back at the living room. 'It's not.'

'It is. Dad –'

'I've watched the security tape. It's not him.'

'You sure?' Caleb asked. It would have been dark at that hour.

A grim smile. 'I know how Tony moves.' She touched Nick's arm. 'Grab my laptop from the kitchen, will you? The video's on it.' She nudged him gently when he hesitated, and he headed down the hall. Ilaria waited until he'd gone, then faced Caleb. 'Wipe it when you're done, I don't want Nick seeing it.'

'So it might have been his father?'

'No, it's definitely not Tony. But Nick's already seen too much damage. I don't want him seeing his grandad getting hurt. I can at least do that.' She lifted her chin, daring him to argue.

He went in to Alberto as soon as Nick returned with the laptop. A cosy room, family photos on the walls, along with a large tapestry of what looked like an Italian village. A portrait of Alberto's late wife in pride of place on the dresser. Alberto lay on top of the blankets in a fleecy brown tracksuit. He sat up as Caleb came to the bed, carefully propping himself against the headboard. Purpling bruises marred his face, his left eye swollen almost shut.

Old. Frighteningly old. Like Caleb's grandfather in the last few months, his once mortar-cracked hands soft and trembling. Tears burned in Caleb's eyes.

'Don't you start,' Alberto told him. 'The boy and his mother have been going all morning.' But he gave Caleb's arm a little rub as he sat on the bed.

'You see who did it?'

'No.' Alberto's head lowered. 'Hit me from behind, and I stayed down.'

A white hot rage. How could anyone have made this man feel ashamed? 'D'you think you're up to watching the tape? It could help.'

'The police have already looked. They said it's too dark for an ID.'

'Worth a try. You might recognise the way he moves.'

'Of course. I should have thought of that.' Alberto levered himself straighter, making a painful show of interest.

The video was set up and ready to go. Alberto's spry figure walking down the darkened alley, someone running up behind him. A blow to the back of his head; he smacked to the ground. Caleb flinched. Too dark to see the attacker's face, but his movements were clear as he raised his arm, brought something long and thin down on Alberto's back. Lashing repeatedly as Alberto curled in a ball, his arms over his head. Eventually the man turned, and walked away, the whip held down by his side.

No, not a whip. Cylindrical, a piece of pliable pipe like a garden hose.

Alberto was ashen. 'I don't know him.'

A garden hose. Someone had mentioned an attack with a hose just the other day. A few seconds to retrieve the memory: Tedesco in the park eating a bowl of kale, talking about his latest case, the murder suspect. Jimmy Puttnam, the loan shark. '... *whipping people with a cut-off garden hose ...*'

A rancid thought oozed into his brain. Smashed windows and threatened arson were all straight from a loan shark's playbook; standard methods when a debtor couldn't pay.

Caleb looked at Alberto. 'He's a loan shark.'

'You know him?'

His tension released at Alberto's blank expression. Of course the man wasn't in debt to Jimmy Puttnam. No loan shark would have sabotaged the deliveries and cancelled the electricity account – too time-consuming, too subtle.

But an owner might, to scam money from an insurance company.

*'I upped the insurance, got top cover on everything.'*

He stood, mouth dry. Alberto couldn't have used him as a smokescreen. It'd be unbearable.

Alberto reached towards him, looking alarmed. 'Are you all right? Sit down, sit beside me.'

Caleb's arms were almost too heavy to sign. 'Why couldn't you have just sold the business if you needed money? Sell the building? Why involve me?'

'What are you talking about?'

'You're in debt to Jimmy Puttnam, trying to con the insurance company to get the money.'

Alberto slumped against the bedhead. 'How could you think so little of me?'

How could Alberto think so little of him?

He left. A glimpse of Nick through the living-room door, the boy's face filled with anxiety, Ilaria huddled with friends in a corner. Not his job to tell them, they'd find out sooner or later. He kept going, closed the front door behind him.

# 37.

Judge Lovelay looked like he'd woken from a long nap, his salt-and-pepper hair matted on one side, cheek creased. Early retirement hadn't suited him. The fit and handsome man from the news reports a few years ago was gone, replaced by someone much older.

He appeared bewildered by Caleb's request for him to turn on the outside lights, even more bewildered at his business card. 'Are you looking for work?' he said, eyes still on the card. A clear tone, with the steady pace of a man used to public speaking.

'No. I'm here about Maggie Reynolds. About her daughter.'

Surprise crossed Lovelay's face. 'I'm not really that close to Maggie. You'd be better off contacting her family.'

Caleb tried to dredge the right words from his mind. Strangely blank, as though he'd just woken from a deep sleep, too. Maybe he had: he'd apparently been walking through his life in a daze. *'How could you think so little of me?'*

Focus. Don't think about Alberto or Frankie or the thin crust of earth cracking beneath his feet, just concentrate on getting Tilda back.

'It's connected to Transis,' he told Lovelay.

'I'm afraid I don't know what that is.'

Caleb hesitated: was he mistaken about the judge's involvement? No wariness to the man's manner, just faint confusion, an obvious

217

wish to be left alone. Maybe the truth was his best bet. 'Maggie's daughter's been kidnapped. Tilda.'

'Oh my goodness.' Lovelay's face drooped.

'I'm hoping you can help. Can I come in?' He stepped onto the threshold without waiting for an answer.

'Oh. Of course. If you think I can be of some use.'

The judge led him to a large sunroom overlooking the backyard. Spotlights illuminated silver birches, bare limbs shivering in the wind. The room had an unused quality; no clutter, just a wilting floral arrangement and a bookmarked biography of Churchill on a side table. Only one of the four leather armchairs was softened by use.

Caleb took the one closest to Lovelay's, waited for the judge to get settled. Whatever the man's role in Maggie's affairs, he seemed strangely open to helping. 'Tilda's in danger,' Caleb said. 'Not just from the kidnappers, but from one of Maggie's clients. They think she knows something incriminating.'

'Oh that poor child. Poor Maggie.' In the light of the sunroom, he looked more than badly aged: rheumy-eyed and shaky, a few bristling patches where he'd missed shaving. 'I'm sorry, but I'm not sure what you want from me.'

'I need Maggie's client list. I know you're one of them.'

'I've got no idea about that. Ask Maggie.' Not denying the connection, but not quite admitting to it.

'Maggie's sick, she can't help. But you've introduced her to lots of people. Tell me who they are.'

'I'm truly sorry, but I don't know anything that could help.' The judge's voice wavered and caught. He pulled a crumpled handkerchief from his pocket and dabbed his watering eyes. 'My apologies. I'm afraid I'm a little weepy these days. The thought of another child –'

*Another child.* The rotting flower arrangement and bloodshot eyes: the man was in mourning. Slow today; should have put that together straight away.

'I'm sorry, have you lost someone recently?'

'My stepson. He wasn't a child, of course – twenty-three – but still so young.'

The tawny-haired boy with Lovelay in all the pre-Quinn society photos. Another death. A man peripherally connected to Maggie. Caleb sat still. 'I'm sorry, had he been unwell?'

'Oh. No. An accident. I'm sure it was an accident. Although I hadn't seen him much in recent years. Not my choice, you understand – I loved the boy.' He wiped his eyes. 'It's quite unbearable, you know. Having unfinished business with someone you love.'

Caleb asked the question, tried to keep the hope from his voice, from himself. 'What was his name?'

Lovelay gave him a grateful smile. 'Jordan.'

# 38.

Jordan's old flatmate was called Ike. Or possibly Mike. Early twenties, squat and thoroughly stoned. After a few failed attempts, he finally understood Caleb wasn't there to see Jordan, but talk to the man's friends.

'Right, yeah, come in,' he said. 'Ben knew him best. Come and –' He wandered into the house, still speaking.

Caleb followed, hoping Ike wouldn't get too distracted on the long walk down the hall. The house was one of the few un-renovated terraces remaining in Carlton. Threadbare carpet and peeling paint, the heady scent of fresh dope and unwashed dishes; not squalid, but giving it a good try. According to Lovelay, Jordan had been studying at nearby Melbourne Uni and living off a 'small trust' provided by his stepfather.

Ike led Caleb to a dim smoke-filled room. Purple velvet curtains and an odd assortment of furniture. What looked like a vintage record player was pumping out a heavy beat. A freckled young man was sprawled on a couch, smoking a bong. Ike flopped next to him.

Caleb stayed standing: dark, loud music, two people. Two very stoned people. 'Can you turn off the music?'

Neither of them moved. He went to the record player and lifted the needle, switched on the overhead light. The students recoiled.

'The fuck?' Ike said.

'Sorry, I need to see.'

'Nah, bro, turn it off. Too fucken bright.'

'I'm deaf, I'm lip-reading.' He braced himself. Young men were usually the worst: too desperate to prove their manhood to let a perceived weakness go unchallenged.

They stared at him, a pair of very relaxed owls.

'Cool,' the freckled guy eventually said, and offered him the bong.

Caleb shook his head. 'You Ben?'

Freckles nodded, his eyes so bloodshot they looked painful.

'I'm here about Jordan. Ike said you knew him best.'

'Guess so.'

'You meet any of his friends?'

'Nah, Jordy kept to himself.'

'He ever mention someone called Maggie or Imogen?'

'Nah.' A pause for thought, or something approaching it. 'Have you got a seeing-eye dog?'

'No. How did Jordan seem before he died?'

'Why haven't you got a dog?'

'Because I'm deaf, not blind. How was Jordan in the last few weeks?'

'Good. Real happy. That's how we know he didn't top himself. Told his dad that at the funeral. Stepdad.' Another long pause. 'Dunno why he was there. Jordy hated him.'

'Why?'

'Rooted around on his mum. Jordy reckoned she died because of it. Had a stroke or something. Couldn't let it go.' Ben looked at his mate for confirmation.

Ike nodded. 'Real Oedipal shit.'

Lovelay weeping in that empty house; a man grieving alone because of his own stupidity. Should hang him on the wall, use him as a warning. Or a mirror.

'Is Jordan's stuff still here?'

'Yeah.' Ben gazed at him. 'What about one of them canes? White ones. You use one of them?'

'Only when I'm driving. Where's his room?'

'Upstairs. Near the balcony.'

Jordan's bedroom was the cleanest thing in the house. A pile of dirty clothes in one corner and an almost-made bed. No computers, but a good-quality printer. The shelves held textbooks and a well-thumbed copy of *Infinite Jest*, uni work with an assortment of high distinctions and fails. In the mix were printouts from real estate sites: not the small family homes Caleb had been leaving for Kat to find, but rambling country properties. Looked like the 'small income' Jordan had been getting from Lovelay's trust would stretch to some significant properly investment. Not bad for a 23-year-old.

Jordan had obviously wanted to punish Lovelay by exposing his dirty money. The question was, who'd taken his laptop – a family member, or someone who'd been in on it with him?

Caleb went back downstairs. The students looked at him without surprise or recognition.

'Who took Jordan's laptop?'

Ben sucked on the bong, searched a distant part of his memory. 'Some bloke.'

'Big guy? Lots of muscles?'

'Nah.'

'Describe him.'

'Um.' Ben looked at his mate for support, got nothing.

Christ, not this again. Was it too much to hope for a simple fucking description? 'Tall? Short? Young? Old?'

Ben jerked back, blinking in confusion.

OK, possibly a bit too much force behind the words. Caleb tried again, hoped he didn't overshoot, end up whispering. 'Can you remember anything about him? What he said? What he was wearing?'

'Oh. Yeah, a baseball cap. Pulled it kind of low. Bit of a dick, really.'

A spark of excitement. 'What colour was it?'

'Blue.' Ben squinted at him. 'Blue's a funny word. Ever notice that? Bluuuuuuue.'

———

He went to use the wi-fi in the uni library. Well after business hours, but a lot of students were still around, sharing study notes and saliva.

A sense he was on the cusp of understanding. If he got Tilda back tonight, she could sleep beside her mother.

The uni wi-fi needed login details, but Big_Dick_Boy_251 had an open hotspot on his phone. Might as well walk around with a neon sign saying 'insecure'. Caleb logged on, resisting the temptation to change the username to It's_Going_To_Be_OK.

One missed video call from Kat, and a forwarded text message.

*Here safe. Yes you missed a call from me but don't stress, everything's OK. No need to call back. xx*

She knew him too well. But he'd still return the call: video meant she wanted to say something face-to-face. She answered after only a few seconds. Sitting on Georgie's couch, looking tired, but well; smiling. 'You beat my estimate by half an hour.'

'That's the Zelic promise – often early, never wrong. Everything OK?'

'Yeah, we solved the public housing crisis on the way down. On to fixing the pay gap now. What's happening with Tilda?' Signing a little too fast, her hands fluttering.

'I've got some good leads. You all right?'

'Yeah, great. Mum and Dad have gone away for the week. Can

you believe it? Can't remember the last time they had a holiday.'
Avoidance was a new technique for Kat, and an obvious one:
averted eyes when she passed baby shops, a change of subject
when anyone mentioned her tiredness or due date.

'Kat,' he said out loud, 'what's wrong?'

'Nothing. Seriously. It's just, I, um, I can feel the baby moving.'

'Oh.'

She'd felt the first stirrings in the second pregnancy, too. Giddy
when she'd told him that time, describing the feeling in breathless
detail.

A sheen to her blue eyes as she kept going. 'I thought maybe
I could the last couple of days, but then in the car, something
about the way I was sitting.' Tears overflowed. 'I'm feeling a bit
weird about it.'

'Yeah.' Say something, sign something. Something joyful and
reassuring, without fear or false hope. No language in the world
could do it. He pressed his fingers to his lips, then the screen; Kat
mirrored the movement.

Perfect stillness, then she dropped her hand. 'I won't keep you,
I just wanted to let you know. Tell me when you've found Tilda.
Any time.'

'I will.'

After she'd ended the call, he sat without moving. Five whole
days until he'd see her again. Too long – always too long, her
absence a hollow inside him. As soon as this was over he'd take
time off, go down to the Bay. They could spend the evenings
together, maybe even the nights. End this limbo and talk about
moving back in together. An incredible lightness at the thought.

He tucked the idea safely away and got to work. One of the
kidnappers must have known Jordan personally if they'd been
aware of the young man's anger and how to manipulate it.
Somewhere, there'd be evidence of their relationship.

Jordan's social media accounts were private, but a few schoolfriends had tagged him in photos after his death. Sullen and awkward, wearing the navy blazer and striped tie of one of the more expensive private schools. A rare one of him smiling, age sixteen or seventeen. The school football team, mud-spattered and victorious, Jordan's arm around the shoulders of a boy with sinewy limbs.

A jolt at the friend's long face and nose. Recognisable even without his swimming cap and tinted goggles – Fawkes the hacker.

Jordan and Fawkes working together.

Lovelay hadn't been the goal, just a bonus. It was all about bringing down Maggie's clients. No wonder the hacker had been eager to get her records. His claim he could ID the customers hadn't been a boast. Tilda must know where the list was. Jesus. Not an organisation or gang, just a twenty-something hacktivist taking on the world, using Tilda to do it. The stupid, selfish prick. Hollywood and his mates must be getting close to IDing him; when they did they'd bust down the door of whatever squat he was hiding in, and slaughter him and Tilda.

Caleb got to his feet, sat back down. Where the hell did he start looking? Even if he worked out where Fawkes was, he couldn't storm a building by himself. No police, no Frankie, no Tedesco.

Imogen. An uncomfortable choice of partner, but she was fearless and driven. And she had a gun.

# 39.

Flinders Street Station was crowded. Shoppers and families going home, couples heading into the city for a late-night dinner. No sign of Imogen yet. Caleb kept a tight grip on Frankie's camera as he went through the turnstiles; all he needed now was a snatch-and-run. He'd bought a memory card on the way and uploaded a single page of Maggie's docs, hopefully enough to tempt Imogen to help. If it wasn't, he was out of ideas.

He stopped around the corner, his back to the toilet wall. Not much ambience but a good view of the concourse. Overhead, a giant television was flashing the day's news; footage of people standing on the roof of their car, muddy water swirling around them. A strong feeling of kinship.

So far he'd only discovered the basics about Fawkes – the name Zack Billington and a former address – but possibly enough to track down his hideout. Just a little luck needed: a speed camera or toll road, a friend's holiday house. If Imogen turned up.

He checked the time on the TV. The image had changed to a news anchor, a man with trustworthy features, the photo of a young girl behind him. Tilda. An old school photo, her hair brushed into unnatural neatness. Words appeared at the bottom of the screen: *Mum's Tragedy*.

Blood drained from his head, his heart. No. Please God, no.

He blocked a businessman heading for the turnstiles. 'Can you hear the TV? I need to –' The man moved around him. Next person, young woman texting. 'I can't hear. Can you –?' She kept walking, not looking up.

Fuck. Fuck. Breathless, pain shearing his chest. His phone was in the car. Borrow someone's, steal it.

Imogen appeared in front of him, talking rapidly.

'Did you hear it?' he said. 'What'd it say?'

'Calm down. People are looking.' She pulled him to the wall, fingers tight on his arm. 'I caught the full bulletin in the car. The idiots are appealing for information, playing the sympathy card about Maggie's injuries. That picture's everywhere.'

He slumped against the wall. Not dead. But not safe. Not with that photo beaming out across the country. A helpful citizen seeing Tilda's photo, realising they'd seen her and that nice young man in the car, the petrol station, the flat next door. Their hotline message going straight to Hollywood and his mates.

Imogen was speaking again. '. . . police?'

'What?'

'Why the hell did you go to the police? She'll be dead by morning.'

He pushed down the rising panic. 'I need your help. I know who took her.'

'It's not my concern.'

'It is. She can help ID Maggie's clients.' He explained about Lovelay and Fawkes, handed her the camera. 'Maggie's records.'

She examined the screen. Her hair was limp today, dark smudges under her eyes. Strange to be with her instead of Frankie; only yesterday the three of them had stood on that pier.

Imogen lowered the camera. 'Where's the rest?'

Under the sole of his shoe, one useful thing Frankie had taught him. 'You'll get it when we get Tilda. Along with whatever she knows.'

Imogen scanned the crowd as she contemplated his words, more open in her stance than usual, arms uncrossed, chin lowered.

'You speak to Billington's family?' she finally said. 'They got a holiday house? Could be there if he snatched her without planning.'

'Not yet, but he went to Melbourne Grammar with Jordan. Call –'

She was already dialling.

Had the kidnapping been spur of the moment? Fawkes might not have known Tilda was Maggie's weak link, but he'd known from the video someone was – he would have been prepared. He wouldn't be in a squat or family home, but a rental property. A house with no near neighbours.

The real estate brochures in Jordan's house – not an investment, but a hideout.

'I've got it,' he said, then stopped. A point of stillness in the moving crowd, the blurred reflection of a large man on the TV screen. Waiting just around the corner by the turnstiles. Hollywood. How? No one had followed him, no one knew he was here.

Except Imogen.

She was working with Hollywood. On the take, or the actual ring leader? Work it out later, just get away as quickly as possible.

She was looking at him, impatience in the set of her mouth, as though she'd waited too long for a reply. 'Where?' she said.

He spoke the first lie that came into his head. 'Lovelay's holiday house. Ring and ask where it is, I need to piss.' He headed towards the toilets. Walking steadily, easy swing of his arms. Into the stream of people flowing around the corner for the trains. Down the escalator and along the platform to the Elizabeth Street exit. Didn't look back.

# 40.

The farmhouse was a couple of hours west of the city, along a turn-off he'd passed hundreds of times on trips home to the Bay. Could have kept driving past it for the rest of his life, never knowing Tilda was there. He left the car hidden in a pocket of trees, phone well wrapped and tucked inside the glove box, then cut across open grazing land. An inky wash of stubbled grass, moon struggling from behind gunmetal clouds.

A stand of tall eucalypts loomed ahead. According to the satellite map, they bordered all three sides of the backyard, with a blackberry-lined creek running along the rear. He hopped the driveway fence near the garage. A kick of adrenaline at the sight of a silver Holden parked nose-in: the car he'd seen outside the pink motel.

Across a wide garden, with overgrown trees and grass. Past the dim shape of a chicken coop to the house, a well-kept weatherboard with deep verandas. An air of desperation to the online listing, the place still furnished, photos showing the wood-panelled room and brown couch from Tilda's proof-of-life video. He circled it, testing the windows. All stuck. Had to be screwed shut, no farmer would put locks on the windows. The front room was lit, heavy curtains drawn. He went past it to the back door. The handle turned easily. Edging it open, breath held.

A jab in his back. Hard, the size of a gun barrel. He froze.

Someone speaking, barking an order. Stand still? Turn around?

'I can't understand –'

The gun pushed him forward. He stepped inside, no sudden movements. Through a darkened laundry and up a long hallway towards a lit room, the gun firm against his spine. Empty rooms to each side, the last on the left closed, a shiny new bolt securing it. A shove towards the open door and into the wood-panelled room from the video. Couch and armchairs, a bright camping lantern on the coffee table, a laptop next to it showing a simple map of the property. Flashing green perimeter lights, a red one where he'd jumped the driveway fence.

He sped up to get a bit of distance between him and the gun. Turned with his back to the window. Fawkes was by the table, resetting the laptop. Some tension left Caleb – Fawkes was an activist, not a killer; he wouldn't shoot in cold blood. Particularly as the young man was armed with a screwdriver and pepper spray, not a gun.

'Jesus,' Caleb said. 'You scared the shit out of me. Could have just tapped me on the shoulder.'

'And have you punch me? No thanks. How the hell'd you find me?'

'Real estate flyers at Jordan's. Where's Tilda? She all right?'

'She's fine. Asleep. Is anyone else here? You got a phone on you?'

'No. But we have to go. People are looking for you, and if I can find you, they can.' He glanced at the bolted door on the opposite side of the hall. 'She in there?' He moved towards it, stopped abruptly as Fawkes darted forward, pepper spray raised. If he got a dose of that, he wouldn't be driving Tilda anywhere tonight.

'Don't move,' Fawkes said. 'Where's Frankie? She out there, too?'

The words hung in his brain without meaning. 'You know Frankie?'

'Course I fucking know her. Why do you think I let you catch me lurking around Maggie's computer? I'm not an idiot.'

Frankie and Fawkes working together. So many thoughts, none of them making sense. He asked the first question he could catch hold of. 'How do you know each other?'

'Maggie kept going on about Frankie stealing the records, so I tracked her down. Finally found her last week. Not that she was any help. The only good thing she did was put me on to you. That lip-reading thing was great.'

Lip-reading. That's why Frankie had dragged him into this – to read the video. *I'm sorry, Cal. I know you're only in this because of my fuck-ups.* Sorrow in her expression, maybe shame. And the kidnapping? Had she known Fawkes was behind it? No – her stricken face and growing terror – she was innocent of that, at least. Like Caleb, she'd been hunting for an organised gang, not an angry young man with a grudge.

Fawkes was talking again, checking the doorway. '... Frankie? She's not answering my messages.'

'She's dead. A Transis cop killed her.'

Fawkes' mouth opened. 'What?' Looking very young now, his weapons like props from a school play. People after him, his hideout discovered, co-conspirators dead.

Now wasn't the time to pity the little fuck. Just get Tilda and go. Caleb stepped sideways towards the door.

Fawkes lifted the can. 'Stop fucking moving. Give me the records and you can take the kid.'

So Tilda had told him where to find Maggie's client list. Good – the sooner they were exposed the better.

'Why didn't you let Tilda go if you've got the names?'

Fawkes looked incredulous. 'Because then Frankie would have had everything. She was trying to play me, thought I was some kind of stupid kid, but she just wanted to make money.

Greedy bitch. Her and her fucking sister.' Spitting the words. Like he knew Maggie personally, hated her.

'You've met Maggie?'

'She killed Jordy.'

And it clicked: Fawkes had hurt Maggie, not Hollywood. Easy to imagine the scene. The young man demanding Maggie's list, distress at his friend's murder fuelling his rage.

'I don't think she killed Jordan,' Caleb said. 'A client did, or maybe –' He stopped. One of the alarm lights was pulsing bright red. Shit, when had that gone off?

'The sensor,' he said quickly. 'Driveway entrance.'

Fawkes didn't look.

'It's not a trick. They're coming.'

Fawkes backed towards the computer. 'There's no gate, sometimes roos set it off.'

A bang.

Slivers of heat, glass flying. Fawkes on the floor, his head gone. A hole in the wall where he'd been standing.

# 41.

Another thud. Plaster dust billowing. Move. Get Tilda. He ran across the hall to the closed door, pulling at the bolt. Large bedroom, blinds drawn, a camping lantern glowing on the floor. Tilda was curled on the bed, somehow still asleep despite the blasts. He scooped her up, one arm under her shoulders, another under her legs.

She stirred and smiled sleepily at him, eyes opaque. A warm hand patted his cheek. 'Caleb.'

'Hey, Turnip. You OK?'

She nodded, but her face slowly crumpled and she began to sob.

He lifted her against his shoulder as he ran to the door. 'It's OK. It's OK, I've got you now.'

Her face pressed against his neck, wetting his skin with tears. Halfway across the room, a dull thump. Glass spraying, tiny shards pricking through his jacket. Fuck, the shooter must have seen his shadow. Another bang. A hole punched in the wall ahead of him.

He hurtled into the entrance hall. 'Just a bit of noise. It's OK. It's all right.'

She was already settling, heavy in his arms.

Front or back? Could be people waiting outside either of them. A jolt, front door splitting. He raced down the hallway and through the laundry. A pounding rhythm – someone inside the house. He flung open the door.

Outside. No moon. Sprinting across a charcoaled landscape to the driveway, Tilda's head on his shoulder, arms loose. He stumbled. Eyes not adjusted after the brightness. A vague shape ahead – chicken coop. Tilda lolled sideways. Had to be drugged. How fast could he run with a sleeping child? Pretty fucking fast.

*Thump*. Dirt sprayed in front of him.

Fuck. How had the shooter seen him in the dark? Faster. Get behind the coop then make a dash for the –

A bang.

Slicing pain.

Falling.

Twisted to land on his back. Stunned; white heat scorching his thigh. Tilda sprawled across him, unmoving. Hurt? Dead? Patting her thin back and limbs, her head. No wounds, just the steady rhythm of her breaths. He kept stroking her tangled hair, trying to slow his own breathing. Searing pain in his leg. Shot? No, front of his thigh, must be shrapnel from the chicken coop.

A light by the house. Hollywood was in the doorway, gazing at a phone, the light illuminating his sculpted cheeks. Was Imogen here? No, she'd be out shooting, too.

Hollywood fumbled with something one-handed. Loading a sawn-off shotgun.

Fear slithered through Caleb and coiled in his bowels. A weapon like that could shatter bone and shred flesh, blast right through him and into Tilda.

Get up.

Go.

Grasping Tilda, sitting upright. Raw, lancing pain. Something sharp in his thigh, length of his hand – metal. Not near an artery. Pull it out. Do it. He gripped the shard and tore it from his flesh. A fist in his mouth to stop the scream. Clammy hot cold, the night folding in on him. Jesus. Fuck. Long seconds waiting for the ground to steady itself.

Hollywood had clicked the barrel into place, was putting an earpiece in his phone.

Get behind the coop. One arm locked against Tilda, digging his good heel into the earth, pushing backwards. Faster. Dig, push, dig, push. Nerves screaming.

Hollywood flicked off the phone. Dark.

Last few pushes, Tilda heavy, slipping. Hoisting her up. And behind the shed. Solid metal and timber, a hole blasted on one side. He leaned against it, hugging Tilda to him. Had to get her to Fawkes' car. Fifteen, twenty metres, too far with a butchered leg. Lure Hollywood away somehow. The man was just visible through the gap in the shed, white shirt pale against the shadows. Cutting across the yard towards them. Slow, cautious steps. Be still. Couldn't see them, not with his night vision ruined by the phone.

But he kept coming. Straight line towards them. As if he knew where they were. He'd known where to shoot in the house, too. Known to come to the house.

Fawkes' words in the pool. *'Everything can be bugged.'*

A tracker. In the alleyway outside the hospital, Hollywood must have planted one. Listening to it now, stalking him. Where? Different clothes then, different shoes.

Same hearing aids.

An image of the man standing over him, phone in his hand. Not texting – connecting to the bluetooth from his aids. Fuck, hadn't occurred to him. Unsecured signal, open to anyone close.

He ripped them from his ears, went to throw them. No. A possible diversion, disconnect the batteries. Scrabbling at the plastic, trying to find the latch. Got it. Now the other one. Hand shaking, couldn't feel the bump.

Hollywood only a few steps away. Coming to a stop.

Caleb threw the live aid across the yard.

The man whipped towards it. A burst of red as he fired.

A second flash and Hollywood took off, faster now, almost running. Quick, get down to the creek, chuck in the other aid. Should give them a minute or two before it shorted.

He laid Tilda gently on the grass, every instinct against it. She didn't stir, face a pallid moon against the grass. Leave her. Go.

He hauled himself to his feet. Swooping dizziness, clutching the shed. No time – go. Stumbling down the slope towards the bank, checking behind every few steps. Jeans sodden with blood, leg giving way. Had to be halfway there, trees just ahead.

Another check over his shoulder. A flash of movement near the house – Hollywood. Moving towards the coop. Towards Tilda.

OhGodohGod. Too far to run back, too far to the creek. Yell, make a noise. He let out a strangled cry, cut it off like he'd fallen. Running, staggering. Down to the murky line of the blackberry bushes along the creek, twigs and leaves smacking his face. The smell of damp soil. Close now, close enough. Pulling the aid from his pocket, hands slick with sweat. Don't look back, just run. The latch, where was it? There. Clicking it closed, lobbing the aid in a high arc.

Hollywood's pale shape still running towards him.

Caleb dropped, bit back a cry as he knocked his leg. On his stomach, arm over his face, peering beneath it. Hollywood kept coming. The aid was cracked open, caught in bushes, dead.

Closer.

Almost on him.

It couldn't end like this, not with Tilda lying alone.

Hollywood swung away. Darted through the trees, parallel to the creek.

Caleb let out a shuddering breath.

He got back to Tilda, somehow hauled her up. Across the yard and into the garage. Leg numb, dragging. The car was unlocked, key in the ignition. Could have wept. He laid Tilda in the rear footwell, eased himself into the driver's seat.

A manual. Shit. Using a clutch with a fucked leg. He got his foot onto the pedal, pressed down. A knife in his thigh, whole body shaking. Into reverse, engine on. The car shot backwards out of the garage.

Lights on, looking over his shoulder, the driveway a thin ribbon between the towering gums. The back tyres slipped from the path. Slow it down. Nearly at the gate, tight gap between the posts.

The windscreen exploded. Crystals of glass, wind in his face. Skewing off the concrete into a tree. Head snapping back, blood in his mouth.

Hollywood was running down the middle of the driveway, raising the shotgun. Only used one barrel – another cartridge in there. Caleb threw himself behind the dashboard.

The car rocked, cloth and foam spraying from his headrest.

Go. Quick, before he could reload. Engine dead. Stalled. Jesus, fuck. Start it again. Foot numb, slipping from the pedal.

Hollywood coming closer, snapping the barrel into place. A car length away.

He stopped, shotgun raising.

Get the clutch in. Shoving from his hip, leg spasming. And in. Engine on, stomping on the accelerator. The car surged forward into Hollywood, slamming him onto the bonnet, gun flying. And down.

Car into reverse, skidding down the driveway, out the gate. A glimpse of Hollywood lying on the concrete. Dead? Injured? Didn't matter. He accelerated away. A narrow road, hills rising on both sides. Only one headlight pushing back the darkness: enough.

# 42.

He reached Resurrection Bay as dawn kissed the sky. No one around at this hour on a Sunday, just an empty expanse of road, houses nestled by a blue-grey sea. Almost there, Georgie's place just around the corner. A computer, bed, Kat. Somewhere Tilda would be safe and cared for while he slotted the last few pieces into place.

Awake for twenty-four hours and counting. A hammering pulse in his thigh, surviving on dregs of adrenaline and drive-through Macca's coffee. But strangely calm. A wobbly moment there, down on hands and knees in the roadside grass, puking and shaking, but he'd pulled himself together for the ninety-minute drive. Patched his leg together too, using a roll of duct tape he'd found on the back seat; a sick feeling Fawkes had used it to secure Tilda. The glass cuts flecking his arms and back would have to wait until he could get something more sophisticated, like a bandaid.

As he slowed for the turn-off, Tilda woke. Sitting upright in the middle of the back seat, looking around like a scruffy meerkat. He'd picked some of the twigs and leaves from her hair when he'd moved her onto the seat, but there were still a lot tangled in it.

He pulled over and turned to her. 'Hey, Turnip, you OK?'

A nod, a little more meerkatting, taking in the demolished headrest and missing windscreen, his ripped clothes. Her eyes still fogged from sleep, but a lot clearer than last night.

She made two fists and tapped her thumbs together. A rending in his chest: he wasn't ready to tell her about Frankie. Never would be. 'Frankie's not here. But she was looking everywhere for you. She was really worried.'

'Did ... me?'

'Hang on.' He eased out of the car and lowered himself beside her. 'Sorry, sweetie, I've lost my aids. You'll have to speak slowly.'

'Did you come and get me?'

'I did. Don't you remember?'

'No.' She inspected him. 'You're very messy.'

'I know.'

'Are we going home now?'

'Very soon. We're going to a friend's house first so I can make sure everything's safe. My wife's there – Kat. She'll help you ring your mum. She's finding the number right now.'

Hopefully. He'd texted Kat from a public phone half an hour ago; she was usually an early riser but might not have checked messages yet.

Tilda's eyebrows drew together. 'Zack said he'd let me go home if I told him about the memory game, but then he didn't.'

An effort to keep the anger from his face. 'I'm very cross with Zack for doing that, but he's gone now and can't come back. I promise I'll take you home as soon as I can. I just need to make sure no one can ever take you again. OK?'

Tilda considered his words. 'OK.'

He hesitated. Now was the time to ask, while she was still relaxed from sleep. 'How do you play the memory game you taught Zack? Is it hard?'

'No, it's easy. You just have to make up a story for all the letters.' She gave him a doubtful look. 'But you might find it hard. Mum has to practise them a lot because her brain's older than mine.'

'Yeah, I'll definitely need your help. What was the story you taught Zack? I could start with that one.'

'Sam ... went to the ... and ... net.'

Too hard without his aids, should have waited till he had a pen and paper. 'Can you say that again. Really slowly?'

'Sam went to the shops. And bought. Seventy-eight teddy bears. And a gold net.'

He repeated it, working it out as he went.

'SWTTSAB78TBAAGN?'

'Yes. I can test you later if you like.'

'That'd be great, thanks. What does your mum do with the letters once she's learnt them?'

'Puts them in the computer.' Her forehead pinched. 'Can we go now?'

He nodded. 'Yeah, we're almost there.'

———

Georgie's house was an old bluestone cottage on the edge of the town. A tangled garden of flowers, veggies and chooks, a banged-up white Volvo in the driveway. Kat ran out as he bunny-hopped the car to a stop. She'd ditched her usual jeans for black leggings, the swell of her belly visible beneath a thigh-length red top. As he hauled himself out of the car she flinched, looking at the duct-taped mess of his jeans. Her hands flew quickly as she signed. 'You OK?'

'Yeah. I really am.' He hugged her, breathing in her morning warmth. 'Did you get onto Maggie?'

'Yeah, she's back home. Happy to know of Fawkes' death and very keen to talk to Tilda.'

'Her phone might be tapped. Did you –?'

'Use a blocked number and false name? Yes. I even let "slip" we were in Sydney.'

Of course she had – Kat knew too well the horrors people could wreak. She squeezed his arm and looked down at Tilda. The girl had climbed from the car and was following their signing with avid attention. 'Hi, Tilda.' She knelt in front of her. 'I'm Kat. Cal said you've had a big couple of days.'

Tilda gazed at her without speaking.

'Do you want to come inside and call your mum?'

'Straight away?'

'Straight away.'

Tilda looked towards the house and slipped her hand into Caleb's. Two pyjama-clad boys were half-watching, half-wrestling, in the doorway: Georgie's son and neighbour. Seven years old, with the kind of energy that could power whole suburbs. Her daughter was probably inside planning an ambush.

Tilda turned to Kat, 'Can Cal come, too?'

'Of course. He needs a shower – looks like he's been rolling around the garden.'

'The car's really messy, too.' She grasped Kat's outstretched hand, and went inside.

———

Tilda sat next to him on the couch while she spoke to Maggie. Crying at first, but gradually settling. The kind of room that soothed: plump, mismatched chairs and multicoloured rugs, a pot-bellied stove burning. Could almost fall asleep. Head back, one arm around Tilda, leg propped on a chair. His thigh throbbed with a sharp intensity, but the painkillers Georgie had given him were kicking in nicely.

SWTTSAB78TBAAGN. What the hell did it mean? A feeling he'd have worked it out by now if his brain wasn't unravelling into a ... A what? Ball of wool? Would you call a ball unravelled?

A touch to his arm; he started upright. Kat was sitting next to him, holding two plates of food: slices of cheese and apple in a fan of alternating colours. A strong suspicion it hadn't been done in his honour. Tilda paused long enough to take a plate and say, 'Thank you very much', then returned to her conversation. She was reciting everything she'd eaten in the past few days – cereal and chocolate bars, by the look of it, a mix of shock and approval in her expression. At least Fawkes hadn't scared her unnecessarily. She'd be distressed about the kidnapping for a long time, but hopefully not traumatised.

Caleb balanced the plate on his lap and slid his arm free so he could sign. 'Thanks. Impressive presentation.'

'Felt I needed to up my game. Georgie's making waffles in between hauling the kids away from Tilda.' Her eyes swept across his face, taking his emotional temperature. She'd been doing that since he'd given her a rundown of last night's events. 'What'll you do when you've got the names?' she asked.

When, not if. Had to love a woman with that much confidence in you.

'Take it to the media.'

She shook her head. 'It's too incendiary. The legal departments will sit on it too long. Give it to Fawkes' hacker friends – they'll get it out instantly. Sammi'll know how to reach them.'

He blinked at her, dazzled by her brilliance. 'Have I told you how smart you are?'

'Not today.'

'You're very smart. Gorgeous, too. Want to come to bed with me?' The edit button on his brain seemed to have short-circuited, an interesting side effect of sleep deprivation.

Kat patted his knee. 'I like your confidence, but the only horizontal thing you'll be doing is sleeping.' An analysis or instruction? Sadly true, either way.

Tilda shifted against him as she started in on his food. She was rating Fawkes' soft-drink collection now: not fond of Coke, but big fan of Passiona.

Kat followed his gaze, signed with small movements, 'Is Maggie going to jail?'

'Maybe not. She's pretty cluey.' Not sure if he was trying to convince himself or Kat. Strange for them both to be hoping Maggie would walk free.

He rested his head on the couch. Warm in here. Kat and Tilda leaning against him. The scents of waffles and coffee, wood smoke. They should get a house with a fireplace; extra bedrooms, too. Big, ramshackle home for whatever family they ended up having. Adoption, fostering, nieces, nephews; lots of different ways of doing it.

Kat touched his arm; he roused himself. 'Sorry, what?'

'Go lie down. I told Maggie you were driving Tilda back from Sydney.'

A twelve-hour trip, more than enough time to work out what to do. Kat was a genius. 'Have I told you how smart you are?'

'Not in the last ninety seconds.' She put her arm around him, and he leaned against her. Maybe close his eyes. Just for a minute.

# 43.

He was woken by a small body ricocheting off him. Georgie's five-year-old daughter, Minta, had got in on the wrestling with the boys. A tangle of small brown limbs; wailing, but no sound. A lot of his parenting might be done with his aids off.

Through the open doorway he could see the kitchen table: Kat sketching, Tilda beside her, hair washed and tied in a neat ponytail, head bent over a large hardcover book. Possibly one of Georgie's law tomes.

How long had he slept? A year, judging by the stiffness in his back when he sat up. A crutch lay on the floor next to him, along with a packet of bandaids and neatly folded towel. Taking it as a hint, he went to shower.

Georgie caught him when he limped out of the bathroom; towel around his waist, crutch under one arm, skin dotted with Mr Men bandaids. The duct tape was still suturing his thigh, a few more layers firmly applied. Georgie gave him a clinical up and down. He clutched the towel a bit tighter. She had a bundle of men's clothes he hoped were for him. 'God, Cal. Do you actually try to get in trouble?'

'Raw talent. Can't be taught.'

'Can obviously be perfected, though.' She gestured to his leg. 'Go … bathroom … bandage … erlee.' A moment to fill in the gaps: *Go back in the bathroom and I'll bandage that properly.* No – if Georgie looked at it, she or Kat would end up driving him to hospital. The wound was narrow but dug into his thigh muscle, a lot deeper than he wanted to think about. It'd definitely need stitches, possibly surgery.

'Thanks, but I'll go to a doctor once I've got Tilda home.'

'I can do it. Half my family are doctors.'

'And yet you chose to be a lawyer.'

Her mouth compressed, but she handed him the clothes: dryer-warm and smelling of eucalyptus. 'You ... die ... dead ...'

Did he want to know? 'Sorry, you'll have to slow down. Haven't got my aids.'

'Huh. I forget you're deaf sometimes. You're usually so good at understanding me.' Her expression gave him half the necessary information most of the time. Right now it was an odd mix of amusement, irritation and concern.

'Some people are easier than others. Can't understand your kids at all.'

'Lucky you.' Her hands went to her hips. 'I'd rather you didn't die,' she said, then stopped. A keep-it-away-from-our-family speech. Definitely deserved; she'd been more than welcoming given the circumstances.

'But I should fuck off now?'

'*But* you need to get life insurance. You need to make sure Kat and the boorai are OK if you take it too far one of these days.'

'Hi, I'm Caleb. Have we met?'

'Sorry, of course – Mr Worst-Case-Scenario. You got top cover as soon as you found out.' She gave an approving nod. 'You might be a fuckwit, but you're a good man, Cal. I hope everything works out.' She strode down the hall, scooping up an abandoned shoe as she went.

*Top cover.* Alberto had used the same words. *'Nick gave me the lecture last week. I upped the insurance, got top cover on everything.'*

Nick had told Alberto to increase the insurance. Nick, who'd been there at every incident, who had direct access to the ordering system. A slipknot of tension loosened – Alberto wasn't involved, just a stupid boy who didn't know how lucky he was to be so loved. Son of a problem gambler, following in his father's footsteps and getting into trouble with a loan shark, screwing over his grandfather to dig himself out.

But it was fixable. No idea how, but it was.

————

He fortified himself with waffles and more painkillers, and took Kat's laptop to the couch. Tilda joined him, carrying a battered *Guinness Book of Records*, hair already coming loose, fringe sticking up. She launched into a quick succession of sign names: the stroked whiskers for Kat, his own simple CZ, Georgie's Hands-On-Hips. Kat had been busy while he'd slept.

'So I guess you're waiting for your sign name?' he said.

'Yes please. It's not culturally appropriate for Kat to give me one.'

He bit back a smile. 'Do you know the word "swede"?'

'Of course – it's a vegetable and what people from Sweden are called. That's why I'm called Turnip.' She paused, examining his face. 'It's a joke.'

'Yeah, thought it might be. The sign for "swede" reminds me of you.' He placed one hand palm down, the other gently pulling tufts of hair into spikes. 'What d'you think?'

A bright-eyed grin. 'Deadly.'

He laughed. Kat had definitely been busy.

He opened the computer while Tilda settled in to read about parasites. Back up everything first. He uploaded Maggie's records and code to the cloud, and sent the links to Tedesco. The email took a bit longer.

—Tilda is safe. Have sent you a link to Maggie's financial records. The code will hopefully disambiguate the names. Imogen Blain is bent. Possibly taking kickbacks from Maggie.

He paused, then typed,

—We both did what we felt right.

A start towards mending the rift. Hopefully a start. He'd lost too many people to bear losing another one.

He opened Maggie's records. Only one more step and Tilda would be safe. SWTTSAB78TBAAGN. A code? Unlikely. According to Frankie, Maggie had changed her security overnight, spooked by a break-in. Had to be something simple, something she could have done on the spot – in the computer, Tilda had said, so a password, or web address.

A web address. That story she'd told had ended in the word 'net'. '... and a gold net.' Could it really be that simple? Just an online file, accessible only with the right address; security through obscurity. He opened a browser and typed SWTTSAB78TBAAG. net, then hit enter. A page of writing appeared, names down the left-hand side, account numbers down the right. Light-headed, as though he'd surfaced too rapidly from a deep dive. That was smart, very smart. Easy to see where Tilda got her sharpness; Maggie hadn't just found the fastest and safest way to store the list, but obviously remembered not to use her own computer to do it. The library maybe, or a burner.

He copied the names across to Maggie's accounts, examined the results. Thirty people laundering different amounts. Judge Lovelay was one of the smaller clients, with enough dirty money to keep him very comfortably off, but not in the big league. Be interesting to know where the cash had come from, but that was a job for the prosecutors. Maggie's top clients were another story. If three months' records were typical, all of them were cleaning around ten million a year.

A search on the three biggest customers revealed they were businessmen with a history of making large political donations. No wonder Transis had been shut down as soon as it touched Maggie. Like throwing dynamite into a pond. How many of them had been after Tilda? Just Imogen? All of them? Didn't matter – once Maggie's records were public, she and her daughter would be safe.

Time to get everything to Sammi. He emailed her the documents, then video-called. A bright smile when she answered, along with a stream of words, something about Kat. No: cats. Must be talking about his scratched face. Not politely, judging by Tilda's abruptly turned head.

'Can't understand you,' he said. 'I've emailed you some records. Can you get them to all the top political hackers, particularly Anonymous?'

She gave a thumbs-up.

'Straight away? It's important.'

A double thumbs-up.

'Out of the goodness of your heart?'

Double thumbs-down.

He sighed. 'Put it on my account.' He should just give her all his money and be done with it. An idea flickered into being, a possible way to help Alberto. 'Delete a name before you send it,' he said. 'Angus Lovelay.'

Sammi gave him another thumbs-up and ended the call. He made the same alteration to his records before doing a general spray to everyone he could think of: police, newspapers, television. Imogen got her own personal email.

—Maggie's docs are now public. There's nothing left to kill for

A reply came immediately. Had she been waiting for his message?

—RING ME

251

He closed the laptop. An almost dizzying wave of relief: it was over. The terror, the lies, the betrayals. Caught between an urge to laugh and cry. Laugh, definitely laugh.

He left Tilda reading about intestinal worms and went to find Kat. She was in the study with Georgie; at the desk, pencil in hand, an open sketchpad showing her project with Jarrah. Eyes alight as she described the bird's wings, its outstretched claws. A rare moment of unburdened joy. No, that wasn't true; Kat was often light-hearted with her family and friends, with Jarrah. Her light only dimmed with him.

Understanding hit him like a physical blow, pain radiating from his chest. They weren't going to make it if they lost the baby. There wouldn't be any ramshackle house. No spare rooms, or dreams, or future. There were too many cracks in the foundations of their relationship to bear another sorrow, too many years of him ignoring them.

He gripped the doorframe to steady himself.

Kat turned at the movement, smile slipping. 'You OK?'

He spoke out loud so he didn't have to meet her eyes. 'It's over.'

# 44.

He borrowed Georgie's Volvo for the drive back to Melbourne, an automatic with mercifully jolt-free suspension. Tilda was reading the *Guinness Book of Records* beside him, turning at each red light to tell him about skateboarding dogs and land-speed records. Surprisingly easy to understand despite the bizarre subjects and his lack of hearing aids. Despite the image of Kat's dimming smile looping through his brain.

It took a bit of doing to get himself and the crutch out of the car while convincing Tilda not to sprint ahead, but they managed it without tears. The loose front door had been fixed; a new security screen and alarm fitted, along with CCTV. None of it went with the airy glass and timber house, but it was all top-of-the-line and very obvious. That Maggie had managed to pull it all together while dazed and injured was impressive.

The ex-army guard from the hospital opened the door. Caleb relaxed: Tilda was in good hands. The man must have IDed them via the monitor, but he still scanned the garden, his open jacket giving a glimpse of his gun.

Tilda slid behind Caleb's leg. He put an arm around her. 'It's OK. He's just one of the helpers your mum told you about.'

A couple of days to make sure word had spread, and her life could return to normal. Or almost normal – she hadn't mentioned Frankie again, but she'd have to find out sooner or later.

She clutched his hand as he followed the guard down the

hallway and into the cream and grey master bedroom. A uniformed nurse was reading a magazine by the window, Maggie sitting in the pillow-plumped bed, phone within easy reach. Smaller bandages today, eyes focused, but she still had the washed-out look of someone fighting a migraine.

Tilda released Caleb's hand and ran across the room. Onto the bed and into Maggie's arms, shaking with sudden sobs. Maggie kissed her, stroking her hair, patting her all over, as though checking she was whole and real. Caleb stood beside the bed, still trying to work out how to ask what he wanted.

When Tilda eventually stopped crying, Maggie raised her head, gave a little start, as though she'd forgotten he was there. She'd be doing that for a long time – forgetting conversations and events, losing time. Was there someone who could care for Tilda while she recuperated? Maybe that great-aunt Frankie had mentioned.

'Thank you,' Maggie said. 'I don't understand what happened, but thank you.'

The same shock at the familiar rhythms of her speech. Have to get over that.

'She seems OK,' he said. 'The guy didn't scare her too much.'

Rage flared in her eyes. 'He's definitely gone?'

'Yes. A shotgun.' He pushed away the memory of Fawkes' grisly body.

Maggie nodded, but her thoughts seemed to have already moved on from the hacker, her expression faltering. 'The police came. About Frankie. Did you tell –?' She angled her head towards Tilda. The girl had snuggled under her arm, playing with her mother's nightgown buttons.

'No.'

'They said you were there.' Tears welled in her eyes and flowed down her cheeks. 'Was she scared? Did it hurt?'

Frankie's panicked eyes, her shock as the bullet slammed into her.

A moment before he could speak. 'No. It was fast. Really fast.'

'Was it money again? She owed someone?'

'Yes.'

Maggie swiped at her eyes. 'Stupid cow. I would've helped her if she'd asked. She knew that.' She grasped his hand with cold fingers. 'I'm glad you were with her. I'm glad she wasn't alone.'

Eyes burning, a terrible pressure building inside. Tilda was looking up at Maggie; her face echoed her mother's distress.

'It's OK,' Maggie told her, 'Mummy's just a bit tired.' She faced Caleb as the girl settled. 'Go now. We'll talk tomorrow.'

'I have to tell you something first. Frankie –'

'Tomorrow.' Steely-eyed now, a glimpse of her hard inner-core.

'It's important. You're probably safe but you should hang on to the guard for a couple of days. I posted your files online to protect Tilda. There's nothing directly linking you to them, so you should be safe from the cops.'

Her mouth gaped. 'You posted them?'

'It was the only way to keep her safe.'

'Get out.'

'I'm going. Just, could I see Turnip if she wants –?'

'Get out!'

Tilda's head jerked up. The guard was behind him, yanking him to the door. Slipping, the crutch skidding on the floorboards. Tilda scrambled from the bed to get to him.

Maggie held her back. 'Stay away from him. He's a bad man.'

Tilda looked from her mother to Caleb, body quivering. He let the guard pull him from the room. Down the hallway to the front door. Outside. He stumbled on the front step, kept going.

———

He drove to his flat and pulled into the underground carpark. A low ceiling, the weight of the building borne by spindly concrete pillars. Five o'clock on a Sunday and most of the parking spots were taken, everyone tucked up inside discussing dinner plans or watching footy, thinking about the full weekend behind them, the busy week ahead. He found an empty space halfway along the wall, turned off the engine. Complete stillness, complete silence. If he closed his eyes the world wouldn't exist.

'He's a bad man.' Of course. What had he thought would happen? That he'd pop around for play dates with a child whose father he'd killed? That he could slip her into a life with Kat and become a happy, makeshift family?

Yes.

Yes, that's exactly what he'd thought.

Should have known better. He'd asked Frankie why she'd gone into business with him, but it was obvious really. They were both destroyers, their lives filled with a long line of people who'd either loved them at their peril or hadn't loved them enough. Perfect for each other; best kept at arm's-length from anyone else.

He pulled the crutch from the passenger seat and got out. Cold. No air movement down here, just the mass of the building above and the stale smell of a place never warmed by sunlight. He headed slowly for the stairwell. Go to his flat and get drunk, take Henry Collins' little pills, face reality tomorrow. Or not.

A slam of pain in his lower back.

Pitching forward, the crutch spinning away. Someone grabbed him and spun him around, slammed him against the back of a van. A forearm on his throat, hot breath in his face. Hollywood's shirt was torn and smeared, face crusted with dried blood. Cold focus in his eyes.

Too big to fight; needed a weapon – keys. He grabbed them

from his pocket, fist rising. Hollywood kneed his wound. A scream ripped from his throat. The world red black slipping sideways.

Hollywood shoved him against the van doors, windscreen wiper cutting into his head. He was saying something, asking something. Too close, too hard without his aids. 'Can't understand you.'

A punch to his thigh, pain spearing through him. Another jab. No. Too much. Panting, cold sweat slicking his body. Hollywood was talking again, getting ready for another blow.

'Slower. Can't understand.'

'Where's. The. Girl?'

Jesus fuck, he was still after Tilda. Imogen hadn't told him.

'It's over. Maggie's records are online. Ask Imogen.'

'... talking about?'

'Everything's public. No reason to hurt Tilda. Call Imogen, ask her.'

Hollywood's face cleared. He released Caleb, reached for his phone. No. Not a phone, a gun. *Cleaning house.* If Caleb was dead, there'd be no one left to identify Hollywood and Imogen.

Hollywood raised the gun. Caleb smacked his head forward. Dull pain, forehead hitting cartilage and bone. The man reeled back, blood streaming from his nose. Wouldn't stop him for long – get something sharp, stab him. Windscreen wiper. Caleb grabbed it with both hands, tugging hard, yanking. He staggered as it snapped. In his fist, turning, ramming the jagged edge into Hollywood's face, scraping along cheekbone and skin into his eye socket.

Hollywood dropped. Hands to his face, mouth contorted in a scream. Still holding the gun.

Get away. Up to the street. Lurching from car to car, leg buckling, hands slipping from the duco, slick with blood. Up the driveway towards the exit and the dying light of day. Nearly there.

A silhouette appeared: Imogen running around the corner into the carpark.

She skidded to a halt when she saw him, lifting her gun. Couldn't get away, nothing he could do. Her feet were spread wide, both hands on the weapon. The same stance as when she'd killed Frankie.

She exhaled and squeezed the trigger. A distant thump.

No punching heat, no bullet.

Imogen was still aiming the gun. Shouting, smacking the air with a flat palm, repeating two blunt syllables. *Get down!* He dropped.

Another dull thud.

Stillness.

His face pressed to the cold concrete, fingertips gripping. Imogen ran past him. He pushed himself into a sitting position, turned. Hollywood was still doubled over clutching his face, the stairwell door open behind him.

Imogen knelt by a sprawled figure, feeling for a pulse, a gun lying a few metres away. Long dark hair spread on the oil-stained ground, fine features turned towards him, slackened in death: Quinn.

His brain ground into gear. Quinn was behind the bloodshed, not Imogen. Quinn with her sharp mind and need to get ahead. Not just Maggie's hireling, but a business partner. Making the most of the opportunities Lovelay had given her. '*He did everything for me. Taught me things, introduced me to the right people.*' Trying to protect herself and her hard-won success by destroying the records and everyone along with them.

Caleb had seen her brightness and still been fooled.

Imogen pulled out her phone, her eyes on Hollywood. Calling the ambulance and her colleagues. They'd come with their endless questions and need to understand; people in uniforms and suits, cotton overalls and latex gloves.

Let them find him.

He hauled himself to his feet and limped towards the fed. 'Thanks,' he said.

He ignored her rapid spill of words and kept going. Past Quinn and Hollywood, past the blood, the gun. He slowly bent to pick up his crutch and made his way to the stairwell. Started climbing.

# 45.

They met at the Vic Market again. The vegetable stall this time, Caleb with his walking stick, Henry Collins with his wicker basket. Only two potatoes in it so far. A rain-washed day, the concrete path slick with mud and rotting leaves, but plenty of people out shopping, coats buttoned to their chins, breath steaming towards the arched steel roof.

The therapist was pawing through the avocados, poking each one as he sought the softer flesh. He looked at Caleb, golden hair flopping across his brow. 'You haven't mentioned the ultrasound.'

'All good.'

Or so the doctor said; he hadn't been able to look at it. Kat had – a first for her. She'd gripped his hand and smiled and cried, and taken a copy home to show her family.

A gentle smile. 'That's good news, Caleb. It's OK to be scared, but it's OK let yourself be happy, too.'

He nodded. Tedesco had said much the same thing during the one stilted conversation they'd had so far.

Henry added, 'You haven't mentioned the coroner's report, either.'

'This "haven't mentioned" thing's a bit passive aggressive for a therapist, isn't it?'

Henry stood waiting, face open and eager. Their fourth session in the two weeks since Tilda, but the therapist hadn't run out of patience with him yet. God knows why; he certainly had. 'Sorry.

There's nothing much to say. Quinn killed a lot of people, and now she's dead.'

Still couldn't quite get his head around it. Bright, funny Quinn behind all that death. The informant, Jordan, had been first; a brutal decision to try and head off any danger from their panicked clients. She must have been terrified when Maggie was attacked, thinking she'd be next, running to hide in the childhood home she'd worked so hard to leave. But she'd still been quick-thinking when he and Frankie had turned up with news of Tilda's kidnapping. Distanced herself from her hit man and decided to kill Tilda, directed their suspicions towards Delaney. The damp solicitor had been the perfect fall guy: a new recruit with no criminal mates to protect him, or obvious links to Quinn. His guilt-induced family holiday had probably saved his life.

Henry had moved on to the cauliflowers. Caleb followed, careful on the wet ground with his cane. A passing thought that the city's original graveyard lay beneath their feet. Bodies never moved, just paved over. Early settlers lost to accidents and illness, the local Wurundjeri people slaughtered and infected with disease. Children. Lots of children. The bones of nine thousand people crumbling in the clay.

Henry was watching him, a robust-looking cauliflower cradled in his hands. No new additions to the wicker basket. 'What are you thinking?'

'That we're standing on a graveyard. You going to buy that or did we come here for two potatoes?'

Henry examined the cauliflower, didn't look up as he spoke. 'Are you having suicidal thoughts?'

'No.'

The therapist turned the cauliflower over to study its underside. 'Are you sure?'

'You think it might have slipped my mind?'

'How would you describe your emotional state?'

Bereft, rudderless, empty. 'Angry.'

'With Frankie?'

'Yes.'

'With yourself?'

'No, I'm great. I made all the right decisions, and everything turned out fine.'

Henry lowered the cauliflower. Direct eye contact now, no waver to his focus. 'A lot of people did terrible things – Frankie, the hacker, Tilda's mother. Do you blame yourself for their decisions?'

Back to this again. Asking for this session had been a mistake; he was too tired to cope with Henry gnawing at his brain. Should have just stayed in the office, buried in mindless paperwork.

The therapist was opening his mouth to take another bite.

No. Couldn't do it right now. 'I'm sorry,' he told Henry. 'I have to go.'

He went down the aisle towards the street. People jostling and talking, stuffing their baskets with produce. At the kerb, a swirling pool of grey water where the gutter had flooded its concrete banks; a dank scent, the rubbish and ruin of the city flowing out to sea. He stood for a moment, then stepped into it and headed across the road.

# EPILOGUE

The marquee was in the alley behind Alberto's. Bigger than Caleb expected, with steepled ceilings and white canvas walls. Flowers and fairy lights, gas heaters warming the air. Only the umbrellas and puddles of water by the entrance hinted at the squalling rain outside. Nick was by the kitchen door, looking his way. Caleb ignored him and escorted Kat through the crowd towards an empty table, grateful he'd left his aids at home. A five-piece band was pounding out a dance beat on the raised wooden floor, amplifiers turned to full. People were already up and moving, most of them barefoot.

Kat stuck in foam earplugs as soon as she sat down: orange to match her headscarf. She was a flash of brightness in a flowing red skirt and slinky top. No more hiding the high mound of her stomach now, at twenty-three weeks.

'I like the outfit,' he told her.

'Wait till you see me dance in it.'

'You're going to dance?' Kat dancing was a gift – free and joyous, with the disco moves of a bad seventies movie.

'You are, too. And don't pretend your leg's too sore, I know you're back running every day.' A gentle nudge: telling him she knew he'd slipped into obsessive behaviour. That he should make another appointment with Henry. That his forced smiles didn't fool her.

She was waving at someone behind him. Alberto was winding his way towards them, back to his usual darting walk; no sign of the bruises that had disfigured his face a few weeks ago. 'My dear,' he told her, 'you look delightful.'

A hug and a kiss for Kat, a hug for Caleb. Not quite a return to his usual rib-cracking enthusiasm, but getting there. Alberto had accepted Caleb's apology graciously, seemed to believe the story he'd spun about Jimmy Puttnam targeting the business due to mistaken identity. Hopefully he'd never discover the truth.

'I'm glad you came,' Alberto told him. 'We wouldn't have made it without you.'

'No more problems?'

'No.'

There shouldn't be: Lovelay had agreed to pay off Puttnam without too much persuasion. Maybe because he'd wanted to help save another family and its wayward son; maybe because Caleb had promised never to mention the judge's name to the police.

Alberto gave Kat a little bow. 'Dance with me?'

'Of course.' She stood, shooting Caleb a look. 'You're up next, Travolta.'

Caleb watched them go, then headed for Nick. Might as well get it over with; Nick had been trying to talk to him ever since he'd told the teenager that he'd fixed things. He caught the boy's eye and went out into the chill night air, Nick following. Tarpaulins had been strung between the kitchen and marquee to protect the waiters ferrying trays. Water pooled on the rubber mats and formed slow drips overhead. Caleb shivered as a splash ran down his neck.

Nick's head bobbed nervously. 'I wanted to thank you. For, you know, what you did. We would've been stuffed without you.'

'I didn't do it for you, I did it for Alberto. But there's no more money where that came from. You get into debt again, you're on your own.'

'It wasn't like that. Wasn't my fault.'

Just like Frankie, blaming everyone else for his problems. No point arguing; people didn't change. Caleb turned towards the marquee, and Nick grabbed his arm. His mouth was trembling. 'It's true. It was Dad's debt. That guy, Jimmy came to the house when Mum was out, said we had to pay now he'd skipped town. He knew all about us. Had it all written down so I'd understand.' His eyes and nose were running; he scrubbed them with a sleeve. 'He said he'd hurt Mum and Grandad. Showed me this video of him bashing, whipping people. Said he'd do it to them.'

It had the ragged feeling of truth. 'Why the hell didn't you tell someone?'

'I couldn't tell Mum. I just couldn't.'

'Then Alberto. He would have helped.'

'He would've sold the business. It would've killed him.'

Maybe, but there was more to Nick's hesitation. The poor, scared, stupid kid.

'You didn't want Alberto to know about your father.'

'Dad didn't mean to get us in trouble.'

As if someone you loved wouldn't hurt you, wouldn't rip out your heart. Destroy you.

'Your father's weak, but you're not. Don't be dragged down by him.'

He left Nick shivering in the walkway and returned to the warmth of the marquee. People signing and dancing, ferrying plates of food and drink, the amplifiers thumping out a Latin rhythm. Alberto had disappeared, but Kat was in the middle of the dance floor, barefoot and flushed, skirt swirling in colourful spirals. He kicked off his shoes and went to her.

A bright smile as she saw him, eyes shining. She flung her arms around his neck, faltered slightly at the stiffness in his shoulders. He clasped her to him and spun her around. Arms wrapped tight, moving with her, the music pulsing through him. Trying not to think about what he'd lost and what he might lose. Just clinging to the moment. Trying to breathe.

# ACKNOWLEDGEMENTS

My thanks to Medina Sumovic for her insight into Deaf culture and watchful eye on my Auslan. To pedantic ghoul Kate Goldsworthy, whose editorial insight made all the difference to me and the book. The Echo team, in particular publisher extraordinaire Angela Meyer for her ongoing support. Janette Currie whose talks of books and darkness spurred me on, and Sandy Cull for the beautiful cover design. Simon Dale and Marcus Viskich for their IT advice, and The Hot Milkers for their writerly chats and laughs. I'm grateful to the Australia Council for giving me the much-needed time to write. And above all to Campbell, Meg and Leni for their patience, love and support; I owe you all a holiday.

# AVAILABLE AND COMING SOON
# FROM PUSHKIN VERTIGO

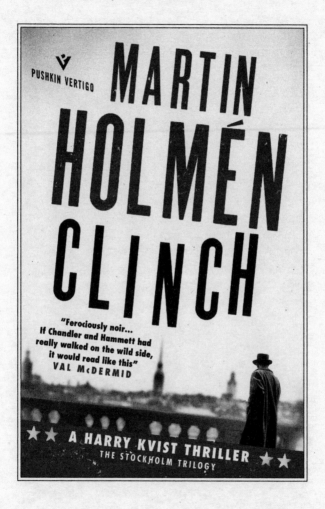

PUSHKIN VERTIGO

# MARTIN HOLMÉN

## CLINCH

"Ferociously noir...
If Chandler and Hammett had
really walked on the wild side,
it would read like this"
VAL McDERMID

★★ A HARRY KVIST THRILLER
THE STOCKHOLM TRILOGY ★★

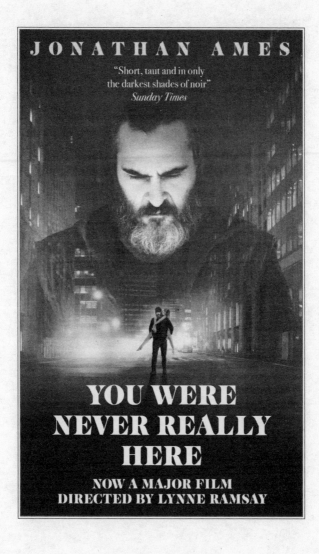

'Ice cold modern noir'

*Mr Hyde*

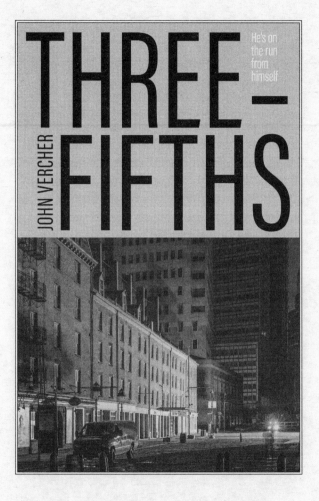

THREE-FIFTHS

He's on
the run
from
himself

JOHN VERCHER

FIFTHS

Set against the backdrop of the simmering
racial tension produced by the LA Riots and
the O.J. Simpson trial, comes this powerful
hardboiled noir of violence and obsession